Leo Kessler is a familiar name to readers of war fiction. In addition to his numerous superselling war series, he is the author of several non-fiction works and of the screenplay *Breakthrough*. A remarkably energetic writer, he lives in Germany between bouts of travelling.

Leo Kessler

Sink the
Scharnhorst

Macdonald Futura Publishers

A Futura Book

First published in Great Britain in 1981
By Macdonald Futura Publishers

Copyright © Macdonald Futura Publishers 1981

ISBN 0 7088 2060 3

Photoset by
Rowland Phototypesetting Limited,
Bury St Edmunds, Suffolk.
Printed in Great Britain by
Hunt Barnard Printing Ltd
Aylesbury, Bucks.

Macdonald Futura Publishers Ltd
Paulton House
8 Shepherdess Walk
London N1 7LW

Live and let live
No matter how it ended
These lose and, under the sky
Lie befriended.

For foes forgive
No matter how they hated
By life so sold and by
Death mated.

Graves: El Alamein, J. Pudney.

Part One: 1939

ONE

The Wellington was dying in the air!
Its port engine was shattered, they could see that, its starboard one roaring at full throttle as the pilot desperately tried to keep the English bomber in the air. But that wasn't to be. Now it was sinking into the packed grey mass of warships a thousand feet below, the brown puff-balls of the 88mm flak exploding all around it, tracer – red, green and white – zipping furiously into the dawn sky.

'They've got the bastard! They've definitely got him, *Leutnant!*' *Obermaat* Thomsen yelled excitedly, letting go of the E-boat's multiple machine gun he had been manning during the raid and watching the British bomber's dive of death.

Leutnant zur See Horst Hartung pushed his cap to the back of his cropped blond head and stared at the stricken Wellington. The cadence of its remaining engine had now changed to a despairing whine as it plunged ever deeper, thick black smoke streaming from its tail. A moment before, his excitement at this first taste of action of the new war had been almost unbearable. Now he could only feel compassion for the pilot of the dying aircraft, as he fought against the inevitable.

'There she goes!' Thomsen bellowed above the frenzied thump of the flak-guns on the 10,000 ton *Prinz Eugen* anchored at the far side of Wilhelmshaven's great naval harbour.

The Wellington seemed to be standing on its nose. Suddenly, a sheet of flame shot outwards from its shrapnel-riddled wings. One fell off and dropped to the sea, twirling down like a great metal leaf. Then, like a stone, the blazing coffin plunged straight down into the harbour. Wild white water erupted in a furious geyser and a mushroom of steam shot into the sky. A moment later all that marked the bomber's death throes was a swirl of oil spreading steadily across the harbour.

Obermaat Thomsen, his broad, north German face wreathed in a happy smile, thrust out his big hand, calloused from his ten years' service with the *Kriegsmarine**. 'May I have the pleasure, *Leutnant*?' he asked, as the rumble of the flak started to die away to be replaced by the thin wail from the sirens of the naval barracks close by and the triumphant wails of the ships' whistles.

'What for?' Hartung asked, adjusting his cap. At eight hundred hours Grand Admiral Raeder himself was to address all officers and the Chief of the German Navy was a stickler about dress.

'What for, sir? Because we've knocked the shit out of the Tommies, sir! I reckon we damaged or destroyed half those Wellingtons.' Thomsen beamed at him. 'That's a real smack in the kisser for those buck-teethed Tommies. They won't be paying Wilhelmshaven a visit so soon again, I'll be bound.'

Hartung smiled a little at the big petty-officer's enthusiasm.

'I wouldn't be so sure about that, *Obermaat*. I know the Tommies. They're persistent shits. They'll be back.' Hartung tugged at his tie. 'All right, check the ship and the crew. See they're all shaved and wearing their number one uniform, just in case the Old Man takes it into his head to come and have a look at *S–34* this morning.'

'Number one uniform,' Thomsen grumbled. 'I thought the Fuhrer said that this was going to be total war, not a

*German Navy.

fashion parade.'

'Tell that to Grand Admiral Raeder, *Obermaat*,' Leutnant Hartung said and touched his cap as the petty officer snapped to attention.

The cobbled streets of Wilhelmshaven were buzzing with excitement. Housewives stood at their doors chatting about the raid and little boys in Hitler Youth uniform were hunting for pieces of shrapnel from the flak and the bombs dropped by the British, most of which had missed the naval targets, with the exception of the cruiser *Emden*. Naturally the SA were out in full force, wearing their World War I medals and looking suitably warlike in their new steel helmets.

Hartung grinned as he strode towards the barracks where Raeder would speak to the officer corps. Most of the big-bellied storm troopers, in their brown uniforms, would probably have a heart attack if it came to any serious physical action. All that the Party rowdies were good for was making bullying noises at Jews and communists – though there weren't many of them left in the old red stronghold of Wilhelmshaven. He stopped to let a *Kriegsmarine* wagon, pulled by a team of horses, go by and stared, momentarily bewildered, at the strange shapes under the tarpaulin in the back. Then, with a shock of recognition, he realized what they were and snapped to attention as a token of respect.

'Tommies,' the elderly SA man standing casually at his side said gloatingly. 'Just pulled 'em out of the harbour.'

'They're the first . . . dead I've ever seen,' Hartung stuttered as the cart rumbled by.

'You'll see plenty more,' the elderly SA man said. 'They say that drunken Jew-lover Churchill, was a passenger on one of the planes. They've already got divers down looking for his fat-gutted body.'

Hartung looked at the SA man, his fat face full of stupid pleasure, and asked himself the old question, the one that

had plagued him ever since he had first met Peter Harding
R.N. back in 1936: were such people worth fighting for?
'They *are* human beings, you know,' he snapped, as the
cart disappeared around a corner, one hand bouncing up
and down from underneath the blood-stained tarpaulin,
as if waving goodbye.

'Human beings – the Tommies?' the SA man said, his
piglike eyes suddenly full of suspicion. 'You should not be
saying things like that, *Leutnant*. That's defeatism,
almost . . . I nearly think I should report it.'

A hot retort sprang to the young officer's lips, but he
caught himself just in time. Back in 1936, in that incident
when he had first met Peter, he had nearly lost his chance
of the naval career on which he had set his heart ever since
he had been a schoolboy. Now that Germany was at war
and there was a real opportunity for the adventure and
glory which his heart desired, he could not risk everything
in another run-in with the Party. So he contented himself
with a precise salute and a polite '*Auf Wiedersehen*',
striding off, with the fat SA man staring suspiciously at his
ramrod-straight back.

'*Stillgestanden!*'

The big damp barracks square echoed and reechoed
with the stamp of one hundred pairs of boots stamping to
attention. In the bare skeletal trees which surrounded it,
the crows rose in hoarse cawing protest.

Standing on the raised platform, surrounded by his
staff, with the white-and-black flag of the *Kriegsmarine*
snapping in the stiff North Sea breeze above him, Admiral Raeder, clad as always in an old style naval frock
coat, complete with stiff wing collar, raised his gloved
hand to his cap and said, 'Gentlemen, please stand at ease.'

There was an outburst of coughing and a shuffle of feet.
Hartung standing in the front rank with his fellow officers
of the E-Boat Flotilla, grinned. Raeder was so old fash-
ioned that he looked like something left over from the

time of Admiral Tirpitz*. No wonder most of the younger officers quipped about their C-in-C that 'as long as the Navy runs on wheels nothing can be any good'.†

'*Kameraden*,' Raeder commenced. 'I do not need to tell you that our friends of the Army and Air Force are achieving tremendous victories in Poland. Their successes have been reported amply in the radio and press – perhaps too much so,' he added with a slight smirk.

There was a rumble of agreement from the senior officers of the cruiser squadron, who occupied the front rank of the centre square as befitted their rank. Hartung smiled to himself and winked knowingly at his neighbour. Everyone knew the cruiser officers were spoiling for a fight, ready to try out their new ships against what they believed was a highly overrated Royal Navy.

'What of the Navy, people are asking. What role has the *Kriegsmarine* played in this war so far and what role will it play in the future? Apart from the bombardment of Danzig three days ago, by the *Schleswig-Holstein*, it looks to the average folk-comrade that – to put it drastically – we of the *Kriegsmarine* have sat on our big blue bottoms and done nothing.'

The ripple of laughter from the junior officers of the E-Boat Flotilla did not quite drown out the mumbled assent from the cruiser men.

'This raid we have experienced will show the general public that the *Kriegsmarine* is taken seriously by England, the world's premier naval power. After all, they lost ten aircraft trying to bomb our ships. But this is not enough, some of you will say. When will our fleet take to the sea?' Raeder looked directly at the cruiser officers and Hartung knew that this whole exercise was being put on specifically for them. 'I shall tell you, comrades. *Not* in this year of 1939.'

There was a soft groan from the ranks of the cruiser

*Navy Minister at the turn of the century.
†Pun on Raeder's name, as 'raeder' means 'wheels'.

officers. Raeder hurried on, his sallow face flushing a little red. 'You all must know that our fleet is not yet prepared for the equivalent of the blitzkrieg at sea. The *Bismarck* and the *Tirpitz* are not yet completed. The *Scharnhorst* and the *Gneisenau* are not fully worked up. All that I can spare for attacks on British commerce is the *Graf Spee*, *Deutschland* and *Scheer*.'

Out of the corner of his mouth, Hartung's neighbour whispered, 'So that's where those three are.'

'Shut up!' Hartung hissed. 'When the Old Man's dealt with the big boys, I'm sure he'll come to us.'

'The Fuhrer agrees with me that our fleet of capital ships must be husbanded until they are properly ready to strike a major blow at the British,' Raeder continued. 'Until that time comes, we of the *Kriegsmarine* must rely on our U-boats to deal with the enemy's merchant shipping in the Atlantic and the Indian Ocean. That has already been taken care of by Commander-in-Chief U-boats Admiral Doenitz. But what of the North Sea, the Channel and the Western Approaches? What ships will we employ there?' Raeder swung round to face the officers of the E-Boat Flotilla, not many of them, save *Flotillenkapitän* Hoffmann, older than twenty-five, and Hartung felt himself tense with expectation. The Old Man was going to tell them they were going to go into action; he knew it with the clarity of a sudden vision!

'The answer is the ships of our newest arm of the service – our Moses, the E-boats*.'

Flotillenkapitän Hoffmann, a hard-faced professional, who had originally learnt his trade in the old Baltic boats where the skippers had enforced their discipline by the boot, the rope or the belaying pin, snapped to attention. '*Herr Grossadmiral*,' he cried in that harsh, rum-thickened voice of his. 'We of the E-boats would deem it an honour to be given even the most dangerous of assignments.'

*In the German Navy the youngest crew-member is called 'Mosēs'.

'Well said, Hoffmann,' Raeder answered, obviously pleased that he had dealt with the cruiser skippers and was now on safer ground with the eager young men of the E-boat Flotilla. 'But do not be so hasty, until you hear your assignment.'

Hoffmann did not hesitate. 'Would you like us to have a crack at Scapa Flow, *Herr Grossadmiral*?' he growled, while the cruiser officers frowned at such temerity.

'Not exactly,' Raeder answered, the smile still on his thin lips. 'But what about Hull to begin with it, eh?'

Hull, the name stabbed into Hartung's consciousness. It had been to the north Yorkshire port to which he and Peter had taken the Jewish girl Anna, in that crazy episode that had nearly cost both of them their careers back in 1936.

'Yes,' Raeder was saying, 'it is time that we of the *Kriegsmarine* showed the gentlemen of the Senior Service, as they like to call themselves, that even their own backyard is not safe. Comrades of the E-boat Flotilla, I will expect a detailed plan of attack from you within forty-eight hours. The public is hungry for news of the exploits of the *Kriegsmarine*. We have a duty to our traditions not to let them wait much longer.'

Someone bellowed: 'Attention!'

As one, the officers clicked their heels. Almost casually, *Grossadmiral* Raeder touched his gloved hand to his gold-braided cap. But there was nothing casual about the look the elderly admiral gave the young eager faces of his E-boat skippers. It was as if he did not expect to see many of them ever again. . . .

TWO

'Nothing doing yet.'

'Looks like another bloody Hundred Years' War to me, mate.'

'Rummiest bloody war I ever knew . . . Fighting it with sodding leaflets! I think Chamberlain *and* Hitler have got the wind-up.'

'It's a war of nerves, chum.'

'War of nerves my arse! All I know is that it's ruddy well boring me stiff. There ain't even no football either.'

First-Lieutenant Peter Harding smiled at the two old codgers grumbling at the back of the 'Mucky Duck', as the 'Black Swan' was known locally. Like the rest of the population of Britain, they had obviously expected all-out war, with bomb and gas attacks causing thousands of casualties and all the rest of the horrors the pundits had been predicting for the last few years. Now everything seemed a kind of anti-climax, with Hitler doing what he liked in Poland, while the Western Allies sat on their thumbs. It was even said that the air minister had refused to bomb the German Ruhr because the German war factories located there were private property!

Peter Harding smiled at himself in the pub's flyblown mirror, seeing a long, handsome face, dominated by clear, blue eyes which were perhaps a little too sensitive for a man in his profession. He drained the rest of his pink gin, picked up his gas-mask case, and went out into Hull's teeming midday streets.

Hull was as dirty and as shabby as always. Unemployed workers, dressed in flat caps and with artificial silk mufflers wrapped around their skinny throats, lounged at every corner or played pitch-and-toss with halfpennies when they thought the police weren't looking. Factory girls, metal curlers showing from beneath their headscarves, were eating fish and chips out of newspaper. Here and there, a local whore stood in doorway, waiting for a customer from the sailors who were everywhere, kitbags slung over their shoulders, their caps perched on the back of their heads at a very unofficial angle, heading for the docks and their ships.

'Hull – the arsehole of the world,' Peter Harding muttered to himself as he showed his pass to the middle-aged policeman at the dock gate, telling himself yet again that he had never thought the real start of his naval career would be at this godforsaken port in deepest Yorkshire. All the same, he thought, as he returned the policeman's salute and entered the busy dockyard, that stank of fish as did most of Hull, he did have his first command – and within three years of leaving Dartmouth.

The tall young officer made his way through the cluttered dockyard, dodging the cranes moving everywhere, working his way through great piles of crates, noting as always the indolent, ratfaced dockers scattering for cover every time someone who seemed to be in authority made an appearance. He shrugged and told himself that Mr Chamberlain was not going to win this new war fast with that type of material.

He paused suddenly and dismissed the scrounging dock-workers from his mind. There, directly before him, lay his ship, *Motor Launch 120*, shabby and old like Hull itself, but *his*! He stood there and stared at her.

He had been working her up for six weeks now, and although the maximum speed her twin Hall-Scott petrol engines could attain was only eighteen knots – half that of the modern German E-boats – *ML 120*'s high free-board and her clean lines made her blessedly dry at sea, which was something her crew delighted in; at that time most fast launches had their crews permanently soaked. His gaze ran along her deck, noting that the crew had now stowed the morning's rations and fresh crates of ammunition, and rested on her three pounder cannon of World War I vintage. He frowned. The cannon and *ML 120*'s two Lewis machine guns mounted aft wouldn't be much use if they ran into any serious opposition on their first wartime mission. But there again the Jerries had so far not shown themselves in the North Sea; indeed the German Navy was keeping remarkably passive. Even the RAF's raid on Wilhelmshaven the day before had not stung them into action. No wonder, people were calling this new conflict the 'phoney war'. He shrugged, and adjusting his peaked cap to the rakish angle favoured by the young officers of the ML squadron, he walked the remaining distance to his ship.

'Had a nice night last night, I did, sir. Tommy bloody Handley on the wireless again! I'd read every bloody paper in the house! The pictures is closed and the missus had her bloody monthlies again. Freedom in peril, old Winnie says. They're bloody well telling me!'

Harding smiled, as the little tirade ended in a snort. Old Chief Petty Officer Hurry was sounding off again to young Rawlings. Ever since the craggy-faced east coast trawler skipper had been summoned back from the Reserve, he had grumbled and grumbled. About his wife who constantly refused him sex. About the sloppiness of the young ratings, all of whom could have been his son. About 'them thieving dockies', as he invariably called the dock-workers. About Chamberlain and his 'ruddy umbrella'. Even the new First Lord of the Admiralty Winston Churchill was not altogether immune from his venomous assault. Yet Harding valued the old CPO. He knew east coast waters like the back of his hand and in the treacherous conditions that always seemed to pertain off that long Yorkshire coastline, the old man's knowledge would prove invaluable.

He clattered up the gang-plank. Sub-Lieutenant Rawlings, a fresh-faced, freckled twenty year old not long graduated from Dartmouth, and Hurry, as leather-faced and sour-looking as ever, came to attention. Harding waved them to stand at ease and said, 'Well, Chief, been enjoying yourself as usual I can hear.'

'Couldn't even get the old woman to go to the chip-shop last night,' he moaned. 'Said she was scared she'd get molested in the blackout.' He spat sourly over the side. 'Molest *her* – that'll be the day!'

Harding winked at Rawlings. 'Total war, you know, Chief, we've all got to make sacrifices, even if it's only fish and chips.' Then he was businesslike again. 'All right, this is the drill, we've got the southerly convoy coming down from Newcastle.'

Rawlings' smooth boyish face lit up excitedly. 'Oh, I say, sir, good show! We might see some action, eh!' he exclaimed.

Harding shrugged slightly. 'It's possible,' he agreed.

CPO Hurry was not impressed. 'The southerly convoy from Newcastle. You know what that means, sir, don't yer? A bloody lot of colliers! We won't get the stink of soft brown coal off the ship in a month of Sundays.' He shook his head. 'What a ruddy war. . . .' And with that he disappeared below to carry out his duties.

Harding grinned and said, 'Well, Rawlings, not the most glamorous of assignments, I suppose.'

But Rawlings' enthusiasm was not to be dampened this day.

'I don't care if we're to escort a bunch of sea-scout canoes, sir,' he cried. 'It's action, sir, and if you're going to win a gong, it's action you want!'

Harding sniffed and told himself that there would be precious little action off the coast of east Yorkshire this day, but he was going to be proved wrong.

Two hours later, *ML 120* had finally cleared the lock and was nosing its way into the debris-littered channel of the Humber. Already Peter Harding, standing on the little

bridge, could feel the keen wind blowing down the estuary from the North Sea and he buried his chin deeper into
the rough, warm collar of the duffle-coat, narrowing his
eyes to slits as the hundred-foot craft started to pick up
speed. Because she only drew a mere five feet fully
loaded, they were able to keep her closer to shore and out
of the tight shipping-lane crowded with traffic from the
new convoys, which had been organized immediately war
had broken out at Winston's orders.

Now the flat, mud-bound coast, dotted here and there
with tiny villages, dominated by the grey gothic spires of
medieval churches, started to slip past more quickly.
Automatically he noted their names – Sunk Island,
Hedon, Patrington – telling himself that he had once
found this coastline ugly, that first time he and Horst
Hartung had sailed into the Humber with the girl Anna,
on that mad-fool escapade which had nearly cost him his
cadetship at Dartmouth. Now there was something almost beautiful about this harsh, northern vista, which
contrasted so strongly with the bright white cliffs and
golden beaches of his native Devon.

For a moment he thought about Horst – that charming,
but very tough German, who had risked his own career
that year – wondering where he was at this moment and
how he could fight for that monster Hitler and his gang,
who had persecuted Anna and her parents so cruelly.
Then he dismissed his long-lost 'partner in crime', as the
stern-faced captain at the court of inquiry had called the
German, and concentrated on the task of getting *ML 120*
around the treacherous mud-bank that ran out from
Spurn Point and into the North Sea. . . .

'*Colliers*!' CPO Hurry said in disgust, as the smudges on
the horizon grew larger and the Aldis lamp from the Hunt
class destroyer which had escorted the half-dozen ships
from Newcastle started to flick off and on. 'I can smell the
mucky sods from here!' He wrinkled up his big red nose. 'I

bet some of the deckies on them haven't had a swill-down since the midwife gave 'em a bath as a baby. Black as the ace-of-spades most of 'em.'

'Give it a rest, Chief,' Harding said, as his own signaller flashed back his receipt for the little convoy, and the Hunt class destroyer started to turn to make her way back to port. Now the colliers' dirty little wooden craft, their decks piled high with coal, thick black smoke pouring from their tall old-fashioned funnels, began to edge their way closer to the coast, while *ML 120* swung out to their seaward side. This was standard operating procedure. It was unlikely that any German sub would be able to penetrate the shallow waters through which the convoy now sailed. The only danger could come from surface craft and it would be the motor-launch's job to ward off any threat. Though at that moment, Lieutenant Harding suspected that what lay before them now was a long, boring crawl along the coast to Hull. And Hurry was right – the colliers did stink!

'Number One,' he snapped.

'Sir,' Rawlings, his eyes still glowing with excitement, answered smartly.

'Take over. You, Chief, come with me. I want to have a look at our artillery.'

'Pop-guns, if you ask me,' Hurry snorted as they clambered down to the deck. 'That lot of rubbish was knackered in the First War!'

Harding smiled but said nothing. He knew the CPO was right. Still, it was all they possessed and he had to be sure that the gun-layers were alert and ready to go into action at once.

But the two of them were not fated to reach the vintage cannon, for just as they dropped to the deck, there was a cry of surprise from the aft look-out which was changed a moment later into a more official-sounding 'Aircraft, sir!'

Harding swung round, raising his binoculars as he did so, a startled gaze taking in the dark shapes coming in slowly across the sea towards the little convoy, while CPO

Hurry, his grumbling forgotten now, tensed at his side, craggy face set and determined.

'Flying boat, escorted by . . . two fighters,' he announced after a moment.

'Flying boat – one of our Sunderlands?' Hurry queried, his voice sharp.

'Don't think so,' Harding replied, busy adjusting his binoculars. 'I can only count two engines and not four . . . Oh Christ!' he gasped, as the first black-and-white cross slipped into the gleaming circle of calibrated glass.

'What is it, sir?'

'Jerries . . . *They're Jerries*!'

'*Oh bollocks*!'

Now the two fighters left the slower flying boat and came roaring in, yellow-coloured nose spinners revolving furiously, their machine guns chattering, violet light rippling the length of the wings.

Suddenly the two men woke up to their danger. 'Give me that sodding gun!' CPO Hurry yelled and wrenched the Lewis-Gun from the hands of the surprised young rating. 'Open fire!' he bellowed at his neighbour who was fumbling with the next one. He pressed the trigger of the antiquated machine gun with its round pan.

The weapon burst into frenetic life, slamming back and forth against the petty officer's shoulder. Tracer zipped through the sky towards the hurrying fighters. Behind an angry, red-faced Hurry, Harding ducked swiftly as a burst of bullets stitched a sudden pattern along the length of the stanchion above his head. And then in the same instant, his ears deafened by the tremendous roar of their engines, the two planes swept over their heads, nearly severing their wireless aerials.

'Rotten buggers!' Hurry snarled and swung the gun round, as the two Messerschmidts started to soar upwards, their speed momentarily reduced by the steep climb. Hurry didn't hesitate. Instinctively he knew the second fighter, which had stupidly positioned itself in the slip-stream of the first one, thus reducing its speed even more, was the better target. He pressed the trigger once more. The second plane staggered suddenly, as if it had run into an invisible wall. A dark piece of metal spurted from its side and then another. CPO Hurry continued to fire at it furiously, his eyes gleaming excitedly. Black smoke started to stream from its engine. There was a blinding flash and then with dramatic suddenness, the Messerschmidt had rolled over on its back and was hurtling towards the sea. The crews of the colliers were screaming across the water: *'You've got him, hinny . . . you've got him!'*

THREE

'How very strange . . . how very strange indeed,' the flag-officer said, and walked to the other end of his big office overlooking Hull docks.

Outside, a company of the East Riding Yeomanry marched past on the way to some troop transport or other and the strains of 'Roll out the Barrel . . .' came wafting its way upwards, while the big, bluff captain stood thoughtfully at the window, with Lt Harding staring at his back in bewilderment. He had thought his news of a successfully downed Jerry plane would have been received with delight by Hull's senior naval officer; instead it seemed to be the cause of great worry. Why?

The captain spun round on him. 'You said the two Messerschmidts were accompanied by a seaplane?'

'Yessir. My number-one, Sub-Lieutenant Rawlings, recognized it as an Arado.'

'Arado, eh,' the captain mused, the thick lines that ran out from the corner of his grey eyes deepening even more. 'Now what the devil would the Boche want putting in an Arado, escorted by two valuable fighters, against a collection of rather unimportant colliers hauling coal from Newcastle?' He flashed Harding a brief smile. 'No pun intended, Harding.'

The young officer answered it with a smile of his own. 'Well, now you mention it, sir,' he ventured. 'I don't really think they were interested in us. We just got in their way and they were virtually forced to tackle us.'

The captain's worried frown disappeared. 'Don't think I've forgotten the Messerschmidt your ship downed, because I haven't. Their Lordships will hear of it. I doubt if it'll get you a gong,' instinctively he threw out his own chest, resplendent with three rows of colourful decorations, 'but it might give you a mention, which is better than nothing . . . All right, if they weren't after you, what or who were they after, eh?'

'Their course would have taken them straight for Flamborough Head, sir.'

'The best landmark on the whole length of the Yorkshire coast. The RAF use it all the time for flights out,' the captain mused. 'All right, where were they off to after they had managed to orientate themselves at Flamborough?'

'It couldn't be Hull, sir, could it?' Harding asked suddenly. 'After all, what other target is there of any military importance in the area? Besides if they were after a land target, why use a seaplane for reconnaissance? They'd probably employ one of those Junkers 88s of theirs for that kind of a job. . . .' He stopped short.

The flag officer sucked his lips for a moment.

'But if you're right – and I think you are – what are they leading up to? A bombing raid perhaps?'

Suddenly Harding had a flash of inspiration. 'Remember Scarborough in 1914, sir?' he said excitedly.

'What!'

'You recall, sir, when the German cruiser squadron suddenly appeared out of nowhere and started pounding the place to bits. I mean, we were caught completely off guard. It was a tremendous propaganda victory for the Kaiser. By the time our chaps arrived on the scene, the Jerries had fled back to Kiel or wherever they came from.'

'Of course, of course!' The captain's eyes narrowed. 'Their fleet has been just too damned quiet – and it's not like the Boche. But all the same, I can hardly see them using their capital ships for an attack on Hull – it's simply not that important. Nor would they risk their subs in the estuary. The Humber is too narrow. They could be detected too easily.' He stopped short and looked hard at the handsome young officer, whose face was flushed with barely contained excitement. 'Are you thinking what I am thinking, young man?' he rapped.

'E-boats, sir?'

'Right in one! E-boats. They've got the radius. They're damned fast and they've got a lot of punch. They could be in and out of that estuary like a dose of salts through my maiden aunt. I doubt if those territorial gunners stationed at Spurn Point could do much to stop them – they're still only half-trained.'

Lt Harding could restrain himself no longer. 'Don't they say in the detective stories, set a crook to catch a crook?' he blurted out.

'And what's that supposed to mean?'

'Give us the job – the ML flotilla, sir.'

'But your old tubs have got half the speed of those modern E-boats of the Boche.'

'Agreed, sir. But we'll have the advantage of being on the spot, and waiting for them, and we do know those waters well.'

The captain pursed his lips and Harding could almost feel his brain racing as he considered the proposition. 'All right, Harding, you and the rest of you fast-boat wallahs are on,' he said, his decision made. 'I'll get right on the blower to Coastal Command to see what kind of support and reconnaissance I can get you.' His voice softened momentarily. 'But don't let the Boche get the advantage of you, young man, or you'll be fish-food before I can say Jack Robinson.'

Hurriedly Harding grabbed his cap and rose to his feet, as if he feared the captain might change his mind. 'Don't worry, sir, old Jerry will have to get up earlier if he's going to catch *ML 120* out.'

'If I know the Boche, they're up already, young man,' and with that the captain picked up the phone and barked, 'Get me Coastal Command – at the double now. . . .'

The flag officer was right. The E-boat Flotilla was already out in the North Sea, refuelling for the last leg of their attack and attending the final briefing on the deck of *Kapitänleutnant* Hoffmann's boat.

To the south-west, banks of cloud were building up black on the horizon, and there was no moon. It was the ideal moment for refuelling. Even the water, unusual for this time of the year in the North Sea, was calm, with only an occasional ripple splashing at the sides of long lean craft moored to each side of the tanker. But Hoffmann was taking no chances. He hurried through the briefing without letting his officers ask any questions; and they all knew why. If the E-boats were caught now, there'd be mass slaughter.

'Weather,' he rapped. 'According to Met, coastal fog is predicted for dawn on that coast. It's common there for this time of the year.' There was a brief rumble of approval from the assembled officers. 'Now final tactics. Air has promised us a sortie against the Tommy batteries on Spurn Point to cover our entrance, as you all know, but if there's going to be fog, I have my doubts. We all know that those flyboys are delicate creatures, easily put off by weather.'

Hartung grinned. Hoffmann was running true to form, although he was under obvious strain. He had no time for any branch of the forces other than the *Kriegsmarine* and even there he had his reservations.

'So, what do we do? We'll use the fog to our advantage. Like this.' Hoffmann reached out a paw like a steam shovel and his second-in-command thrust a glass of *Korn* into it. He drained it in one and continued with hardly a pause. 'Go in individually at five minute intervals. If we can, we'll tack on to a merchantman entering the estuary, putting the ship between us and the batteries. If they spot us then, they're not going to shoot for fear of hitting their own people. Besides, everybody knows the Tommies can't shoot. Think of the Skagerrak* and the shitty mess they made there.'

*The German name for the Battle Jutland, 1916.

'That's over twenty years ago, *Kapitänleutnant*,' Hartung said. 'They've probably learnt a little since then.'

'Not the Tommies, Hartung,' Hoffmann snapped confidently. 'Remember what that Jew scribbler Heine once said when asked where he wanted to be on the Day of Judgement? England, because everything there happens a hundred years later than elsewhere!' There was a ripple of laughter, in which Hartung joined, although he was mildly surprised that a ruffian like Hoffmann had ever heard of Heine.

'All right, once in, beat up the whole damned estuary. According to those pansies in Intelligence, most of the Tommy's naval shipping is in the George Fifth Dock. That means it'll take them at least twenty minutes to get a craft out of the dock and through the lock. The real danger might be their aircraft. So in quick, shoot up as much as you can, and use your fish if you can spot anything worth expending a valuable torpedo on.' He paused momentarily. 'Now for all of you, this will be the first time, the very first time.' He looked around the circle of tense young faces illuminated by the pale yellow of the dipped lamps. 'It won't be anything at all like you've anticipated. I was at the Skagerrak as a lad of sixteen, and I know. When the shit hits the fan, anything and everything can and probably will go wrong. So, gentlemen,' Hoffmann fixed them with a hard look on his tough, wind-reddened face, though Hartung could see the look of concern in his eyes, 'I want you to do your best. Knock out as many Tommies as you can. But I *don't* want any dead heroes. All right, enough talk. Back to your ships . . . Give 'em hell. . . .

One minute later, the great Maybach engines were spluttering into life everywhere. Hartung flung a last glance over his ship, as the tanker began to edge away from the powerful, lean ships, waiting there with their engines throbbing like racing dogs eager to be let off the lead. Everyone of the deck crew was at his allotted position. It was time to be off.

'Ahead port! Ahead starboard!' he commanded.

The two wing engines roared. The whole boat shuddered with the strain of restraining nearly 2000 hp. Down below the chief mechanic thrust the throttle levers forward. The sound was deafening. The stink of burning diesel instantly filled the ship. Suddenly the sharply cut bow lifted clear out of the water. At thirty knots an hour the nine E-boats slashed through the dark-green sea, leaving a great V of wild water foaming white behind them, racing westwards towards the battle to come. . . .

FOUR

'Damn this fog!' Peter Harding cursed, coughing a little as the cold, wet damp penetrated his throat. 'Can't see a hand before your damned eyes.'

'Sea-rook, that's what they call it along this coast.' Hurry commented as he stood there next to Harding on the bridge, muffled up in the hood of his duffle coat so that. he looked like a hard-faced nun addicted to the communion wine.

'I don't care what the hell they call it, Chief. All I'm concerned with is that if the Jerries are coming, they could easily slip in through this little lot.' He peered out at the rolling waves of white and told himself visibility was not much more than fifty yards. For all he knew, the whole German fleet could be out there. 'And if I let them through, seeing I'm the one that got the squadron into this, Howling Mad Lucas has promised to have me keel-hauled.'

There was even a shadow of a smile on Hurry's usually gloomy face at the mention of their big, bearded commander who was known behind his back as 'Howling Mad' on account of his habit of baying like a mad hound when he was enraged, which was often, 'Ay, he's the lad most likely to do it, sir.' Hurry commented. 'But there's one consolation.'

'What's that?' Harding asked, gaze concentrated on his front, as the motor launch crept at a snail's pace through the fog, ears cocked to pick up the slightest sound. 'We'll hear them before they'll hear us.'

Harding swung round on the petty officer. 'And how the devil can you know that, Chief?'

'If you'd had as many nights out in Brid Bay as I've had,

sir, with the wind freezing yer bollocks off, so that a bloke wondered if he was ever going to get his John Thomas up again – that is providing his missus were prepared to spread the pearly gates, which mostly she weren't –'

'Oh get on with it, Chief!' Harding interrupted, knowing that with half a chance, the gaunt petty officer would be off on yet another tirade against his wife's lack of sexual willingness.

'Well, if you'd have suffered like me out here, you'd have known well enough from which direction the prevailing wind hereabouts comes, cos it's always sodding freezing. It's a north-westerly. Now do you get me, sir?'

'Of course! It would carry the sound from the general direction the Jerries must come to us.'

'Ay, that's right, sir.'

'So, if we closed down the engines altogether,' Harding said urgently, 'we'd have even a better chance of hearing – that is if they're coming and they're coming our way.'

'Ay, sir. Only one thing, if we're caught out here in Brid Bay with our drawers down, while old Jerry is coming in from another direction, yon Howling Mad Lucas'll have something to say, mark my words, sir.'

'The bark of Howling Mad Lucas is worse than his bite, Chief,' Harding said with more confidence than he felt.

'Famous last words,' was Chief Petty Officer Hurry's gloomy comment. . . .

'Starboard side, *Leutnant*,' *Obermaat* Thomsen hissed. 'Two of them I think.'

Hartung knew it was useless to attempt to use his night-glasses. In this pre-dawn pea-souper they would be no good. He'd have to rely on his own eyes and ears. 'Bring about forty-five degrees,' he ordered *sotto voce*, as if whatever was out there might hear him. 'Engine-room – half speed.'

Almost immediately the lithe lean craft's sharp bow dropped into the water and the usual high-speed buffeting ceased, for which Hartung was profoundly grateful. Even after three years with the *S-Boote** he had still not been able to overcome the stomach-upsets and violent vomiting that the usual dash at thirty knots occasioned.

In tense silence, the two men on the bridge peered through the white wet fog, trying to make out the dark shadows now looming out of the mist. To Hartung, they appeared to be merchantmen of perhaps three thousand tons, seemingly loaded right down in the water and steering a north-westerly course.

'What do you make of them, *Obermaat*?' Hartung asked at last.

'My guess Ellerman Wilson Line – two coastal freighters. Pre-World War One by the look of those funnels. Coal-burners too. Can't you smell 'em, *Leutnant*?'

Hartung sniffed the damp air and nodded his agreement. He knew, of course, that they couldn't be German, so close to the enemy coast; yet at the same time they could be one of the neutrals, Swedish or Dutch, plying their trade with Hull. Orders were not to sink neutral shipping if it were not absolutely necessary. 'All right,' he hissed, as they sailed on, unaware that their progress was being observed by some eighty pairs of keen eyes. 'We'll tag on to them. It's obvious they're heading for Hull. They might just be the fellows we're looking for to get us past that gun battery.'

'*Jawohl, Herr Leutnant*!' Thomsen snapped, bringing the wheel round and steering a new course after the two merchantmen, which were almost invisible again as the fog clutched them once more in its white clutches, 'And what about the Flotilla Leader? Do we inform him.'

Hartung chuckled. 'Let him know so that he can rake in all the glory and grab a piece of tin to stick on his big chest while we scratch our arses out in the cold! Never in this world, Thomsen. Absolute radio silence now and let the Old Man find his own way into the estuary. . . .'

---

*German name for E-boat.

'Rum up, sir!' Chief Petty Officer Hurry grunted and thrust a steaming mug of tea-and-rum at the frozen officer who had now been on the bridge for six hours.'

'A little drop of Nelson's blood is just what the doctor ordered,' Harding said and clasped the mug in both gloved hands, grateful for its warmth, feeling the steam thaw out the end of his nose.

'Don't make it like they used to do. Now in the first lot at Jutland –'

'Jutland!' Harding exclaimed, taking a first tentative sip. 'Don't tell me you were at Jutland, Chief?'

'Course I was. I was a three-striper in those days. Mind you, some of those cheeky sods of ratings think I was with the Admiral at Trafalgar.'

Harding grinned, savouring the hot drink. 'Then you could have got out of this lot if you had wanted, Chief? At least you'd be eligible for a nice cushy desk job, instead of freezing out here.'

'Might as well be here, getting me goolies frozen up,' Hurry grunted. 'For all the snake I get in bed back home. I swear my missus wouldn't let me have it, except on Saturday nights naturally after our bath, if I was the last man on –' He stopped short. 'What was that, sir?'

'What was what?' Harding asked, lowering his mug.

'Out there – to starboard!' Hurry said urgently, peering through the white gloom.

Harding forgot the drink, eyes narrowed to slits, his ears already aware of the soft throb of powerful engines, lots of them. 'There!' he said, pointing to the first sinister black outline looming out of the fog. 'And another!'

Hurry's mouth dropped open stupidly, as yet one more long lean shape appeared. 'Am I dreaming, sir?' he said weakly.

'No you're bloody well not!' Harding answered, sensing a sudden weakness in his legs and realizing that he was breathing very rapidly. 'They're Jerry E-boats all right!'

'What now, sir?' Hurry asked.

For a long moment Harding didn't answer, as the E-boats sailed by them like grey ghosts. Ever since he had first entered Dartmouth as a thirteen year old, he had been training for this moment; yet he hesitated, for he knew he was hopelessly outnumbered. One word from his mouth and it would all commence: the slaughter of war, which would leave no one untouched. It was a terrible decision to make in cold blood, but it was one he knew he had to make.

Hurry seemed to read his thoughts. 'Sir,' he whispered, 'no one would blame yer for not tackling that lot all by yerself. Even Howling Mad Lucas –'

'Report the enemy's position to HQ, Chief!' Harding interrupted him, his voice unnaturally harsh. 'Start engines!'

'Start engines it is, sir!'

With a tremendous roar the engines started up. Now Harding knew there was no use attempting to conceal their presence in the bay.'

'*Engage enemy*!' he bellowed above the racket and grabbed hurriedly for the nearest stanchion as the craft hurtled forward, two white waves curling up high above the *ML 120*'s bow.

Almost immediately the gun crew opened up. The little craft reeled under the shock. A tracer shell howled through the fog and a spurt of water erupted, boiling a furious white, yards away from the nearest boat.

There was instant reaction from the Germans. A star shell sailed into the sky. *Crack*! It exploded above the sea between the two opponents, bathing the fog in an eerie glowing white. At once the E-boat commanders recognized the enemy who had stolen so close to them. Furiously, the coxswains swung to left and right, attempting to avoid the wildly speeding launch.

Green and red tracer came streaming towards *ML 120* like a myriad, swarming dragonflies, criss-crossing in mid-air, converging on the craft heading straight towards them on a collision course. Grimly Harding stared at what seemed a solid wall of tracer, telling himself that his

Lewis-guns were going to be little use against the Germans' quick-firing 20mm Oerlikons, knowing that if his gun crew didn't strike lucky in a moment, he would have to break left or right or crash into the nearest E-boat.

Again the gun thundered, making the whole launch shiver. A shell screamed towards the E-boat closest to them. Quite distinctly Harding heard the thud of its striking home. Next moment the forecastle of the E-boat disappeared in a thick burst of brilliant scarlet flame. The vessel seemed to stop, as if it had just run into an invisible wall and then it was limping forward once more, its bow crumpled like a banana skin, little figures starkly outlined against the flames, running wildly up and down its deck.

'Hard to port!' Harding screamed and grabbed for support as *ML 120* heeled wildly and came roaring round in a tremendous flurry of white water, her aft Lewis-gunners already sending a stream of tracer towards the enemy, while behind them the sea churned and frothed crazily, the air suddenly full of the stink of cordite.

The battle had commenced.

FIVE

The long, lean E-boat slid into the entrance of the Humber. Above, the unsuspecting merchantman towered, so close that Hartung could see the rusty patches and flaking paint of her hull. In spite of the mist, which was thinning now, it would only take a deck look-out one glance over her side to spot the unwelcome guest. Hartung tensed as they edged their way by the unseen gun battery on Spurn Point, feeling the sweat break out all over his body despite the dawn cold. All around his silent crew, their faces white and drawn, did the same. They knew the danger they were in. At this range, even the poorest gunner couldn't miss; they'd be blown out of the very water!

Now the first of the two merchantmen had cleared the entrance and was beginning to gather speed a little as it entered the main channel, marked by unlit sound buoys. Hartung gave a small sigh of relief. Now it was their turn. Slowly, maddeningly slowly, the old tub worked its way through the entrance.

'*Grosse Kacke am Christbaum!*' Thomsen cursed bitterly at Hartung's side. 'That old pot can't be doing more than five knots!'

'*Shut it!*' Hartung hissed, feeling his heart thumping away like a trip-hammer. *Were they going to pull it off?*

The seconds passed leadenly. Now the mist was thinning even more. Instinctively Hartung knew that it could be a matter of moments now before they were discovered.

Before them, a tiny figure in white had appeared at the stern of the first merchantman, with what looked like a tub in his hands. Hartung was transfixed as the man lifted the container to the guard-rail and prepared to throw what was probably trash from the galley overboard before they reached their berth. As if by magic, the gulls dropped out of the mist and screaming hysterically, dived for the trash. Angrily the man in white waved his hand at them. Abruptly he stopped, mouth opened stupidly as he spotted the long white craft hiding in the lee of the second merchantman.

For what seemed an age, he just stood there, rooted to the spot. Suddenly he dropped the can over the side and bellowed.

'*Full ahead*!' Hartung cried, tightening his stomach muscles instinctively to withstand the shock which would come soon. With a great roar, the E-boat lurched. Abruptly its nose was high in the air, a huge white sweep of water on both sides of the stern. In an instant the torpedo-mate, his black leather coat soaked at once and gleaming, steadied himself over his firing lever. Behind him the oerlikon gunner glued his eye to his sight, as the first wild star shell burst in a gleam of hard silver over the estuary, hollowing out Hartung's sharply handsome face into a death's head. . . .

'Great balls of flaming fire!' Howling Mad Lucas threw back his head and bayed with rage, while Sparks fearfully cowered at the side of the little bridge.

Roxburgh, Lucas's second-in-command, said in that mild-mannered, if anxious manner of his, 'I say, sir, do you think they've got it right?'

Lucas, his face almost purple with rage, a vein ticking furiously at his temple, thrust the signal Sparks had just brought up at him, as if he would have liked to have shoved it in Roxburgh's chubby, bearded face. 'Of course it's right, you silly sod. Harding's fighting what appears to be the whole sodding Boche navy and now one of their E-boats has sodding well got into the Humber – or so they think. The balloon's gone up, Roxburgh and we're out here like sodding virgins at a dance keeping our knobbly knees together so that no nasty sailorman can put his nasty paw up our skirts –' Howling Mad broke off, gasping for breath.

'I say, sir,' Roxburgh breathed, his fear, tinged with respect. 'You do have a way with words, don't you?' Howling Mad glared at him, his eyes bulging out of his purple face, as if they might pop out at any moment. 'What's the drill now then, sir?' Roxburgh asked hastily.

Instead of answering his question directly, Howling Mad swung round on the signaller who was trying to make himself as small as possible against the bulkhead. 'You Sparks.'

'Sir,' he quavered fearfully, knowing that in his rages Howling Mad had been known to toss offending ratings over the side of the ship. 'Get a message off to Flag-Officer, Hull. Tell him I'll detach one of my ships to wait for the Jerry coming out of the estuary.' In spite of his rage, Howling Mad grinned, showing a mouthful of to-bacco-stained, sawn-off teeth. 'A couple of Jerry shells into Hull can't do any harm, probably scare the shit out of those lazy dockies at least. Might make 'em work. The rest will go to the assistance of Mr Harding. Got it?'

'Yessir.' Sparks disappeared hastily, glad to have got away so lightly.

'Bunts,' Howling Mad bellowed, leaning over the bridge to where the signaller tensed over his Aldis lamp. '*BUNTS*! Signal the squadron, new course . . .' Hastily he gave the rating the course bearing.

At his side, Lieutenant Roxburgh beamed, as the squadron swung round in a great curve of wild water, and the engines began to whine ear-splittingly at full power. 'Here we go, sir,' he chortled. 'Tally ho, what!'

'Oh shut up, you silly sod!' was all he got back from his commander. . . .

ML 120 reeled again as a shell slammed home nearby. Water drenched the bullet-pocked bridge and down below, the gun-layer, bleeding from a terrible scalp-wound, pulled the lanyard. A three-inch shell howled flatly across the gap between the motor-launch and the racing E-boats – and missed. Instantly the enemy's oerlikons began to chatter again. Tracer streamed towards them in a blinding brilliant scarlet, cannon-shells exploding into the sea all around, whining off into the thinning mist.

'Torpedo to port!' Rawlings screamed urgently as the E-boat broke off to the right and went roaring away, throwing up a tremendous wake.

Furiously Hurry swung the wheel round, while Harding stared horror-stricken at the tell-tale flurry of bubbles which marked the torpedo's path, his hands gripping the bridge-stanchion, white-knuckled with tension. It hissed by with mere inches to spare. Moments later it exploded somewhere on the hidden shore with a thunder of noise.

But Harding had no time to think about the near miss. The next E-boat was coming in, oerlikons spitting white fire, two dark figures crouched over its torpedoes. Harding swallowed, praying that the three-inch gun would rattle them enough to make them miss. Below on the shell-littered, soaked deck, the gun-layer slumped over his breech, unconscious from loss of blood. Rawlings didn't hesitate. He sprang forward, thrust the unconscious rating to one side, and commanded: 'Load – for Christ's sake!'

The loader slammed home another shell. Rawlings sighted frantically. He pulled the lanyard. The cannon erupted. Burnt cordite surged upwards to the bridge. Harding closed his burning eyes. There was a huge roar and Harding gasped as he flashed open his eyes again. The nearest E-boat had come to a sudden stop, her whole superstructure a blazing shambles, her wireless masts snapped off and trailing in the water like broken limbs, most of her bridge shot away with panic-stricken sailors – those who were not lying dead or dying in the tangled confusion of the deck – springing over the side into the icy water.

'We've got her!' Rawlings cried jubilantly. 'We've –'

His cry ended in a scream of absolute agony in the same instant that the hammerblow smashed into Harding's shoulder and he felt a searing pain that sent him reeling against the bridge, all breath knocked from his lungs, only barely aware of Chief Petty Officer Hurry sinking slowly, very slowly, at his side.

Through clouded eyes, as if glimpsed through the opaque waters of an aquarium, feeling the stricken motor launch coming to a slow stop and beginning to slant to port for some reason he could not quite make out, Harding watched as Hurry fought death on the deck at his feet, which for some strange reason was now turning bright red.

'I'm knackered,' the old CPO groaned, 'proper knackered. . . .' Then after what seemed an age, with his white head bent, one weak hand trying in vain to keep him upright there, he said, 'Now she'll never let me have it. . . .'

'Chief,' Harding tried to say, fighting off the wavering red haze which threatened to overcome him at any moment, but somehow he couldn't get any further than 'Chief. . . .'

The Chief's head hit the deck and he turned with infinite weariness and looked up at the young lieutenant wavering back and forth above him. Drops of red dripped on his gaunt upturned face. For the life of him, Harding could not understand how they got there. Only later, much later, when he had time to think of Chief Petty Officer Hurry's death in the naval hospital, did he realize it must have been his own blood which had stained the dying man's face.

'Lieutenant,' Hurry croaked, his faded eyes pleading now. Harding could not do anything but incline his head.

'Don't let me . . . die . . . at sea,' he coughed thickly and bright red blood started to seep from the corner of his mouth and join the film which was beginning to cover his face. 'Take me . . . home. . . .'

His head fell to one side and he was dead. It was the last thing that Harding saw before he slumped unconscious to the deck. . . .

The E-boat was hitting the water at seventy kilometres an hour now. It was as if she were striking a series of solid brick walls. On both sides of the vaguely glimpsed estuary, the sirens were howling and searchlights were cutting the grey dawn gloom, trying to pinpoint the flying, leaping boat.

To their left, the crew of the racing craft saw a series of dull brown barges plodding wearily on their way up the Humber, heading for some inland port. Their decks were piled high with great drums of oil. 'Burst from the oerlikon!' Hartung screamed, saving his twin torpedoes for a better target. The gunner swung his twin-cannon round. At a thousand rounds a minute, the white tracer shells converged on the tug. In an instant, the tug's structure disappeared beneath that tremendous blast of flying metal and the crew were flinging themselves over the side, struggling crazily in the water in a desperate attempt to get away before the fuel went up. That wasn't to be. There was a tremendous flash. Scarlet flame split the grey sky in crazy, zig-zag streaks. A wave of burning oil rolled towards the swimming bargees and engulfed them with fire. For a couple of seconds they seemed to swim on, dripping fire from their burning arms, and then they disappeared underneath the water for good. Hartung turned away hastily, sickened. The E-boat raced on.

'*Attention front, sir*!' Thomsen yelled in warning.

Hartung flung a wild glance in the direction he had indicated. Before them, the lock gate which let into George Fifth Dock was beginning to open to allow what looked like a small armed trawler to emerge, with men already running forward to take the tarpaulin from the hooded gun on the vessel's foredeck. Hartung reacted immediately. 'Gunner,' he ordered, 'target twelve hundred – *fire*!'

The gunner hit the elevator pedal. The two thin air-cooled barrels of oerlikon dropped immediately. The running men leapt into the centre of his ring sight. He pressed the firing button. The twin 20mm cannon pounded crazily. Red and white tracer shells zipped through the air, dragging a glowing trail after them. They riveted a sudden line of gleaming silver metal along the trawler's bridge. The glass splintered into a crazy spider's web.

'Down! . . . For hell's sake, *down*!' Hartung screamed as the British dragged off the tarpaulin to reveal what looked like a six-pounder.

The gun layer dropped from his perch like a bird hit on the wing, as the oerlikon gunner's second burst ripped open his chest. Next to him the loader threw up his arms, as if he were climbing up an invisible ladder, in the same instant that the armed trawler smashed into the side of the jetty and came to an abrupt halt, black smoke streaming out of its shell-riddled funnel at a dozen spots.

In a wide insolent sweep, the E-boat roared off, leaving the stricken vessel to its fate. Behind it on the jetty, an infuriated sentry started to blast individual shots from his rifle at the wildly bucking German craft. Hartung laughed. But he knew now that time was running out. He had to plant his torpedoes and get out while there was still a chance to do so. Already he thought he could hear the drone of aircraft engines, somewhere above him in the mist, and they could only be that of a Tommy; their own air strike had obviously been cancelled, as Hoffmann had predicted it would be.

'Ready you, torpedomen, with your fish?' he bellowed above the roar of the engines.

'*Fertig, Herr Leutnant*!' each man cried back, as they huddled precariously over their deadly 'fish', both filled with two thousand pounds of high explosive.

'Targets?' he yelled to Thomsen, as the E-boat zig-zagged across the Humber, racing towards the low hills on the Lincolnshire side of the estuary.

'*There*, Lieutenant!'

Hastily Hartung followed the direction of the petty officer's outflung hand.

Barely visible through the greyness, was the long thin outline of what appeared to be a large tanker, scuttling for what cover the far bank offered.

'Difficult!' Hartung roared, his face wet with flying spray.

'Tempting though, sir!' Thomsen yelled back. 'Looks like a ten thousand tonner. Put a lot of Tommy cars out of commission if we sink her!'

Hartung nodded, doing a rapid calculation, knowing that the petty officer was right; the fleeing tanker was worth a torpedo. 'We'll have to come in from the quarter,' he said. 'Bad deflection angle. Hell, the fish could simply cannon off her without exploding.'

'Can be done, sir!' Thomsen persisted.

'*Natürlich*,' Hartung. '*Los hinterher*!'

Rapidly the flying E-boat began to close with the other vessel. The Lincolnshire mudflats below the hills started to loom ever larger. From some concealed pillbox, a slow machine gun started to spit tracer at them, hacking away like an ancient, bad-tempered wood pecker. At the bows of the E-boat one of the torpedomen yelped with pain and dropped to the heaving deck, hugging his wounded shoulder.

Hartung wasted no more time. It would have to be now or never. '*Feuer*!' he bellowed above the scream of the engines and the slap-slap of the boat hitting wave after wave. The remaining torpedoman pulled his trigger. Nothing happened!

'The mallet!' Hartung screamed. '*Hit it with the mallet*!'

The torpedoman smashed home the mallet kept for such emergencies. In that same instant, the machine gun on the other bank swept the bow with a burst of slugs. The torpedoman screamed shrilly, threw up his hands and fell over the side. Hartung momentarily sickened turned his head, not wanting to see what came out at the other side, as the screws churned up the unfortunate man's body, ripping it into bloody chunks.

'The fish . . . she's running straight on course!' Thomsen yelled, unaffected by the terrible death of his comrade.

Hartung stared in awe as the white frothy wake revealed the torpedo's path as it flashed towards the fleeing oil tanker, knowing that the tanker still had time to manoeuvre out of danger if a look-out spotted the torpedo in time.

'She's spotted it!' Thomsen seemed to read his mind. 'She's turning, the bitch . . . she's turning!'

Hartung held his breath. Which way would she turn? Into or out of the racing torpedo's path?

Slowly the big tanker started to turn inwards. Hartung slapped Thomsen on the back hard. 'Right into the shit!' he yelled. 'Nothing'll save her –'

The rest of his words were drowned by a tremendous explosion. The tanker trembled violently, but continued to move onwards. Suddenly a plate fell from her side and another. There was a terrible groaning sound as metal rent and bent and ripped apart. The look of triumph on Hartung's face vanished instantly. He was too much a sailor to take pleasure in a fine ship going down. Suddenly the tanker seemed to leap out of the water. Later Hartung would swear he had been able to see her screws churning quite clearly. Next instant she smashed down again and simply fell in two parts. Almost at once she started to sink, bow first, while aft great flames shot upwards like a gigantic blow torch. Hartung had seen enough. The tanker had had it. 'Come on,' he roared above the cheers of his crew and the crackle of burning material on the stricken tanker, 'let's get the hell out of here . . . we've done enough. . . .'

Rawlings slapped his face again. Harding barely felt the blow. He shook his head, ignoring the burning pain in his arm and side. 'Again,' he said thickly. Rawlings, his face streaked with blood and cordite stains, gritted his teeth and did so.

Abruptly, everything jolted into focus and Rawlings' anxious young face, as he stared down at the skipper sprawled on the shattered, debris-littered bridge next to the dead Hurry, became quite clear.

'What . . . what's the situation, Number One?' he asked weakly, forming his words with care, as a series of shudders racked the dying craft and a wave of heat from below hit him in the face.

'The Jerries have sheered off . . . Looks as if Howling Mad has engaged them.' Rawlings indicated the muffled rumble of gunfire somewhere further out at sea.

'And the ship?'

'We've taken some terrible punishment, Captain. We've got a flash-fire down below and we're pretty badly holed.'

Harding inwardly groaned and thought dejectedly that he had made a ballsup of his first action. What would his father, the admiral, say? He raised himself painfully. 'What have you done, Number One?'

'Done?' Rawlings asked a little stupidly. 'I thought sir, you'd make the decision . . . Abandon ship, I thought.' He lowered his voice, as if the very words were obscene.

Harding looked at Hurry's craggy dead face and remembered the dying chief's last words to him. 'Abandon ship?' he said with real anger. 'I'm not abandoning *ML 120*. Here, help me up.'

Willingly Rawlings raised him to his feet.

Harding gripped a stanchion with blood-wet hands and gasped as he saw for the first time the extent of the damage: the debris-littered deck, the smashed wireless masts snapped off like broken matchsticks, the great hole in the bow through which black smoke escaped in thick billowing clouds, tinged with oil.

'Number One,' he commanded, holding on as the boat lurched once more and nearly threw him down, 'get that damned fire under control. Tell the engine room crew to get up to top.'

'Yes, Captain.' Stepping over CPO Hurry's body, the young sub-lieutenant relayed his order swiftly and stepped back to the captain, who hung to the stanchion as if his very life depended upon it. 'What now, sir?'

'Lighten the ship . . . throw everything over the side. We've got to keep her afloat so that we can beach her.'

'Even the torpedoes sir? They cost two thousand quid a piece!'

'Even the torpedoes!' Harding grunted through gritted teeth, feeling the waves of pain threaten to overcome him again. 'This ship is worth more than those damned torpedoes . . . Now get to it!'

Hartung gripped the bridge rail, his nerves jingling, as he watched the merchantman start to sink, while the guns of the Spurn Head battery thundered over her holed bows trying angrily to reach the E-boat concealed on the other side. Now that he had used his last torpedo to sink the Tommy and thus escape from the estuary, he was practically defenceless, save for the twin 20mm cannon – and they were no match for the heavy guns of the battery.

On the water, the flames of the burning oil grew ever larger, relentlessly advancing on the men swimming everywhere. The first sailors were enveloped in it. A man threw up his arms and leapt clean out of the water. Another folded his hands, as if he were praying. The searing flame swept on. Hartung caught one last horrifying glimpse of a group of sailors doing a frenzied dance of death in the water, their burning bodies galvanized into violent, agonized action by the unbearable heat; then the E-boat was through, in clear view of the gunners in their steel turrets only half a kilometre away. Heavy calibre shells began to rain down about them at once, rocking the ship from side to side and drenching the bridge in spray.

Hartung frantically thrust the helmsman from the wheel and grabbed it himself as the engines raced to full power. He violently flung the wheel back and forth, sending the deck crew scrambling for holds, steering the heeling craft in a series of zig-zags, trying to out-think the gunners on shore, hoping against hopes that his tactics would unsettle them until the mist banks swallowed him up.

Now steel and water rained down on the lone enemy craft. The superstructure was ripped apart and gleaming holes appeared everywhere in the metal. A wireless mast crashed to the deck, engulfing it in a mess of sparking, crackling wires. Hartung flung the wheel round hard, the threshing screw churning the struggling men in the water into bloody pulp. Hartung no longer saw or cared. His whole being was now concentrated on the white line of boiling water where the sea struck the river emerging from the estuary. It was the token of his escape – *he must make it*!

Time and time again the boat rocked as a near miss sent it heaving with its shattered masts almost touching the water. Now Hartung could smell burning. He didn't care. He had to reach that thin line of water. Next to him Thomsen screamed shrilly, like a shocked, hysterical woman. He sank to his knees, as if in supplication, his spine gleaming a bright white in the mess of blood that had been his back. An instant later, his head hit the metal deck with the sound of a coconut being split open by a heavy hammer. The E-boat roared on.

And then with the clarity of a sudden vision, Hartung saw he was making a fatal mistake. He was letting the Tommy gun-crews out-think him. They knew he was heading straight for that line of boiling water that signified the open sea. But why should he? The S-3s* had the most

*The most common make of E-boats used by the German Navy in 1939.

shallow draft of all. He didn't need deep water to make his escape, as the Tommy gunners thought he did.

Crazily he laughed out loud. '*Gedacht . . . getan!*'* He roared at the dead Thomsen. 'Bring her round – closer inshore!'

'Inshore, sir?' the helmsman yelled back. 'But the shallows, sir, we could easily run aground!'

'Here – give me the wheel!' As yet another six-inch shell howled over their heads, Hartung thrust the man away from the wheel and took over himself. He swung the ship round violently. The fabric screamed in protest. At the stern the screws thrashed the water to a white boiling fury and then they were off, racing along the coastline with the enemy shells falling hopelessly out of range behind them. They had done it!

Harding, a dirty towel held to his side, to staunch the flow of blood from the great tear which had been rent in his flesh, listened to a black-faced Rawlings making his report, at the same time surveying the chaos of the deck. From below, the sailors' metal lockers had vomited their contents and now letters, photographs and books were swimming around in the confused mess of the tangled wiring and shattered superstructure that lay on the deck.

'Thanks Rawlings,' he said when Rawlings had finished. 'You've done a good job. At least the damned fire below is out.'

Rawlings wiped the sweat off his blackened forehead with the back of his hand. 'And what now sir?'

Harding stared at the smudge of coast just visible through the grey mist. To judge by the brown cliffs instead of white chalk ones characteristic of Bridlington Bay, their position must be somewhere south of the resort town. 'I think we've got to be between Bridlington and Hornsea, Number One.' He made a quick calculation.

*Roughly – 'thought – done'.

'Don't think we'll make Hornsea in this condition.'

Rawlings nodded his head in agreement. 'Yes, we're only taking on water slowly, sir. But without any power, we'd go down before we could make Hornsea.'

'My thoughts, Number One. But she'll steer. So,' Harding shrugged. 'We'll try to beach her. We owe it to the dead. We – well, you understand, Number One?' he ended a little lamely.

'Of course, sir. That beach doesn't look too far away and the tide's running our way. Sir,' he looked at Harding in sudden alarm, as the captain swayed against the bullet-pocked bridge, his face ashen and his eyes closed for a moment, 'are you all right?'

Harding thrust away Rawlings' hand. 'Yes . . . all right, Number One,' he breathed weakly. 'Just a dizzy spell . . .' He laughed. 'Can't stand heights, I suppose.'

'But sir –'

'No buts, Number One, let's bring her round . . . and detail somebody to set off signal rockets. It looks like the end of the world out there, but there might be some farmer or other who'll see them.' He winced. 'Come on, give me a hand.'

Slowly the battered ship began to shift towards the muddy shore. It was nearly over now.

'Signal rockets to port, sir!' the look-out sang out.

Leutnant Hartung flashed a look in that direction, and glimpsed the exploding rocket, a faint pink through the greyness. He bit his bottom lip. What did it mean?

For the last half hour, the lone E-boat had been making its way along the East Riding coast, keeping well into the shelter of the shore, taking advantage of the mist which still clung to it. Hartung knew from the intelligence briefing at Wilhelmshaven, that the RAF had two bomber fields close by at Leconfield and Driffield, and he reasoned that their aircraft would be ranging further out into the North Sea, where visibility would be clear. As long as he clung to the coast he would be relatively safe. Then, when the heat was off, and the RAF fliers would be returning, he'd make a high-speed dash for the safety of Dutch territorial waters. From there he'd sneak back to Emden, the closest German naval base.

For a moment or two Hartung pondered what to do next, as the sky ahead was illuminated once again by a red signal rocket; then he made his decision. 'Half speed, engine room!' he ordered. 'Gunner!' The oerlikon gunner swung round on his perch. 'What have you got left in the way of ammo?' Hartung asked hastily.

'About two thousand rounds, sir.'

Hartung frowned. Enough for a couple of minutes' firing. 'All right,' he said. 'Stand by to open fire.'

'Sir!'

At half-speed the lean E-boat crept forward through the still water, every man in her crew tense and anxious, knowing now that they were in grave danger. Below Hartung could hear one of the petty officers handing out grenades and machine pistols to the deck crew. It was good thinking, he told himself, but such small arms would be of little use against a regular Tommy warship. Now his ears became aware of the sound of what appeared to be water slapping against a hull. He wiped the sweat from his creased forehead. Was there a ship moored out there barring further progress? But why the signal rockets? For a moment he was tempted to order full speed and make a run for it, but he restrained his impulse in time. That might just be fatal; it would be a long haul to Dutch waters with the RAF bombing all the time. At his temple a vein began to tic.

The strange sound became suddenly louder, interspersed by the type of creaking that is made when metal is subjected to severe strain. Completely mystified, Hartung hissed at the look-out, straining his eyes through the mist, 'Can't you see anything yet, man?'

'No sir, I – *sir*, there!'

Hartung followed the direction of the excited sailor's

outstretched hand. A faint dark shape was looming out of the mist. Hartung swallowed hard. Was all his success in the estuary going to be for nothing? There was no mistaking it. The grey paint and the shape gave the vessel away – it was a naval craft of some kind.

The deck crew raised their weapons, some of them with stick grenades held high. At the twin-cannon, the sweating gunner clicked off a catch and strained his head forward, trying to make out the details of the strange craft, which seemed to be motionless.

Then, with dramatic suddenness, the mist clouds billowed to one side and the vessel lying there was clearly revealed to the tense sailors.

'Holy strawsack!' a petty officer gasped. 'What a mess!'

'What a mess indeed,' an astonished Hartung echoed under his breath.

The Tommy motor-launch was wallowing in the troughs, the small waves breaking over her shattered, battle-strewn deck, dead sailors lying among the debris like broken dolls, with her torn white ensign lying limp at her holed stern.

'Heaven, arse and cloudburst!' a sailor cried on the deck, lowering his hand grenade in awe. 'What the shit's keeping her afloat?'

'Prayer, I shouldn't imagine,' Hartung breathed and then in his usual harsh decisive voice. 'All right, let's close up. Gunner, stand by!'

The E-boat swung round and Hartung, his face set like the hunter he was, prepared for the easy kill.

'E-boat sir . . . E-boat. . .!' Dimly through the red mist which threatened to engulf him again, Harding clinging with the last strength to the stanchion, as he willed *ML 120* to make the shore, heard Rawlings' cry of alarm.

He opened his eyes. For an instant everything was blurred and vague. He blinked several times, now aware of the roar of high speed engines.

A lean shape was racing towards them, a white bone in its teeth, and even in his weak, semi-conscious shape he recognized it – an S-3 type of German E-boat. His heart sank. Even as Rawlings staggered to the last remaining Lewis-gun and started firing, he knew it was hopeless. They hadn't a chance against the German. His gaze fell on the dead body of Chief Petty Officer Hurry at his feet, the faded blue eyes still open and staring upwards. 'Sorry, Chief,' he said weakly, slurring his words like a drunk. 'I'm afraid we're not going to make it this time. . . .'

Now they were within fifty metres range. Hartung could see every detail of the wrecked Tommy absolutely clearly, even to the look of frustrated rage on the blackened face of the barehead young officer who was struggling furiously with the jammed machine gun to aft, up to his ankles in sea-water. How the Tommy craft had survived such a terrible beating was beyond him; he was going to do them a favour by sinking the ship.

He cupped his hands around his mouth and flashing a look at white, helpless faces of the British sailors standing there, their shoulders bent in defeat, waiting for the slaughter like dumb animals, cried in English, 'Abandon ship . . . I'll give you sixty seconds . . . Come on, abandon ship!'

The oerlikon gunner swung his twin cannons round so that the deadly barrels were directly aimed at the vessel's pock-marked bridge. Out of the corner of his eye, Hartung could see the knuckles of his hands begin to whiten as he prepared to fire.

'Come on!' Hartung called, more gruffly now. 'Your time's nearly up . . . Gunner, prepare to fire!'

'*Jawohl Herr Leutnant*!'

Hesitantly, one of the Tommy ratings picked up a float and flung it into the water. Behind him another man started to take off his shoes. They were going to do it, Hartung told himself.

Suddenly, a familiar face, admittedly pale with a trickle of congealed blood running down the side of his head from a scalp-wound, appeared over the edge of the wrecked bridge. Hartung gasped audibly. *It couldn't be*! It was. There was no mistaking those eyes and that lean tall figure. It was Peter . . . Peter Harding!

'*Peter*!' he gasped.

Below, the crew members stared up at their captain, as if he had suddenly gone mad.

'Peter,' Hartung raised his voice. 'It's me . . . Horst!'

The wounded man on the other bridge moved his head terribly slowly as if it were worked by stiff wires, trying to locate the sound, but the eyes were vacant, too dazed to recognize the speaker.

'Captain, aircraft engines!' the look-out called briskly. 'Coming in from the west!'

The cry broke the heavy silence. Hartung realized their own danger. Below the gunner called out. 'Shall I sink her, sir?'

'No!' Hartung rapped.

'*What*?' the gunner called incredulously.

Hartung ignored him. The sound of the aircraft somewhere above in the low cloud was getting louder by the second. 'Full ahead!' he yelled.

The gunner seemed for a moment as if he might disobey Hartung's order; the target at that range was too tempting. But then reluctantly he spun his twin cannon round and pumping the pedal started to elevate them to meet the new danger from the sky. Next instant, the engines thundered at full power and the E-boat surged away, racing for the east at thirty knots an hour. . . .

Exactly thirty minutes later, the crippled *ML 120* gently nudged into the sand-banks off the little resort village of Aldborough, their immediate front lined with empty green-and-white painted railway coaches dragged there as holiday homes by fresh-air enthusiasts in the late twenties. Rawlings went over the side first and gasped with the shock of the cold water which reached up to his waist. He waded the fifty yards or so to the beach proper without difficulty and then, satisfied that it was safe, returned to organize the others, while the *ML 120* started to settle by the stern, wallowing back and forth at the whim of the waves.

First the wounded were brought ashore, then the secret papers. The dead followed, lined up like so many pieces of driftwood on the wet, chill sand and covered hastily by a blood-stained tarpaulin.

Then and only then, did Lieutenant Peter Harding allow himself to be carried to the shore where with the rest, he watched the end of his first command, as the motor launch's bow rose almost vertically for one long moment before she slid into the water and disappeared from view. There was a ragged cheer from the men standing on the beach and then, supporting their wounded, each man wrapped in his own thoughts, the survivors started to limp up through the wet sand towards the houses. . . .

Part Two: 1940

ONE

The sea sparkled in the sun. Up on Dartmoor the snow still lay thick. But here, down at the coast, the January day was pleasantly warm and the grass around Slapton-Mere was already a spring-green.

Peter Harding took in the scene with pleasure as always and drew a deep breath for the last hundred yards he would run to Torcross. For three weeks now, ever since he had been discharged from the naval hospital at Portsmouth on convalescent leave, he had imposed the self-discipline of this four mile speed-march between Slapton and Torcross upon himself every morning. After three months in hospital, he knew he needed it if he were ever going to get back on sea-duty and be given a second command. Run a hundred yards, march a hundred yards, that was his system, and he was already feeling the benefit from it, in spite of his mother's morning protestation that he was 'overdoing it', and his father, the admiral's grunted comment over the edge of his *Times* that all a naval officer needed to keep fit was to 'keep his bowels open and believe in God'.

'Here, we go,' he said to himself and began to run towards the cluster of white-painted houses grouped around the local pub which made up the hamlet of Torcross. It was then that he spotted the Riley parked on the gravel path outside the pub and the lean figure clad in navy uniform leant against it, pensively drawing on a cigarette with an elegantly leather-gloved hand. It was only when he came almost level with the man that he saw to his astonishment that he was smoking his cigarette in a long black-and-white ivory cigarette-holder! The sight of a lieutenant-commander using such a thing stopped him in his tracks.

The officer looked at him with his long sardonic face and slowly removed the object from between his somewhat cruel-looking lips. 'I thought you young tigers of the fast-boat service trained on bad women and even worse whisky,' he said in a slow Etonian drawl.

Peter Harding giggled. 'Two pink gins are about my limit, sir. After that I start singing.' He came to the position of attention. 'Peter Harding, sir,' he said formally.

The strange lieutenant-commander looked up and down as he stood there in his white cricket sweater and baggy old flannels, his cheeks glowing a ruddy healthy hue. 'Yes, I know,' he said, obviously pleased with what he saw. 'My name is Fleming, Ian Fleming. I'm from Room Thirty-Nine, personal assistant to Admiral Godfrey.'

'Naval Int –' Harding started in astonishment.

'Room 39,' Lt Commander Ian Fleming said firmly and taking out the stump of his cigarette, screwed in another of his three-ring Moorland Specials, lighting it with the still glowing end. 'Filthy habit. Can't stop though. No will power, I suppose.' He took Harding's arm and steered him to the beach away from the pub. 'We can sit down here against this boat. You might lend me your towel to sit on. Uniforms cost a packet these days.'

Bewildered and confused and wondering why this strange and somewhat affected officer with his Etonian drawl had come all the way from the Admiralty to see him, Peter Harding drew the towel from around his neck and placed it on the shingle.

Carefully Fleming lowered himself on it and took out a silver flask. 'Malt,' he announced. 'Care for a drop?'

'No thank you, sir. I'm in training.'

'Good. The stuff's getting terribly hard to find now in London.'

He screwed off the cap and took several delicate sips, seemingly very interested in the ducks sweeping in and heading for the Mere. Finally he put the flask away carefully and opened the magazine which bulged from his greatcoat pocket. 'Read German, Harding?'

'No sir. I did French and Spanish at Britannia.'

'I see. No problem. I do, fluently as a matter of fact.' He tapped the magazine with the end of his cigarette-holder. 'This is the German Forces' weekly, called *Der Signal*. It's very glossy and nicely turned out production. Full of propaganda, of course, but it's required reading at Room 39.'

'Yessir.'

'Now do you recognize this particular teutonic hero?' Fleming opened the magazine to reveal a well-remembered face flashing a white-toothed triumphant smile at him from underneath a naval cap set at a rakish and decidedly non-regulation angle.

'Why, sir . . . It's Horst . . . Horst Hartung!'

'Exactly,' Fleming gave him a cool sardonic smile, as if he had achieved something, though a surprised Harding could not imagine just what that was. '*Leutnant zur See Hartung, der Held von Hull*,' he coughed, 'the hero of Hull, as the text has it, and proud winner of the first Iron Cross, First Class – mark you – to be bestowed upon a member of *Kriegsmarine*'s fast boat service. Your old pal is well on the way to becoming a second Priem.'

'You mean the chap who sank the *Royal Oak* in Scapa Flow last October, sir?'

'Yes.'

Harding whistled softly.

'Quite a hero.' Fleming's voice hardened suddenly and now his companion could see that behind the sardonic, somewhat affected personality there was a very hard, even ruthless individual. 'Now when did you last see this Boche?'

'In the summer of 1936, sir,' Harding blurted out, wondering where all this was leading. 'Well, not really. I *thought* I saw him just before I passed out last year during the raid on Hull. But I couldn't be sure . . . I was in a pretty bad state due to loss of blood.'

'Well, it got you a good gong, Harding. Gongs will be money in the bank after the war, mark my word . . . Yes, you definitely *did* see him that morning.'

'But how could you know, sir?' Harding asked incredulously.

'This, told us that you had.' Out of an inner pocket, he produced a wrinkled, worn envelope that looked as if it had passed through many hands and gave it to Peter, who gasped with surprise when he saw that it was addressed to him, care of The Admiralty.

Fleming chuckled. 'Yes, our hero is an enterprising sort of a chap. Go on, read it. It's in English. Besides it is addressed to you.' He took out his flask once more and started to sip at the contents delicately, while Peter fished out the letter with fingers that trembled slightly.

'Dear Peter,' he read. 'It is now six months since I wrote to you. That summer I think you understand it was better that I, as a German officer, did not write any more. . . .'

'His style is a little strange, isn't it?' Fleming commented, not taking his gaze off the ducks zooming in low over the sparkling sea. 'But it's not bad – for a Boche.'

Peter said nothing, but read on with growing excitement.

'. . . but I could not resist from writing to you, after I had seen what had happened to you and your ship that morning. Friends who go to Holland, will post this for me. Are you well? Have you recovered? Please answer to this address – *Willemsstraat* Groningen, the Netherlands. They have me a hero now and it would not be good if you wrote to me direct. Your friend Horst. PS. What news of the *Hoellenkatze*?' Peter flashed a glance at the date. It was the 15th October 1939.'

For a moment he sat there, too stunned to react and just

as he opened his mouth to ask the questions which were now racing through his mind in a confused jumbled mess, Fleming reacted for him. 'You are wondering what this is all about, aren't you, Harding?'

'Yessir.'

'I shall tell you.' Fleming put away his precious flask once more. 'Your letter was intercepted two months ago by the censors and in due course passed on to Room 39 for vetting.'

'But why, sir?' Peter protested, suddenly angry at the high-handed manner with which his personal mail had been treated.

'Why not?' Fleming countered unruffled. 'After all, it is somewhat strange, don't you think, that a serving officer of the Royal Navy should be corresponding with a Boche officer – and a hero to boot – during wartime?'

'But *I* wasn't corresponding, sir. He was writing to me.'

Fleming ignored the objection. 'Besides that little PS with the mention of the '*Hoellenkatze*' – German for 'hell-cat', if I'm not mistaken, has worried – and still does – some of my colleagues.' He looked directly at the red-faced young officer next to him with his green eyes hard and flashing fire so that instinctively Peter drew back. 'What does it mean?' he rapped harshly.

'It's the name of a girl . . . a girl who both of us knew once,' Peter shuddered. 'A sort of a nickname be-. cause . . . this girl was a decided fury when she was roused . . . That's all, sir. All quite harmless, sir, I assure you.'

'A German girl?'

'German-Jewish, sir.'

'And why should a Boche officer be enquiring about a Jewess?' Fleming persisted, his gaze boring into Peter's red, embarrassed face. 'Come on – why?'

'Because sir, she's in London . . . and she used to mean a lot to Horst, I mean Lieutenant Hartung.'

'What did she mean to him?'

Harding swallowed. 'I suppose you could say that

he . . . er . . . loved her, sir.' His face went an even deeper red.

'You mean he bedded her?' Fleming sneered, cynicism written all over his long face.

Peter nodded, but said nothing.

'But I always thought the Boche were like dogs? They make love, go away and don't write.'

Peter remained silent again.

'But this one does and that interests us too in Room 39. He writes to you, our Boche hero, and he enquires about a Jewish girl in London. Very interesting . . . very interesting indeed.' He tapped his front teeth with his ivory cigarette-holder. 'I think, young man, we'd better repair to yon tavern up there. I think you've got a story to tell me . . . Undoubtedly it will be a long one and to prevent *ennui* overcoming me entirely, I shall need the assistance of a whisky bottle.'

His mind suddenly full of the events of that summer in Wilhelmshaven, a completely confused Peter Harding let himself be led to the pub. . . .

TWO

It was what the Germans called 'Fuhrer weather'. The sun shone with remarkable brightness for that northern coast and the sea sparkled brilliantly. Everywhere the nineteenth century villas that lined the promenade had been painted and polished in honour of the Olympic Games, which were being held that summer in Berlin, making the normally grey, somewhat drab naval base of Wilhelmshaven appear gay and welcoming. There were even striped umbrellas outside the cafes. Although the women indulging themselves in *Kaffe und Kuchen*, tackling the mountainous cakes, piled high with cream, with typical north German seriousness, were not as elegant as those the British cadets had encountered in the Mediterranean training cruise of the previous summer, they were decently dressed and obviously prosperous. Germany, it was obvious to Cadet Peter Harding, taking in the sights with half-a-dozen others from *HMS Devonshire* had pulled itself out of the depression. In contrast, England looked positively shabby. This new Fuhrer of theirs, Adolf Hitler, whose scowling-faced portrait was even above the strangely named *abort** at the railway station, had put new life into the country within three short years, though the cheap papers back home were full of nasty stories of the methods he was using to do so.

Wilhelmshaven on this pleasant, lazy summer Sunday was peaceful enough, though. Of course there were fat-bellied Brownshirts everywhere, their jackboots highly polished and their chests heavy with the medals of the Old War, strutting around importantly; but the Party bully-

*toilet.

boys did not seem to be taken very seriously by the German sailors in their big floppy caps with the ribbons dangling behind, and their officers studiously refrained from answering the Brownshirts' polite salutes.

As the gunnery officer in charge of the Dartmouth cadets, a huge, bearded, bad-tempered lieutenant, known behind his back by the 'matelots' of *HMS Devonshire* as 'Howling Mad' Lucas (for some reason known only to them) had remarked before allowing them on shore-leave. 'The German Navy doesn't like these Party wallahs – at least the old officers don't. They won't even have them aboard at a wardroom shindig. But that doesn't mean you lot of snotties can get uppity with them.' He had wagged a finger like a hairy pork sausage at the assembled cadets, all of them dressed in their number-one uniform. 'You are guests of the German government and you represent the Royal Navy, and don't you forget it. I don't want any drinking. I don't want any political trouble. I don't want any sky-larking. And above all, I don't want any of you chasing after skirt and getting in trouble with the locals. Clear?' He had frowned down at their smooth youth faces, coal-black eyes blazing from a face that seemed covered with curly hair.

'Do you think we might dare to buy ourselves a bag of sweeties?' 'Jumbo' Wilson, who was fated to go down with the *Hood* within five years of leaving Dartmouth had asked. 'Sir!'

'Comedian!' 'Howling Mad' had barked and dismissed them.

Now they were out on the town, taking in the sights, mentally absorbing the impressions that would form their picture of Germany for the rest of their short lives, before ships sailing from this same port would end them.

It was 'Jumbo', the big, fair-headed cadet from Edinburgh, named thus on account of his enormous nose, who made the suggestion which started the whole disastrous affair. 'I don't know about you laddies,' he said stopping under what looked like a band rostrum decked out in huge

red and black swastika banners, 'but two weeks on board ship have made this particular sailor decidedly randy.'

The others laughed rather self-consciously. For the most part, their sexual experience had been limited to rushed, shabby little encounters with the whores who performed for thirty shillings in the backstreets of Pompey and Plymouth.

'They don't call me Jumbo just on account of my nose, chaps,' the big Scot carried on. 'I'm a laddie who's got a lot of weight to carry around with him. If I could lighten that load a bit this day, I'd be a happy man.'

Again his companions laughed and someone said, 'And where exactly do you propose to lighten this said burden, my cock-o-the-north, eh?'

'Och, man, you know these continental ports. They've all got some sort of knocking-shop district near the docks. Follow yer feet and ye'll find it. That's Jumbo's motto.'

Jumbo's big feet led them to the sleezy district behind the fish docks, away from the freshly painted and be-flagged houses of the bourgeois, teeming with sailors from half-a-dozen nations strolling in groups, looking at the hard-faced, heavy-bosomed whores who hung from every window or stood posed in what they obviously believed were seductive attitudes in the alleyways, asking with professional concupiscence, thickly made-up mouths opened in fake passion, *'tu viens, chéri?* . . . *wollen wir eine Nummer machen, Kleiner?'* . . . You want jig-jig girl, sailor . . . in half-a-dozen different European languages.

'I say, Jumbo,' Peter protested, 'they do look very ropey. I mean a chap could get a nice little souvenir from something like that.' He pointed to the dyed red-head leaning out of an upstairs window with her breasts almost bursting from her low-cut artificial silk blouse, who looked every day of sixty, 'And they're not exactly Greta Garbos either.'

'Close yer eyes, laddie, and think of mother,' Jumbo

quipped, but there was disappointment in his voice and after a while even he agreed that they'd have a drink of beer and call it a day.

Bei Anni was a typical waterfront *Kneipe* of the area, a long dark room, dominated by zinc-covered bar awash with beer suds in which wet cigarette-ends swam unlovingly, packed with drunken sailors enjoying themselves without restraint, while the *musikbox* beyond the bar thumped out military marches and sea-shanties in what purported to be English, though none of the cadets could understand a word of the growled chorus.

With difficulty, they pushed their way to the bar and ordered beer from the enormously fat woman who affected a little clay pipe and a blonde wig, and who obviously ran the place.

'Anni, no doubt,' someone said.

'All I know is that I wouldna like to buy her by the pound,' Jumbo quipped and raised his dripping glass of *Pils* in toast, 'Cheers, old dear.'

'*Prost, mein Sohn,*' the old woman croaked and slipped the money they had given her for the beer, with startling speed for her age, into a money box just below the bar as if she were afraid that someone might attempt to steal it there and then.

It was about then that the drunken Greek sailor volunteered to eat a razor-blade, an offer which was received with a loud burst of applause from those around him, who were obviously expecting some sort of blood-bath. But the olive-skinned seaman chewed and masticated the razor-blade without apparently any ill effects, washing down the gleaming bits of steel sticking to his tongue with a swallow of beer. Emboldened by his success and flushed with beer, he offered to do it again, this time with two blades at the same time.

'Christ,' Jumbo said in disgust, 'the things some folks'll do to get into the limelight.'

Peter grinned. 'Surprised you're complaining as a Scot, Jumbo. After all it's free entertainment, isn't it?'

Deliberately the Greek placed the one blade carefully on his tongue and then the other on top of it. He winked at his suddenly silenced audience and tapped the side of his huge beak of a nose, as if indicating that he was exceedingly wise and careful and that nothing could possibly happen to a smart Greek like himself. Slowly, very slowly, he crunched down with his long yellow teeth. Peter shuddered at the sound of metal being broken. Next to him Jumbo said, 'Yon fella gives me the willies. I vote –'

But Jumbo never finished his sentence, for it was just then that the drunken sailor with the pom-pom of the French fleet on his head hit the Greek in the small of the back and said, '*Ça suffit, sale con . . . ça suffit. . . .*'

The Greek yelped with pain and spat a bloody mouthful of broken razorblades from his lacerated mouth. He spun round, blood trickling down his unshaven chin, a knife suddenly in his hand, dark eyes glittering dangerously. 'Why you do?' he asked in broken German, spitting blood and metal as he did so.

The French sailor shrugged with Gallic eloquence. '*Ne comprends pas*' he answered carelessly and picked up his glass again.

The Greek's hand lashed out. The beer splashed into the Frenchman's surprised face and trickled down the front of his blues. The Frenchman reacted with surprising speed for someone so drunk. In one movement he picked up his mug and flung it at the Greek. He ducked. The mug smashed into the face of the big white-blond Dane. He roared with pain and flung back the table at which he was sitting, upsetting the many glasses on it.

In a flash all was excited noisy confusion, with the old hag behind the bar screaming '*Polizei*' . . . *Polizei*. . . !' in a cracked voice, as the place erupted in drunken violence, with mugs and chairs flying through the air and men of half-a-dozen nations rolling and writhing on the sawdust floor flinging wild punches at each other.

'Oh, my sainted aunt!' Jumbo exclaimed, hanging on to

his precious glass of beer with Scottish canniness, eyeing the crazy scene in disbelief.

Peter put down his own mug and ducked as a bottle hurtled through the air and shattered the big mirror behind the bar, showering Anni with glass. 'Come on, Jumbo, let's get out of here. We don't want to be found in here by the police. Old Howling Mad'd slaughter us.'

'But I haven't finished my dram yet,' Jumbo protested, 'I canna waste –'

His words were drowned by the scream of brakes outside and the shrilling of police whistles. 'Shore patrol!' a sailor at the door yelled.

'Buckets of fire, now we're for it!' a cadet yelled in alarm. 'If they take us in, we're finished.'

'Come on!' Peter cried above the racket. 'There must be a back way out. Follow me, chaps!'

In a solid phalanx, the cadets battered their way through the struggling cursing men everywhere, dodging wild punches, ducking whenever bottles or mugs came sailing their way, heading for the thick felt curtain at the back of the place and the legend '*Pissecke.*'

Behind them the door flew open. Green-clad police in flat helmets and steel-helmeted naval policemen burst in, wading into the mob with their rubber clubs, while Anni screamed in German, 'Watch my furniture . . . oh, watch my furniture. . . .'

They flung back the curtain and ran outside into a high-walled yard, one wall painted black and stinking of generations of male urine. 'Oh Christ, that's torn it! How in heaven's name are we going to get up those?' Peter moaned.

'Like this,' someone said.

As one they spun round. A handsome blond youth with a tough-looking happy face, clad in the uniform of a naval cadet complete with ornamental dirk, straddled the wall directly above their heads, dangling what looked like a silken female nightdress towards them, while above from a bedroom window a completely naked whore grinned

with obvious pleasure at the scene. 'Come on, Tommies, do not be afraid. It'll support your weight. Hurry, the head-hunters'll have you in a minute . . . *Los, schnell Leute.* . . .'

THREE

'So you met our tame Boche hero in what appears to have been a bordello eh?' Fleming said, and signalled the barmaid to bring him another whisky, although she had told him twice in her thick south Devon accent that whisky was reserved for 'regulars only'. Face set in obvious disapproval, she brought him it and waited, hand outstretched, until he had paid her the necessary one shilling and threepence it cost.

'Yes, the chap who got us out of that little mess was Horst Hartung. Though, I wonder if he would have done so,' Peter Harding's handsome face wrinkled into a frown at the memory, 'if he had realized just what a big mess he would get into by meeting up with me.'

Fleming ignored the comment. 'How well did you get to know him in Wilhelmshaven?'

'We were only there for seven days, but well enough I suppose. When you're eighteen you make friends fast.'

Fleming's face grew moody, as if he were thinking of other, unpleasant things. 'Suppose so, Harding. What was it Scott Fitzgerald said? "When you're in your twenties you need friends, but when you reach your thirties nobody can help you any more."'

Harding gave him a look and wondered what private sorrow occasioned the remark before continuing. 'Well, sir we went sailing together and we did the sights on that coast. A couple of times he invited me and my shipmates to their training cruiser the *Schleswig-Holstein* and that sort of thing. Jumbo Wilson called us the 'Two H's' we were together so often.'

'I see,' Fleming sipped his whisky reflectively. 'And

then came the business with this Jewish girl – the Hell-Cat – I presume?'

'Yessir, Anna.' Peter flushed for reasons known only to himself. 'But may I ask why you are so interested in her?'

'You may not!' Fleming snapped. 'What kind of girl was she? How did you and our tame Boche hero first meet her?'

'Outside a shop sir to be exact. Her parents had a furriers in Wilhelmshaven.'

'And what was she doing there?' Fleming asked.

'Hitting an SA man with an umbrella, sir!' Peter answered.

'*What*?'

'*Juden raus . . . Juden raus . . . Kaufe nicht bei Juden . . . Juden raus!*'

The cries had met them as they had sauntered down the street enjoying the late afternoon sunshine and, although Peter had not understood what they had meant *then*, he had realized from the look on Horst's handsome face that something unpleasant was taking place. Then they were round the corner and she was there, facing the crowd of chanting workmen, beating the middle-aged brownshirt, whose paint and brush lay in the gutter, the words he had been attempting to write on the shop window half finished, with a sun-umbrella. Horst, with his usual verve, had leapt into action at once. Pushing between the couple dodging the girl's blows as he did so, he barked something in German at the brownshirt and indicated with a jerk of his head the puzzled Englishman standing there watching the ugly little scene.

The chanting stopped as if by magic. The brownshirt picked up his paint and brush and without another glance at the girl, who had been just belabouring his head, slunk off, followed by the crowd of shabby workers, leaving the girl standing there, her breast heaving prettily with rage and exertion.

Peter came across, touched his hand to his cap, and stared at the words painted on the window, only being able to make out the one – '*Jude*' – which he knew by now meant 'Jew'. Meanwhile Hartung had addressed the girl, his face flushed a little angrily, in rapid German, of which Peter could only make out the word '*Engländer*' a couple of times. But instead of being subdued by Horst's angry outburst, the tall blonde girl with the bright blue, laughing eyes, said in slow but quite clear English. 'But why should I not hit back?' She indicated the name above the furrier's shop 'Hurwitz'. 'That is my father's store . . . and I am a Jew.'

Horst gasped. 'You?'

'Yes, I.' She gave Peter a sweet indulgent smile and he fell hopelessly in love with her there and then. 'They have the instruction in their schools and in the Hitler Youth on how Jews should look. Dark, small, hook-nosed and preferably humble.' Her beautiful face hardened. 'They find one who is tall and blonde and fights back and they won't believe it.'

'I am sorry,' Peter blurted the words out unwittingly, realizing immediately what a stupid, tactless remark he had just made.

'You need not be sorry,' she said quietly, while he blushed hotly, wishing the ground would open and swallow him up. 'I don't mind being a Jew. In fact I'm proud of it.' And with that she had turned and disappeared inside the shop, leaving the two young men to stare at each other in bewilderment.

'What then?' Fleming asked. Even he had been impressed by the story of the Jewish girl hitting back and had commented. 'Now I can see how she got her name. A redoubtable female. A woman one could perhaps use – but not in the way you *think*, Harding.'

'Well, sir. Horst gave me a long lecture on how the Jews had always throttled Germany since the First War and

although perhaps there had been unpleasant incidents
with the Nazis, such as we had witnessed, the authorities
were making serious attempts to enable the Jews to emi-
grate to Palestine. Indeed, he said, that one of the major
obstacles to their emigration was the British mandate
government who didn't want them.'

Fleming nodded, but remained silent.

'But I could see even then – and I must admit I was a
little innocent – that he'd been struck by the girl. Later,
of course, I realized that he had been seeing her secretly,
although I'm sure he must have realized it could hurt his
naval career if it came out. Why else would he have stuck
his neck out when the balloon went up that summer?'

'The balloon?' Fleming queried.

'Yes sir. When we heard what she had attempted to do
to the Assistant *Gauleiter* of Schleswig-Holstein.
Gauleiter, sir, is Party official –'

'I know what a *Gauleiter* is, Harding,' Fleming interrupted him hastily. 'But what did this Hell-Cat of yours
attempt to do to him, pray?'

'Nothing much, sir,' Harding attempted to be flippant,
but failed badly. 'Only do him in with a stolen pistol.'

Fleming whistled softly.

FOUR

Horst's face was pale with shock as they stood there in the yellow light cast by the dockside lantern, listening to the steel-shod tramp of heavy boots and brisk orders of the sergeants, as the police and their helpers from the brownshirts spread out across the town looking for their quarry. All afternoon the loudspeakers clustered around the lamp standards in the centre of Wilhelmshaven had been blaring out Anna's description every thirty minutes and requesting the population to remain calm – the *Gauleiter* was out of danger now, after an emergency operation – but to report immediately to the nearest police or SA post if they saw the girl, who was believed still to be armed and dangerous.

'Why in three devils' name did she do it, Peter?' he groaned, slamming one clenched fist into the open palm of his other hand, miserably. '*Why?*'

Peter shrugged. 'God knows, Horst, old chap. Despair, perhaps? Or maybe she wanted to show the world, or at least Wilhelmshaven, that the Jews could fight back. You know her temper.'

'But why now, when her parents had a visa and permission to leave the country for Palestine?'

'Had they?'

'Well, that's what the local paper says,' Horst answered dejectedly. 'But what does it matter now? Both of them have been arrested and taken away. Protective custody, the papers are saying.'

Peter sniffed, but said nothing, listening to the shrilling of whistles in the darkness and the gruff cries. Everywhere there were the flickering little lights of the searchers' torches as they looked for her in the maze of

sheds and cargo stores. Anna was in serious trouble; there was no doubt about that. 'What will they do with her when they capture her, Horst?' he asked.

Hartung looked at him. 'Listen Peter, we in Germany have been through some terrible times in these last few years. Why in this very town it's only five or six years ago since the communists and the national socialists battled each other to the death. In these very docks, my father, as a lieutenant-commander of the Imperial Navy, had his epaulettes pulled off and was spat upon by his own crew in 1919 during the troubles. He never got over it. He shot himself on account of the disgrace only two years later, when I was a little boy.'

'Yes, but what has this –'

'Listen Peter,' Horst said desperately. 'You must understand this is not your nice safe little island England cut off from the troubles of the rest of the world. We are a nation fighting for survival. We have seen desperate things and have been forced to take desperate measures.' He paused momentarily, his face miserable under the yellow light. 'They won't treat her with kid gloves when they capture her.'

'What is that supposed to mean?'

'It means that she will disappear! This is the year of the Olympics, so they will not want a public scandal, the golden pheasants – that's the name we give to our high Party officials – but they cannot allow a Jewess to get away with the crime of attempting to murder one of their own. So,' he shrugged helplessly. 'It will mean *Nacht und Nebel*,' he clicked his fingers irritably at his inability to find a phrase in English to explain. 'She'll vanish and that's that.'

Peter Harding's face hardened. 'Then we can't allow them to find her, Horst!' he snapped.

'But what can we do?'

'Find her first and get her out of the country before your authorities do.'

'How?'

'Listen, it just happens there's a tramp steamer in the harbour returning to its home port Hull –'

'Where's that?'

'In northern England.'

'Of course, now I remember, Peter. Go on.'

'At first tide. Now the Captain is in the RNVR – Royal Naval Volunteer Reserve. He came over to the wardroom of the *Devonshire* for a drink a couple of times. He's a fine type. He's ripe for anything. And Horst, he's not particularly keen on Germans. I'm sure he'd cock a snoot at them, if he had a chance.'

Horst looked at Peter in the light of the lantern, a gleam of hope in his blue eyes. 'You mean, he'd smuggle Anna, our Hell-Cat, out of the country?'

'I'm sure, he would.'

'But what then? I mean – your authorities.'

'Let's worry about that later Horst.' Peter thrust out his jaw pugnaciously. 'Are you on?'

'Of course, I'm on.'

'Then what are we waiting for? Come on. . . .'

All that night they tramped the streets of the naval base, avoiding the patrols which were everywhere, seeking the missing girl. As Horst said, the police had thrown an immediate cordon around the port as soon as the crime had become known; therefore Anna would have been unable to leave Wilhelmshaven. Besides, the surrounding countryside was flat, empty farmland with only isolated farms in which it would have been virtually impossible to find a hiding-place; Anna had to be in Wilhelmshaven.

'But where, Horst?' Peter demanded desperately as the clock on the townhall struck midnight with hollow finality and they still had not found her.

Horst rested against a wall, painted with the usual Nazi slogan of *Broth und Arbeit** and frowned. 'God knows,

*Bread and Work.

Peter. All the obvious places where people can take a dive as we say in German – the station, the parks and so on – are watched by the police, as you've seen. She can't hide there.'

'Relatives?'

Horst shook his head. 'Too obvious. If she has any, they'll be under police supervision, believe you me, Peter.'

'In the old days, fugitives sought sanctuary in a church,' Peter said a little wearily. 'It would have been easy then – Christ, Horst, that's it!' He snapped with new energy in his voice.

'That's what?'

'The place in which she might be hiding.'

'But where?' Horst forced himself to keep his voice low with an effort.

'A church – a Jewish church. What do you call 'em?'

'A synagogue, Peter.'

'Yes a synagogue. Is there one in Wilhelmshaven, Horst?'

The German shrugged. 'God only knows.'

Peter chuckled, knowing somehow or other, he had to be right.

'Yes, probably he does. Let's find a telephone kiosk. They'll have a telephone book. It'll be there.'

'Over there,' Horst said, infected by his companion's excitement.

'Where it says – *Fernsprecher*.'

Five minutes later they had it: '*Jüdische Synagoge, Bahndamm 5*'.

Bahndamm Number Five, as its name implied, was a dingy little cobbled street to the rear of Wilhelmshaven's main station; a couple of the usual shabby hotels found near railway stations in all continental towns, a factory, and beyond the line of warehouses, a small, incongruous building with a domed roof. The synagogue.

'What do you think, Horst?' Peter asked in a whisper, as they surveyed the building, its windows boarded up, as if they had been recently smashed, with around the door and its Hebrew scrawl, the black painted swastikas and the usual legend of '*Juden Raus*!'* 'Do you think there'd be a caretaker or anyone living in the place?'

'Doubt it. The Jewish community here is probably too small and poor to pay for one.' He laughed hollowly. 'Besides, you'd need to be a brave man to live out here by yourself at night when any drunken brownshirt, who fancies a bit of fun, could start throwing stones through your windows.'

'All to the good then,' Peter said with more enthusiasm than he felt. 'It would be an ideal place for her to hide, with no one to bother her.'

'Perhaps.'

'Come on, let's have a look-see.'

Together they crept round the building, noting that the broken windows had been firmly boarded over everywhere and that planking had been nailed over the rear door too.

'Not much joy here,' Peter said with a sigh. 'She couldn't have got through that little lot.'

'What about there?' Horst said suddenly.

'Where?'

Horst pointed to what appeared to be a coal shute, covered only by a thin wire grating. 'That would not be too difficult to remove, Peter.'

'What are we waiting for?'

In thirty seconds flat they had removed it and were peering into the cellar which smelt of age, coke, and the sour odour given off by ash. 'Got a match, Horst,' Peter whispered, realizing for the first time that he was committing a crime – breaking and entering, they called it back home. 'I'm going in.'

They dropped into the heap of coke that filled the floor

*Jews out!

of the place, crunching over it the best they could to the door, which they opened and closed carefully behind themselves before Horst lit his match.

A little frightened and a little awed they stared around the place, which looked to Peter more like the gallery of a theatre than the kind of church he was accustomed to at home. 'Shall we risk it, Horst?' he said in a little voice.

'Damn,' Horst cursed as the match burnt his fingers and went out.

'Yes, call her name.'

'Anna, it's us . . . Peter and Horst' the Englishman called, while a cursing Horst fumbled with the matchbox.

There was a spurt of blue flame. The interior leapt into view once more, and there she was, her beautiful face pale, but determined, a stool raised in her hands, as if she were prepared to defend herself to the last.

'Anna!' Horst gasped.

'What do you want?' she asked in English for Peter's sake.

'We've come to rescue you, Anna,' Peter said softly.

For a moment the determined look remained on her face, as if she didn't believe them, standing there in the well of the church below, their young handsome faces outlined by the flickering light of the solitary match; then slowly she lowered the stool and began to cry. . . .

'What happened then?' Fleming broke the heavy silence, as Peter recalled that tense moment of four years before.

Peter shook his head, as if attempting to wake up from a heavy sleep. At the bar, the girl rang the bell a little too loudly and called, 'Last orders . . . and there's no more whisky.'

Fleming ignored her as he waited for Peter to reply.

'Then, sir?' Peter grinned a little uncertainly. 'The balloon went up – and how! You see, sir, we smuggled her off the docks at Hull and took her down to some distant relatives she had at Leeds. Then, after a couple of days we had to – what's the word – declare her to the

authorities. All hell broke loose. Horst was arrested for illegal entry and I was placed under open arrest. I can tell you, sir, both of us thought that we'd really had it, as far as our careers in the navy went. Fortunately for us the cheap papers got on to it, especially the *Mirror* and the *Herald*. The way they told it, we were heroes. Damsel in distress and all that bull. So in the end, all I got was a severe reprimand and one hell of a ticking-off from the chief at Britannia, not to mention from this chap Howling Mad Lucas, when *Devonshire* arrived back at Pompey.'

'And our tame Boche hero? I can hardly think the Nazis were too happy about one of their officers-to-be rescuing a Jewish girl, especially one who had attempted to take the life of one of their *Gauleiters*.'

'I don't suppose so, sir. But the Olympics helped tremendously. Long afterwards, when it was all over, Horst wrote and told me that the whole affair had been hushed up and that he, too, had been given the same treatment as me. Besides, the secret court-of-inquiry the German Navy held into the affair was packed with officers who had known his dead father in the First War, so that was in his favour.'

'The Boche old-boy network, what?' Fleming quipped, though his mind was obviously elsewhere.

'Probably sir, but after all the fireworks were over –and I'll admit I was really sweating it out for a time – both of us survived. But sir, I've told you all this at some length. Now can I ask why you wanted to know?'

Fleming hesitated for a moment, while behind him the sullen girl loudly banged the shutter down over the bar, as if to signal that it was about time they left. 'Yes, Harding, I suppose you have a right to know,' he said thoughtfully. 'You see this Horst Hartung has become an important chap and, if he survives, which is doubtful, he'll go far in the Boche navy. He's the kind they like over there – bold and dashing and good-looking to boot. Ideal for Goebbel's propaganda machine. Well, it would be jolly, if we had an opportunity of using a chap like that. Room 39

could use the information he could give us, I can tell you that.'

Peter looked at Fleming aghast. 'You wouldn't get anything out of Hartung sir,' he stopped short, realizing the full import of the Naval Intelligence man's words. 'Do you mean – I should be used to pump him?' he cried.

'Just keep your voice low, Harding,' Fleming hissed. 'We don't want this to be all over south Devon, do we?'

'But sir,' Peter said, his face shocked, 'I couldn't be expected to attempt to make Horst betray his country, even if he were prepared to, which I know one hundred per cent, he isn't. Horst might not particularly like the Nazis, but he *is* a German and he *is* a patriot. That would be quite out of the question, sir.'

Fleming looked at him with those cynical green eyes of his. 'Are you quite sure, Harding?'

'Yessir!' Peter snapped defiantly.

Fleming rose and buttoned his elegantly tailored great-coat. 'This girl – this Hell-Cat – of yours,' he said with studied casualness. 'Do you happen to know where she is living in London now?' He put on his cap at a rakish angle.

Surprised by the question, Peter told him before he realized what Fleming was after. 'Somewhere in Hampstead, sir. The last I heard from her, she was working in the area. For a publisher, I believe, sir.'

'Thank you.' Fleming extended his hand.

Peter took it. It was cool and hard.

'Good luck Harding and thank you once again for your time. I think you'll be finding a letter from the Admiralty in your post tomorrow.' For the first time since they had met, Lt Commander Ian Fleming smiled faintly. 'I imagine you'll be pleasantly surprised by its contents.'

And with that he was gone back to the little Riley, a man with a slightly affected walk, passing out of Peter Harding's life for ever, though long after Peter was dead, the sullen barmaid, now middle-aged and blowsy, would bore her customers with her tale of the day she met the man who wrote James Bond. . . .

FIVE

'The Navy's here!'

'*Peter*!' Lt Commander Roxburgh exclaimed in delight. 'How good to see you again!' In his usual enthusiastic way he took Peter's outstretched hand and pumped it, his plump face, now adorned by a trim black beard, wreathed in a broad grin. 'It's splendid to have you back with the squadron – we certainly can use you. Most of my skippers are snotties, with no experience to speak of. We've had casualties.'

Peter flashed a glance at the gleaming MTBs* which had replaced the old motor launches; they looked powerful and tough.

'Bad?' he queried, as Toby Roxburgh took him by the arm and started to walk him away, out of earshot of the ratings busily engaged in getting the boats ready for their next sortie.

Over on the other side of the Solent, Peter could see the gleams of silver as a battalion of marines, with fixed bayonets, marched along the front to the thump-thump of a big drum. 'Yes,' his new squadron commander answered. 'The E-boats can still outgun us and outrun us – and they're less prone to catch on fire with those diesel engines of theirs. So we've not fared too well in our encounters with them. That's why I'm in charge now. You know old Howling Mad bought it two months ago, don't you?'

Peter nodded sombrely, his mood of happiness at being back with the MTB squadron gone momentarily. 'Yes, I read his obituary in the *Times*.'

*Motor Torpedo Boats.

Toby forced a chubby-faced smile and tugged at his new beard.

'He bequeathed me his whiskers,' he said and the two of them laughed as they walked along the front, savouring the spring sunshine and the sights and sounds of a busy naval harbour preparing for another day of war, though to Peter's experienced eye, it seemed that Portsmouth was busier than usual. 'Something up?' he asked after a while.

Roxburgh stopped and flung a glance over his shoulder in that melodramatic manner of his that made Peter grin and say, 'You look as if you expect Funf* to be following us, Toby?'

'Can't be too careful,' old boy,' the other man replied. 'Naval security is very hot at the moment and although I am the soul of discretion as you know –'

'Of course, everyone knows *that*!' Peter said sarcastically.

'I might just let something slip in the wrong place and really blot my copy-book for good.'

Peter was intrigued. 'Are we in on it?' he asked quickly.

'You bet your life we are!' Toby exclaimed. 'I virtually went on my knees and crawled to the Admiralty to get in on it. I'm sure there'll be gongs in it, plenty of 'em.' He thrust a thumb at his own chest, devoid of ribbons. 'And Lt Commander Toby Roxburgh is feeling decidedly naked up in that region at this time.'

Peter chuckled. 'What's the drill?'

'All very hush-hush you know. Swore my life away that I wouldn't tell anybody. Shouldn't at all.'

'But you will, of course.'

Toby stretched up on his toes and pressed his mouth close to Peter's right ear. 'Norway,' he whispered excitedly. 'We're going into Norway!'

'But Norway's neutral.'

'I know, but tell that to old Winnie.'

'Yes, I know what you mean. But come on, spit it out.

*Funf was the comic German spy in the Itma show.

What's our role in the business?'

Again Toby gave one of his cautious looks to left and right before answering. 'Well, according to my briefing, the Huns are about to go into Norway, and we're going to beat them, if possible. In the meantime, the Navy's been given the job of mining the waters off northern Norway, in particular off Narvik.'

'The big iron-ore port?' Peter said.

'Yes. The idea is to stop the Huns from capturing it by knocking out their troop transports with mines. To cover the minesweepers, their Lordships are sending out the Second Destroyer Flotilla under a chap called Warbuton-Lee. Now it's going to be our job to back up the destroyers.'

'How exactly?' Peter asked, making a quick calculation and coming to the conclusion that northern Norway was well beyond the range of the MTBs unless they were refuelled at sea, which seemed highly unlikely.

'We've got a sort of roving brief, Peter. If and when the Huns make their appearance off the fiord that leads up to Narvik, we're going to have first crack at them, harassing them until Warburton-Lee's merry men appear.'

'And if they don't appear?' Peter asked.

Toby grinned at him. 'One doesn't ask that kind of question, Peter, old boy.'

Peter returned his commander's grin. Nothing seemed to worry Toby, or if it did, he never seemed to show it. 'All right, last questions, how are we going to get there – and when are we off?'

'It's surprises all the way today, Peter. We're going out with the destroyers from Plymouth by fast transport. We'll be off-loaded, fully fuelled up and so on, off north Norway so we're ready for instant action . . . And when?' He paused dramatically and Peter could hear the hoarse cries of the marine NCOs coming over from Southsea, as they urged the marching men to 'swing them arms . . . bags of swank now'. Then in a hushed voice, Roxburgh said, 'Tomorrow night . . . evening tide.'

'Goodbye Gestapo!' the sailor called down at the grim-faced naval policeman on the dock, as the transport started to pull away. 'Don't bother to kiss me goodbye.'

Next to him his mate started to sing, '*Bless 'em all . . . Bless 'em all. The long and the short and the tall. You'll get no promotion on this side of the ocean. So cheer up my lads, bless 'em all. . . .*'

Peter Harding grinned. 'The boys seem in good form, Toby,' he said to his companion on the rail. 'You wouldn't think that most of them are going into action for the first time.'

'We spread the buzz that we're going to the Med, Peter. Most of them probably think they'll be enjoying the doubtful pleasures of Port Said's red-light district in due course.' He shuddered and his chubby cheeks wobbled. 'Perish the thought.' He straightened up. 'Come on, Peter, I'll treat you to a pink-gin in the wardroom.'

'Thanks, but not just yet, Toby, if you don't mind. I'll stay on the deck a bit longer.'

'Suit yourself. My guess is the gin won't last out the trip. I'm getting mine now.' With that he left, leaving Peter to his thoughts.

Now the spring dusk began to close in. The circle of hills around Plymouth started to change from purple to black. In the channel the buoys lit up, sparkling in the growing darkness.

Peter stared out across the Sound to Drake's Island, taking in the battle wagons which were everywhere, re-alizing yet again just how powerful the British Empire was, and feeling a sense of pride that unimportant as he was, he was still a member of that mighty fleet.

His thoughts wandered as night descended over the water, which was becoming choppier by the second, churned up by Warburton-Lee's destroyers and the ever increasing wind coming from the sea. For a while he thought of that strange lieutenant-commander from Naval Intelligence; his prediction that he would be hear-ing from the Admiralty soon had been proved right. The

cable posting him to Toby's squadron had come the very
next morning. But why had Fleming been so interested in
Anna? Had he plans for her? Peter laughed softly to
himself. If he had, he'd find the 'Hell-Cat' a tough proposition.

For a few minutes he lingered with Anna, feeling envious of Horst because of that night in Leeds when he had
heard the German steal to her bedroom and he had heard
the whispers and sighs through the thin wall that separ-
ated her room from his and could have indicated only one
thing – that they were making love. Then he thought of
Horst and wondered where he was at this very moment.
Was he too setting off on some perilous mission, and
would their paths ever cross again as they had done so
dramatically off Bridlington in 1939?

Suddenly Peter Harding was seized by an almost unreasoning fear. What would he do if he had to face Horst
Hartung in combat again? Would he – *could he* – give
the orders that might mean Horst's death? He shook his
head, as if physically trying to dismiss that overwhelming
question and attempted to concentrate on the singing,
now subdued and a little sad, coming up from the ratings
below. '*There's a long, long trail awinding to the land of
my dreams*,' they were singing softly, indulging themselves in that poignant little song of the old war. Behind
them the darkness had fallen over England, and now they
knew they were alone with the sea and the unknown
dangers which lay ahead.

Wrapped up in his thoughts, Peter stared out at the
dark heaving mass of the sea. What did the future hold?
Inside him a little voice whispered cruelly only one word
as an answer. *Death. . . .*

SIX

Daylight came late, almost reluctantly this April morning. The sky tinged a sullen grey and the last wisps of fog drifted and then finally the pale yellow sun peered over the mountainous crags of Norway's coast and lay there as if too feeble to rise any further. Peter Harding buried his head deeper into the collar of his bridge coat and thanked God it wasn't January; April was bad enough in these northern waters.

All night long they had been scouring the waters between Bergen and Narvik searching for the German Battle Fleet. The Germans had beaten the British yet again. Her troops had already invaded Denmark, Oslo, Norway's capital was being bombed from the air, and the Admiralty had signalled Germany's biggest ships the *Gneisenau* and *Scharnhorst* were sailing north, plus several other heavy cruisers, to protect the troop-carrying transports bound for the northern Norwegian ports. The order was: stop the Germans until the Home Fleet arrives.

Now the MTB squadron, with Toby's ship in the middle, was spread out in a large V, covering a mile of water, zig-zagging at low speed near the coast, knowing that the German ships would probably hug the land as close as possible in an attempt to hide from British reconnaissance planes. What the German command did not know was that Britain's total air power in the area was one antiquated seaplane!

The grey-green, heaving sea remained obstinately empty. Time and time again, a hollow-eyed unshaven Peter, whose stomach rumbled loudly with hunger, swept the area to his front with his glass. In vain! The northern

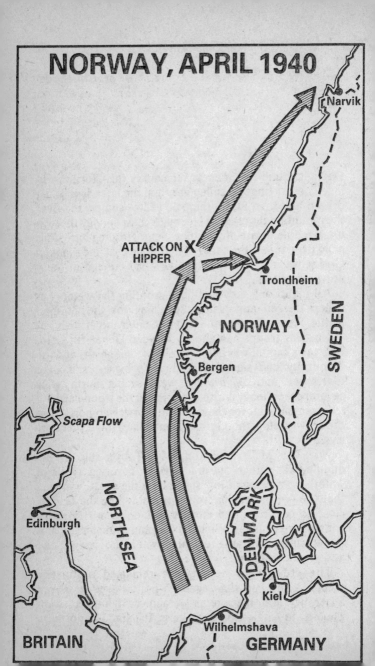

waters were as deserted as they must have been on the day of Creation. Had the Germans decided to go further out after all and risk the chance of being spotted by the RAF? He accepted the cup of coffee and a thick clumsy bully-beef sandwich gratefully, and realized for the first time he had not eaten now for over twelve hours.

'Signal coming in, sir,' the duty signalman's voice cut into his thoughts.

Peter jerked up his head. The Aldis lamp was blinking on and off on Toby's boat.

'How does he read, Bunts'? he asked the smart-looking cockney leading-signaller.

Hastily the man finished scribbling on his message pad and handed it to Peter, whose mouth was still full of corned-beef and bread. He swallowed it and read the message. 'We'll split, Peter. I'll take two craft and head out to sea. You take Number Five and Six and continue on the present course.'

Peter nodded his understanding. In Toby's place he would have done the same, though he felt a little envious that Toby would probably see some action while he'd be stuck with the boring chore. 'Bunts, acknowledge please and wish Commander Roxburgh good luck and gongs.'

'Ay, ay, sir.' The rating began to work his lamp, as the squadron began to split up with the two craft assigned to Harding's command sweeping out to port to cover the same area as that of the whole squadron. Peter watched them do so with approval. Both the sub-lieutenants commanding MTB Five and Six were rookies, but they were learning fast. The search continued.

It was about midday when the look-out yelled, '*Aircraft! Bearing. . . .*'

Peter swung up his glasses. Two dark shapes slid silently into the gleaming circles of calibrated glass. Hurriedly he adjusted the focus and gasped. They were German. Instinctively he knew they had struck oil. They

had to be the scouts from the German fleet. 'Bunts,' he commanded. 'Signal Five and Six. Enemy Aircraft!'

'Sir!'

'Stand by for enemy air attack!' Peter yelled unnecessarily, for the gunners were already scuttling for their machine guns, swinging them upwards, while their mates prepared to feed the ammunition belts into them.

Now Peter could make out the German planes quite clearly. They were Heinkel 115s – torpedo bombers. They weren't the most modern of planes, but they were fast enough and after all the MTBs were armed solely with anti-aircraft machine guns.

Now the twin German planes spotted them. Watching them through his binoculars, Peter could see how the leader wiggled his wings, the signal that he had seen the three craft far down below.

'They've seen us!' he cried. 'Stand by now everywhere!' He flashed a look to the other two boats. They were keeping well apart, which showed their young skippers were using their heads – that way the target was spread out for the enemy – and their anti-aircraft gunners were already crouched behind their weapons ready for action.

'Here they come!' the look-out sang out, raising his voice above the roar of the German planes, as they started their run-in.

'Lead into them . . . lead into them, gunners!' Peter cried urgently, knowing that the greenhorns could be rattled easily, once the torpedo bombers came closer. 'Now . . . *Fire!*' The four machine guns opened up at once. Suddenly the grey sky to their front was peppered a dark brown, the barrels of the chattering guns steaming in the cold. The torpedo planes dropped fifty feet. The first bursts of tracer whizzed harmlessly above the pilots' heads.

'Smart bastards!' Peter cursed aloud. The pilots obviously knew their stuff. Now they were coming in at almost wave-height. At times the blue-grey Heinkels were almost obscured by the tossing waves and marring

the sweating gunners' aim, but there was no obscuring the twin torpedoes they each carried below their ugly bellies.

Suddenly the gunners of MTB Five struck lucky. The lead plane staggered visibly as it took a long burst of slugs. Pieces of metal flew from its fuselage. Almost instantly, a thin white stream of glycol began to pour from its port engine.

'Hell's bells!' a rating cried almost incredulously. 'They've got him!'

Vindictively the other MTB gunners concentrated their fire on the crippled German seaplane. Multi-coloured tracer stitched the sky in a deadly morse. Now flames were roaring up from the Heinkel's fuselage and through his binoculars Peter could see the pilot slumped across the controls, back littered with gleaming pieces of shattered perspex.

With a tremendous bang the plane hit the water. For a moment it was obscured by the spout of boiling water, followed a second later by a blinding flash. The plane was ripped apart. An instant afterwards there was nothing left of it save a lone wing slopping back and forth in the green swell.

But in their excitement, the inexperienced gunners had forgotten the other plane. Now it shuddered in mid-air, as the two thousand pound torpedo it was carrying between its wheels dropped to the water only fifty feet below. One of the gunners turned his machine gun on the Heinkel, but the pilot was already making his break, zooming upwards unburdened now by the weight of the torpedo.

Peter forgot the escaping plane. He swung his glasses round. There it was. The tell-tale trail of bubbles exploding on the water's surface, running straight for Number Five. He grabbed the loud-hailer. The MTB was heading straight on a collision course!

He pressed the catch. '*Hard to starboard*!' he yelled as the torpedo sped ever closer to the unsuspecting young sub-lieutenant intent on firing at the escaping plane, '*For chrissake, hard to starboard, man!*'

But it was already too late. At the very last minute the young skipper saw the deadly fish hurrying towards him in the water. Peter gripped the loud-hailer, knuckles white with tension. Would he be able to swing the MTB round in time? The great, hollow boom of the torpedo striking home told him the attempt had failed.

Suddenly the MTB's stern rose straight up in the air. A horrified Peter could see her twin screws turning purposelessly. A gunner flew from his perch as the whole craft trembled furiously. With dramatic abruptness, the stern hit the water again and the next instant the MTB broke in half, her bows immediately disappearing under the water, while the stern, belching thick black oily smoke, started to settle more slowly.

'Cease firing . . . cease firing,' Peter commanded urgently. Next to him the helmsman anticipating his order swung the MTB round and they started to head towards the sinking MTB, moving more slowly through the oil-covered water, the waves subdued now by the spreading slick. 'Stand-by with the boat-hooks,' Peter ordered, clambering down to the main deck himself to supervize rescue operations personally, knowing as he did so, that there could be few survivors from that tremendous explosion.

'There's one sir,' a rating cried, pointing at a spot in the middle of the bobbing mess of debris that was coming from what was left of the MTB.

Peter grabbed the excited rating's boat-hook and, as carefully as he could, turned the figure in the water over. Next to him the rating gasped with horror. The man's face looked as if someone had thrown a pot of red paint at it and where the eyes should have been there were two holes. Hastily Peter disengaged the boat-hook and mercifully the body turned over again to hide that monstrous face. They moved on, their bow gently nudging aside the mess bobbing up and down on the surface of the water. Now the stern was almost gone. A blackened arm raised itself weakly from between a floating kapok mattress and

what looked a large dart-board. 'Help,' someone called feebly, 'help shipmates . . . please.'

'That's my oppo,' the ashen-faced rating next to Peter gasped. 'Old Scouse Kelly.'

'Well, give your oppo a bloody hand,' Peter cried in exasperation, born of the frightening realization that most of MTB Five's crew had been killed. He thrust the boat-hook into the man's hands. 'Here, get on with it!'

A minute later, they had hauled the gasping Liverpudlian over the side to let him lie on the wet deck gasping like a stranded fish, saying weakly over and over again, 'Christ Almighty, I thought I'd never see Pompey agin. . . .'

He was the only survivor.

It was two hours after the sinking of MTB Five that the still shaken crews of the remaining two motor torpedo boats spotted the German fleet.

A mist had begun to creep across the sea from the land, but further out visibility was still adequate. Thus it was that the two MTBs were fortunately hidden from view as the first long lean shape of what was unmistakably a German destroyer of the *Moewe* class, slid into sight directly to their front, to be followed almost instantly by another – and then another!

Peter swallowed hard as he ran his binoculars over them. There were six in all of the most modern type laid down since the London Naval Treaty between Hitler's Germany and Britain, almost equal in speed to the MTBs and bristling with quick-firing five-inch guns.

His first instinct was to flee even deeper into the ever thickening fog of the coast. His second was to think of some suitably Nelsonian slogan and then dash in for what undoubtedly would be sheer suicide. His third instinct was to wait and see, for it was obvious that the Germans had not spotted the two British craft. Besides, Peter was curious. What was the purpose of so many destroyers

together – were they, perhaps, the escort the capital ships steaming north would need to protect them against underwater attack?

For nearly an hour, the two MTBs, confident now that the fog was effectively covering them, sailed northwards on a parallel course to the six unsuspecting German destroyers, but falling deliberately behind a little for safety's sake. And then Peter saw the two ships, which one day would bring about the end of his short life.

They were unmistakable. He had studied their silhouettes a hundred times on the identification tables. There they were, each one of them over 30,000 tons, potent, mighty, frightening, the most modern capital ships afloat in the world this April morning: first the *Scharnhorst* and then the *Gneisenau*, each of them escorted by two destroyers. Next to Peter on the bridge, the waiting signaller Sparks croaked. 'Jesus, it's *them*!'

Peter forced himself to remain calm. 'Yes, indeed, Sparks,' he said, hardly recognizing his own voice, as his awed gaze took in those great steel monsters sailing before him. 'Take a signal.'

'Break radio silence, sir,' Sparks gasped. 'But they'll pick us.'

'I know, Sparks. But we've got to inform their Lordships.' He hesitated momentarily, trying to think of something suitably heroic to mark this great moment, but he could not. Instead, he said. 'Sighted *Gneisenau* and *Scharnhorst* off Ofotfjord, steaming on a north-easterly course. Will shadow. Await your Lordships instructions . . . then the usual, Sparks.'

'Usual, sir!' Sparks echoed in awed disgust. 'There ain't gonna be any more usuals for this lot of ruddy matelots once Jerry picks up the signal and starts looking for us.'

His decision now made, Peter Harding was calm. 'I 'spect you're right, Sparks. Now cut along and get it sent!'

The drama had commenced.

SEVEN

'*Verdammte Scheisse!*' Horst Hartung cursed yet again and glared around at the grinning officers of the *Hipper*, mixed with those of the Third Mountain Division which the 10,000 ton cruiser was carrying to Norway. 'What a way to go into battle in a tub of this size, complete with hot and cold showers and as much *Korn* as you can drink!'

Traubl, the lean, bronzed Major of the Third Mountain Division slumped in the big leather wardroom chair next to him and grinned.

'What are you complaining about Hartung?' he asked. 'You've got *your* bit of tin,' he indicated the Iron Cross on Hartung's chest. 'Give us greenhorns a chance to grab a little bit of glory. I bet after the photograph of your ugly mug appeared on the front cover of the *Signal*, you couldn't save yourself from eager young girls wanting to bed you?'

Now it was Hartung's turn to grin. 'Yes', he rubbed his chin with fond memory. 'For three days after the Fuhrer gave me it, I didn't get out of bed, except for the normal human functions, and I wasn't alone all that time.'

'How many?'

Hartung held up his right hand, fingers outstretched, including the thumb.

Major Traubl whistled softly, suitably impressed, 'Five . . . *Alle Achtung, Hartung*! They'll be sending you to one of those SS stud-farms there's all the gossip about next.'

'Anywhere, but this big slow tub,' Hartung grumbled, his bad mood returning once more. 'Fancy sending an experienced E-boat officer as an observer on this one! Old Raeder must be losing his grip!'

'It'll do you a bit of good to see how we field-greys have to live, Hartung,' Traubl said. 'We can expect the Norwegians to resist when we go ashore, so when I'm looking at the turnips from below two metres of Norwegian earth, you can write a nice report for that Admiral Raeder of yours on what the field-greys did wrong in the landing.'

Hartung grunted and relapsed into silence. He guessed Raeder had picked him to accompany the mountain troops which would be landed at the Norwegian port of Trondheim, because he did not want an experienced E-boat captain to risk his life in the dangerous operations that would be carried out in the narrow confines of the Norwegian fiords once the landings had commenced. Raeder hadn't said that much, but he had mentioned the need to 'preserve a nucleus of experienced skippers' during the briefing. In a way he supposed he ought to be grateful to the Old Man for his concern; yet every time he looked at the excited mountaineer officers who would be going into action soon, he felt a twinge of envy. They'd be in the thick of it, while he would be sat on his big bottom watching them like a spectator at a boxing match.

'Gentlemen, your attention,' snapped the precise voice of the *Hipper*'s signals officer, a man who affected a pince-nez and a stiff wing-collar and one to whom Hartung had taken an instinctive dislike. The officers ceased their chatter and stared at the signals officer as he stood there, framed in the entrance to the wardroom. 'I should like to inform you,' he said in that prissy, schoolmaster manner of his, 'that Group One – the *Gneisenau* and the *Scharnhorst* that is –'

'Oh, get on with it, you old woman,' Hartung snorted in disgust and some of the field-greys laughed.

The signals officer flushed. 'Well, I was just going to say that Group One have picked up enemy radio signals in the immediate area. We are working on breaking them at this present time. Met has also just informed us that we can expect a Force Eight gale at twelve hundred hours.'

There were groans from the army officers and now it was Hartung's turn to grin.

'In short, gentlemen,' the signals officer concluded, 'the Captain tells me to inform you that one way or other we are in for an exciting time in the next few hours. Good morning.' And with that he was gone.

Hartung grinned at Traubl. 'Shall I get you a bucket, Traubl?' he asked.

Traubl shook his head grimly. 'Not just yet, thank you.'

By two o'clock that day, the dark-green sea was heaving violently in the wind down from the Arctic, buffeting the big cruiser every few seconds, so that the wardroom was full of green-faced soldiers, hands clasped to their mouths, white enamel pails brought in by grinning orderlies, gripped between their feet.

Hartung walked jauntily on the heaving deck, experiencing a little *Schadenfreude* at the sick state of the elite mountain troops suffering down below, noting with satisfaction that even some of the *Hipper*'s crew were looking queasy. 'Don't know what real weather is,' he told himself. 'This big tub's hardly moving.'

'Ship off starboard bow!' the cry rang out from the deck above him.

Hartung swung round, eyes narrowed against the freezing wind. A lone craft was tossing and pitching out there, half a kilometre away, black smoke pouring from her two funnels. 'My God,' he exclaimed to no one in particular, 'she's a Tommy! D-type destroyer!'

It was obvious that *Hipper*'s captain had made the same identification, for in that very moment, a seaman hauled the swastika down hurriedly and ran up the blue and yellow ensign of neutral Sweden.

Hartung grinned. It was quick thinking, but he doubted very much if the *Hipper*'s captain would get away with the ruse. He was right. The next instant, there was a flash of bright light at the Tommy's forward turret. To the

Hipper's port, one of the escort destroyer's reeled violently, her radio masts almost touching the waves. Thick, oily smoke belched into the grey sky and the destroyer, obviously badly hit, retreated into the nearest fogbank, as the *Hipper* turned to take up this impudent little David's challenge. Hastily Hartung grabbed the deck rail, as above him in B-turret the *Hipper*'s twin cannon thundered and the cruiser shuddered with the shock.

Automatically he opened his mouth to prevent his eardrums being smashed by the blast and watched as the great one hundred pound high explosive shells raced towards the tiny Tommy destroyer. It shuddered violently and abruptly its stern sagged, as tons of furious white water swept through the tremendous ragged hole that had been ripped open there.

'Good shooting!' Hartung yelled excitedly, as thick black smoke began to belch from the stricken destroyer's funnels. She was making smoke; she was obviously going to make a run for it under the cover of a smoke screen. What would *Hipper*'s captain do now, he asked himself. Hopefully nothing boring like breaking off the action.

Hartung's fears were unjustified. He had tasted blood; he was not prepared to let this little David who had challenged him so boldly get away. Slowly the 10,000 ton Goliath started to swing round and take up the chase. Five minutes later they were in the midst of the smoke screen, with the deck ratings and Hartung coughing thickly as they strained to make out the destroyer's position in the black gloom.

'There she is!' someone screamed suddenly.

'Watch out for torpedoes!' someone else yelled. 'She's coming straight at us!'

Abruptly she appeared, racing full speed towards the huge cruiser, a white bone in her teeth, forward turrets flashing fire and Hartung was yelling at the top of his voice. '*She's going to ram us . . . she's going to ram*!'

Everywhere the alarm sirens shrilled and the gongs clanged. Along the whole length of the cruiser, the mul-

tiple flak cannon and the banks of machine guns chattered
and thudded, pouring a solid wall of tracer shells and slugs
at the gallant little Tommy. Time and time again she was
hit, but still she came on with dogged persistence, the
shredded white ensign flying boldly at her stern, most of
her superstructure wrecked, her B-turret holed and
ablaze.

Up on the bridge, the furious captain of the *Hipper*
yelled at the helmsman to bring the cruiser round, but the
10,000 ton monster answered only sluggishly to the helm.
Hartung realized at once she was not going to make it.
The two ships were heading on a collision course. He
grabbed hold of a stanchion and waited for the inevitable.
In mid-turn, the dying British destroyer struck the *Hipper*
a terrible blow. There was the rending sound of metal
being ripped away, as the destroyer sheered the length of
the cruiser's side, tearing away a great gaping hole of
nearly forty metres in length. Trailing fire behind her the
Tommy, sinking rapidly now, headed for her grave, her
crew already tossing life-rafts overboard and frantically
attempting to free the jammed life-boats.

There was a tremendous explosion. The destroyer was
torn apart and had disappeared almost before the staring
German crewmen had understood what had happened.

Now they were picking up the survivors. Everywhere the
little red lights attached to the Tommies' lifebelts bobbed
up and down in the oil-covered swell, as the handful of
survivors coughed and gasped, too weak to call out for
help, as the *Hipper*'s sailors fished them out one by one.

High above on the deck, Hartung watched the operation appalled at the sight, as man after man was dragged
up from the water by rope, retching oil from their diesel-
filled lungs, gasping their thanks as the waiting sailors laid
them out on the deck and covered them in grey issue-
blankets, piling them on until finally the wretched survivor stopped trembling.

Now they were almost all up. Down below the sea was left to the flotsam of war, and the bodies floating purposelessly to nowhere, somehow obscene in their oily nakedness.

'How many survivors?' Hartung asked the MO his arms black with diesel up to the elbow, as he passed out instructions to the busy sick-bay attendants.

'Thirty-eight out of one hundred and sixty.'

'Officers?'

'Only one, a sub-lieutenant. The Captain went down before we could reach him.'

'He was a gallant man. The Tommies will give him a medal, perhaps their Victoria Cross.'

The MO, a skinny, bespectacled reservist from somewhere in the Catholic south, looked at Hartung. 'You're young, *Herr Leutnant*, very young,' he said, as behind him one of the survivors started another fit of coughing, vomiting blood tinged with oil.

Hartung flushed. 'What do you mean?' he asked gruffly.

'Medals, you say. I say, the man is dead. What good is glory now, Lieutenant, eh?'

It was a question to which Hartung had no answer. Instead he turned and looked gloomily over the railing at a dead Tommy in the water below: an old sailor by the look of his grizzled head, already stiffened by rigor mortis: a pitiful relic of the sea, doomed to go on floating forever until the gulls got him or his flesh became so waterlogged that he sank. Suddenly Hartung was overcome by a mood of black gloom, as he thought that that might well be his own fate: to sail some godforsaken stretch of water forever like a modern-day *Flying Dutchman*.

For what seemed a long time he stood there, only half hearing the whimpers and groans of the Tommies stretched out on the deck behind him, his nostrils full of the sickening reek of diesel oil, staring out at the enormous green waste of that cruel sea.

And then the alarm sirens were wailing once more and all along the starboard side of the cruiser the flak and the banks of machine guns were chanting their song of death, as the two lean shapes started to hurtle in on their first torpedo-run.

To Peter, on the bridge of the first MTB rushing at the *Hipper* at thirty knots an hour, the prow smacking each wave with a kick that made his stomach want to throw up, his adversary seemed enormous. It towered above the MTB like a great steel wall and its length appeared to fill the whole horizon so that he felt puny and insignificant in the cruiser's presence. Had he really a chance of doing any damage to such a colossus?

The signal from the Admiralty had been brief and brutal. It had given the *Hipper*'s position, reported by the unknown operator of the sinking destroyer just before she had gone under. '*Glowworm* sunk. Engage *Hipper* immediately. She must be delayed.' Even as Sparks had read it out to him, Peter had realized that it was a virtual death sentence. The last word had told him everything he wanted to know. Their Lordships knew that he could do nothing but delay the cruiser until, hopefully, the Home Fleet arrived in Norwegian waters. What happened to him and his ship was of no concern to them.

But now, his blood running wild with the excitement of combat, Peter forgot the danger and his inevitable fate, as the MTB surged forward, zig-zagging madly, getting ever closer to the steel monster which almost blotted out the light, her machine guns chattering, the torpedo men intent on their target, undeterred by the solid wall of fire coming their way. Now gouts of crazy white water shot into the air on both sides, cascading down by the ton on the heeling little craft.

The distance between the little boats and the giant narrowed rapidly. Peter could see the little figures of German sailors, the ribbons of their caps flying behind

them, running along the deck and the tense faces of the machine-gunners of the multiple batteries as their weapons thumped bullet after bullet at the two craft below. 'Get ready with those tin fish!' he bellowed above the crazy din. 'Get ready!'

At his side the helmsman, soaked with flying spray, braced his legs ready to swing the flying boat to port immediately the torpedo had been fired.

'*Fire one*!' Peter yelled.

The MTB shuddered and with a loud hiss of compressed air, the torpedo shot from her bows and started speeding directly for the cruiser.

Peter made a quick decision, his mind quite clear now and drained of fear. He would never succeed in making another run like this. It was now or never.

'*Fire two*!' he commanded.

Again the MTB shuddered violently, as the two thousand pounds of high explosive slapped into the water and then the MTB was racing round, white boiling spray flying high into the air in the same instant that there was a great hollow boom of metal striking metal.

Peter flung a look over his shoulder, ignoring the shrapnel howling everywhere, and gave out a yelp of sheer delight. The first fish had found a target! Behind him, flame spurted high into the air, illuminating the scene with the searing incandescent clarity of a photographer's flash.

But his delight turned to horrified shock when he saw the result of that explosion: fear-crazed German sailors, their dark uniform suddenly bright with fire, tugging at their clothing with hands that dripped flame themselves, rapidly being turned into blackened claws, as the flames from the exploding fuel tanks rose higher and higher, slumping onto the holed deck, where the paint already bubbled furiously, their faces contorted terribly until they lay still, while the greedy flames consumed them.

Pursued by those terrible screams, Peter sped away into the cover of the nearest fogbank, accompanied by the

second MTB, which had no luck at all. They had no further torpedoes. Now it was up to the Home Fleet.

So the crippled *Hipper* sailed on, belching black smoke and trailing fire behind it, its deck littered with pygmy-like shrivelled dead, their limbs arched stiffly in that final agony; and the survivors writhing with pain, screaming horribly as the sick-bay attendants began the awful task of removing the charred cloth from the burnt flesh, including the crumpled figure of a young lieutenant, whose tunic bore the Iron Cross, First Class, its enamel still bubbling faintly with the after-effects of that tremendous heat. . . .

EIGHT

'You know, you really are a jammy bugger,' Toby Roxburgh said in mock anger, and banged the *Times* with his
chubby fist, from which he had just been reading the
official notice of Peter's new decoration aloud. 'Twenty-
four, with the D.S.C., a mention in Dispatches, and now
you've had the audacity to go and win the Distinguished
Service Order!'

He crumpled the paper and dropped it to the quay on
which both of them sat enjoying the May sunshine, while
waiting for the alarm bells to ring once again. Peter
Harding took his gaze from the sailors, most of whom
were stripped to the waist and lounging below on the
MTBs lined up along Dover's South-West Quay, playing
cards, reading the *Picture Post,* or snoring as they caught
up with their sleep.

'If this business of E-boat alley keeps up much longer,
Toby, you're bound to get a gong. I mean, we were in
action three times yesterday against them and by the look
of the sky, they'll be out in full force again before this
afternoon is much older.'

'I damn well hope so!' Toby snorted, his face flushed
with the sun and the sea breeze which always seemed to
blow off Dover. 'Otherwise I'm going to be a lieutenant-
commander for the rest of my career, and one has to
consider one's pension, hasn't one?'

Peter shook his head and kept back the sudden answer
that had leapt to his lips. The way things were going on the
continent this bright sunny May of 1940, there seemed
little likelihood that any of them would survive to draw a
naval pension. On the tenth, the Germans had launched

their great offensive westwards, and now they were sweeping down into northern France, driving the routed Anglo-French armies before them. The Belgians and the Dutch had already surrendered, and although the official propaganda artists were making reassuring noises about the decisive battle to come on the Somme, it was pretty clear to those in the know that it wouldn't be long before the B.E.F.* had either to stand and fight it out to the death, or flee back across the Channel.

The Germans obviously thought the same. Ever since the squadron, or what was left of it, had arrived back at Dover from the Norwegian fiasco, their E-boats had been making sortie after sortie into the Channel from their new harbours in Holland and Belgium, obviously out to dominate the twenty-odd miles between Dover and Calais. Their objective was as clear as the big red nose on Toby's chubby face. They wanted to prevent any attempt by the British to withdraw their troops in France across the Channel.

Down below the music of Ambrose and his band had ceased, to be replaced by the carefully cultivated voice of Alvar Liddell. 'Do you want to hear the news, sir?' one of the ratings sang out at the two officers perched in their wickerwork chairs on the quay above them.

'Not really,' Toby replied a little gloomily. 'It's always the bloody same these days – *bad*!'

'Yes, we do,' Peter overruled him and obligingly the rating, his skinny hairless chest adorned with a heart, pierced by an arrow and the tattooed pledge that '*I love my Mum*', turned up the volume.

As Toby had predicted, even the Ministry of Information could do little to conceal the dire news coming from the Continent; it was the story of one defeat after another. The old familiar names of the First World War cropped up time and again – Ypres, Arras, Amiens, Sedan – and they were all in German hands.

*British Expeditionary Force.

'Hell's bells,' Toby cursed. 'Is there nothing capable of stopping the swine?'

All that Peter was able to give by way of an answer was a small, helpless shrug.

The BBC news reader hesitated a moment. Peter wondered what was coming. Perhaps another fighting speech from the new prime minister, who had left the Admiralty to take over from Chamberlain on the day the great attack westwards had commenced. He had certainly been able to set the blood racing with his promise to the country that he had 'nothing to offer but blood, toil, tears and sweat' and his injunction to 'go forward with our united strength'. But the pause did not herald a new exhortation from Churchill. Instead, the news reader went on to announce that according to 'usually reliable neutral sources', the British Expeditionary Force was attempting to group in the area of Dunkirk-Calais along the Channel coast and this was seen by some observers as a prelude to an evacuation.

Peter flashed Toby a look.

Toby sucked his teeth for a moment, while below, the serious note vanished from his voice now, the BBC started to read out the latest sport results, as if it were peacetime and not war with some 300,000-odd British soldiers fighting desperately for their lives not more than twenty miles away. 'I think it's a calculated leak, Peter. The Ministry of Information is preparing the populace for the inevitable.

Peter nodded glumly. 'My guess exactly. They're preparing us for what is to come.' He stared across the still, green sea at the faint white smudge which was France, as if he were already visualizing the beaten men in khaki, streaming down to the beaches in their thousands, pleading to be taken off, waiting for vessels that never came, while the *Stukas* screamed down on them, their bombs smashing the packed bodies below to pulp. He shuddered suddenly in spite of the day's warmth.

'Someone walked over your grave, Peter?'

'Something like that, Toby.' Peter's voice rose, as below Flanagan and Allen went into the current favourite, *Run, Rabbit, Run*, on the wireless, 'What do you think, Toby? What would be the drill?'

'If there were a mass evacuation of the B.E.F.?'

'Mass confusion, I'd think,' Toby answered. 'Where have we the craft for that kind of job? Troop transports need harbour facilities. They couldn't use the beaches, and Dunkirk isn't too well supplied with docks at the best of times, not for over three hundred thousand men and their equipment that is.'

'Hm,' Peter grunted, absorbing his friend's analysis. 'So?'

'So, old pal,' Toby said, rising lazily to his feet, beads of sweat forming on his red face, 'if you want the Roxburgh verdict, it's going to be a ballsup – one flaming hell of a ballsup. . . .'

On the evening of the 20th May, Vice-Admiral Bertram Ramsay, a big bluff man, who had always seemed to Peter Harding to be somewhat aloof, now the new Flag-Officer-in-Charge, Dover, faced the assembled officers of his command in the deep galleries of the east cliff below the castle. Almost to the word, his sentiments echoed those made two days before by Toby.

'Gentlemen, let me say from the outset,' he announced in a voice that boomed through the cavernous Dynamo Room, 'that the operation we envisage will be a ballsup.' He frowned at a couple of the younger officers who giggled at the words. 'Our job is to prevent it becoming a *very* big ballsup.' He let his words sink in glaring at the circle of younger officers, as if daring them to make any comment. 'All right what is this operation?' he continued. 'I shall tell you. It is the evacuation of our army from France, code-named after this room – Operation Dynamo. Now what time have we got and what resources? Not much of either. The War Office thinks we've got about forty-eight hours

before the Huns put in a full scale attack at the three major ports which are still open to us, Calais, Dunkirk and Boulogne. My personal estimate is that we can't get more than ten thousand men per twenty-four hours from each port, a total of sixty thousand men in all.' He frowned, as if he were just realizing himself for the first time the scale of the problem on his hands. 'Of course,' he went on, 'that simply is not good enough. We can't allow the bulk of our army to fall into German hands. So what are we going to do?' Again Ramsay answered his own question. 'In addition to every available Channel ferry and packet, and the forty destroyers which have been placed at my disposal for this operation, I am summoning every weekend sailor and idiot who likes messing about with boats along the south coast to give us a hand. As I speak to you now, they are being requested to volunteer themselves and their craft to help with this evacuation.' For the first time since he had begun his briefing the Vice-Admiral's tough face cracked into a smile. 'And by God, if they don't volunteer, I can tell you there'll be ructions. By God there will!'

Now the officers listening to him laughed and the tension was broken, the planning could continue without the ever-present, almost overwhelming knowledge that the fate of a whole British army, perhaps even of the Empire itself, depended upon what happened here this evening paralysing their minds.

'So what have we got, gentlemen? We've got a lot of fools – brave ones, admittedly – but fools all the same, mucking around in everything from a paddle-steamer to a dinghy on whose ability the brown jobs will have to depend. Now we must make certain that these fools don't come too badly unstuck. Day,' he barked at the commander standing slightly to his rear, 'tell 'em what you've worked out.'

'Sir.'

The dapper, middle-aged hydrographer stepped forward, pointer already in his hand, and tapped the big map

of the Channel on the cave-wall.

'Gentlemen, I've planned the crossings like this. Speed as you have just heard is the essential factor, so we must use the shortest sea-crossing between France and Dover. So we have Route Z – here – from Dunkirk to Dover, some thirty-nine miles in length. That is going to be our number one. But we'll need alternative routes as well. Thus I've selected Route Y – here – an eighty-seven mile dogleg going from Dover to the Kwinte Buoy off Ostend before veering to approach Dunkirk from the east. And here, the fifty-five mile long Route X, which crosses the Ruytingen Bank and joins the deep-water channel half way between Dunkirk and Gravelines.' He paused and let the information sink in.

Next to Toby, Peter visualized the three routes in his mind's eye and realized that the hydrographer was being careful. If the Germans managed to seize the large heavy-gun French coastal batteries at Gravelines, Route Z would be at the nasty end of the stick. From Gravelines, the Germans could menace all the shipping on the shortest route.

The admiral took over again now. 'As you can see, gentlemen, our ships are going to be very much extended trying to protect the amount of shipping which will be ferrying troops back over those three routes, and make no mistake.' He raised a finger like a small sausage in warning. 'Once the Huns tumble to what we are about they're going to throw everything, including the proverbial kitchen sink, at us. There'll be dive-bombers, long-range artillery, submarines and those damned E-boats of theirs. Now you destroyer captains will cover Routes Y and X. They appear to be not as dangerous as Z and we simply cannot afford to lose any more destroyers. I mean we started this war with two hundred and now we're down to a hundred and fifty and some of those are out of commission due to damage. So,' Ramsay looked at the young innocent faces of the sub-lieutenants grouped around Roxburgh and Harding, 'it's going to be up to your chaps,

Roxburgh,' he said grimly.

'You mean we get Route Z, sir?'

'Exactly. Your MTBs are the fastest craft we have and, if I may be brutally frank, a loss of an MTB, although serious, is not the same as the loss of a destroyer, you understand?'

'I understand, sir.'

'Good. All right, gentlemen, from now onwards you and your crews are on a one-hour alert notice. There will be no leave, not even compassionate. If anybody goes sick, see if your sick-bay attendants can look after the man in question. Then, as soon as you get the signal, Operation Dynamo is to commence. I want you out at sea, because every hour will count.' His hard-eyed gaze lingered on the youthful faces of the MTB skippers, as if he were trying to memorize their features for some reason known only to himself. 'The fate of the British Army, perhaps even the British Empire, will depend on you. Thank you, gentlemen.'

'Atten-*shun*!' a staff officer barked.

The captains thrust back their chairs and sprang to their feet. The big bluff Admiral touched his hand to his gold-braided cap and went out, followed by his staff, leaving the captains standing there, faces wooden, limbs rigid in the position of attention, but with their minds racing at the thought of what now lay before them.

NINE

'This is your first trip, isn't it, gentlemen?' Peter asked, staring around the faces of the assembled skippers in the blue light of his little cabin. There was a rumble of agreement from the civilians, most of them amateur sailors, save for two dour tugboat skippers down from the Clyde. 'All right, let me tell you it won't be cakes and ale by any means,' Peter continued, telling himself that the men facing him were going to be in for the shock of their lives once they saw Dunkirk. He had been over four times since the 26th and each time the corpse-littered beaches and the burning town beyond had looked worse. 'But if we can get across and loaded up by dawn, we could possibly make it to the open sea before the dive-bombers arrive.'

'It's Route Z then?' one of the Scots asked, looking at Peter with his canny eyes.

'Yes.'

The Scot sucked his cold pipe reflectively. 'They say them Jerry batteries at Calais are pretty hot.'

Peter forced a laugh. 'Now then, Captain, you don't want me wetting my knickers, do you? After all, they tell me you can get knocked down crossing the road in Glasgow.'

'Ay that ye can,' the Scot replied, obviously unconvinced, and returned to sucking his pipe.

'Now any questions?' Peter asked and without waiting for anyone to reply, went straight into the final and most unpleasant part of the hasty briefing of these assorted 'volunteers'. 'Now as you go out, I want each of you to take a revolver from that table there. Each one is fully

loaded. It's just a precaution, but I must tell you this.' His face grew grim at the sudden memory. 'It's a jungle over there and the laws of the jungle prevail – the survival of the fittest. Discipline has broken down and the men will just swamp your craft, if you don't watch them.'

The Scot with the pipe said, 'Then we're to shoot the sodjers if they attempt to rush us or board us after we've got our maximum load?'

Peter nodded, his face set. 'I'm afraid so. It's the only way you see.'

'I see.'

But it was the middle-aged businessman from the Guildford stockbroker belt who broke the tension of that little meeting. 'I say,' he said, as his companions started to file out, picking up their revolvers gingerly as they did so, 'then there won't be any time for a coffee break on the other side, what?' He flushed and looked surprised at the burst of laughter which greeted his remark.

Five minutes later, the strange collection of tugs, yachts and motor launches, guarded by the solitary MTB, slipped away from Dover's south-west Quay, into the dark waters of the crowded harbour. Day Three of Operation Dynamo had commenced.

To their front, the dunes rose like lines of hump-backed camels, dotted everywhere with the blacker shapes of abandoned vehicles, half-buried in the sand, twisted into burnt grotesque skeletons by the bombs. Everything was silhouetted against the angry red glare coming from the burning city beyond.

Now, as his little fleet started to nose its way carefully through the dead bodies floating everywhere in the still water off-shore, Peter could hear the drunken shouting of the looters, the calls for help from the wounded lying somewhere in the jumble of the bombed wreckage, and the harsh commands of lone officers trying to keep their battered formations together in this confused chaos.

'*A Company, Green Howards – over here, now!
. . . B Company, East Yorks, stand fast! . . . Rally on
me, lads, rally on me, West Yorks. . . .*'

Once again as the MTB came to a stop, its engines
throbbing steadily, ready to burst into action at a
moment's notice, Peter was overwhelmed by that sense of
despair that had attacked him every time he had come to
this terrible beach. The British Army was a beaten rabble.
Organization had virtually broken down and immediately
he felt himself surrounded by a deadly evil atmosphere,
compounded by the horrible stench of blood and muti-
lated, decaying flesh that hung over the place in the
breathless air. It was as if he now found himself in some
huge slaughter-house. He loosened his revolver in its
holster and commanded the ratings standing on the deck
in pairs, one armed with a boat-hook, the other with a
loaded rifle complete with fixed bayonet: 'Stand by,
lads . . . and use your weapons, if they get rowdy
again . . . Here they come now. . . .'

On the beach, silhouetted by lurid scarlet of the flames
leaping up over Dunkirk, three long lines of waiting men
started to protrude into the water, now that they had seen
the arrival of new ships. These were the men who were
still under the command of their officers, who had been
standing there for days, orderly waiting their turn to be
taken off. But it was not these survivors of the great
debacle in northern France who worried Peter. It was the
soldiers hiding among the dunes to his immediate front:
men who had become animals and who would wound and
murder to get a place in the little boats before it was too
late. They were so crazed with fear that they could easily
overturn a boat or sink it under the weight of their
numbers.

Now the first survivors from the orderly lines began to
come aboard, many of them exhausted and dazed with
blank staring eyes, swaying like drunken men as the
ratings huddled them in blankets, thrust a lit cigarette
between their lips and escorted them below.

Peter left his deck ratings to get on with it, while he surveyed the progress of his little fleet. His amateurs were doing well, packing the survivors into every available inch of space, making a regular count, as he had told them to, and singing out the number to the man at the wheel. He turned his attention to the town itself. The German guns at Nieuport and Calais were beginning to shell it yet again and the flames and smoke plus the night itself mingled together to make a terrible panorama of death and destruction. The whole front was one long continuous line of blazing warehouses and factories, a high solid wall of fire, roaring and darting in tongues and greedy flame, with the smoke pouring upwards and disappearing into the black velvet of the sky.

Peter frowned. As always the flames would attract the E-boats lurking off the port, for they would silhouette the shipping leaving the place. And it wouldn't be long now before the first Stukas of the day appeared, to blast huge gaps in the massed ranks of the brown queues below.

'Let me on, let me on, I say . . . Can't you see I'm a senior officer? I'm needed at the War Office immediately!'

The angry, upper-class voice cut into Peter's gloomy reverie. He swung round. A couple of ratings were staring down perplexed at the man standing up to his shoulders in the water below, looking at them with a well-fed, infuriated face.

'What's the matter there?' he called, seeing at once that the speaker had pushed his way to the front of the patient line of dazed survivors.

'Are you the captain?' the man in the water asked in a voice used to giving orders and having them accepted.

'Yes. Who are you?'

'I'm Colonel Hughes of the Royal Army Service Corps. I must get back to the UK at once. I'm urgently required in London to report on the supply situation over here. Now let us not waste any more time, captain, *please*!' He grabbed the rope ladder and before Peter could react he

was aboard, shaking himself like a wet dog, while the two ratings looked at him helplessly.

'Give me a cigarette, man!' Hughes snapped. 'Don't just stand there like a spare part.'

Peter clattered down to the deck. 'What credentials have you for being given priority, Colonel?' he asked, as one of the ratings fumbled for his cigarettes and lighter.

'You have my word for it, Captain.' Hughes, whose face underneath the red-banded cap of a staff officer, turned out to be ratlike with curious, untrustworthy yellow eyes. 'That should suffice.'

'I'm afraid it doesn't, Colonel,' Peter said. 'Unless you can give me some auth –'

He never finished his words. As by magic, a big service revolver appeared in Colonel Hughes' hand and in a voice that was now pure cockney, the man snarled, '*THIS* is my authority, mate! Now shove off. I've had enough of this sodding place – and the Stukas'll be back within the hour.'

Down below, the men standing up to their necks in water began to cry out piteously, as they took in the tense little scene on the deck, knowing that this might well be their last chance to get away before the slaughter of the new day. 'Don't leave us . . . please don't leave us!' they cried, some of them in tears, holding up their arms pleadingly.

'Be quiet!' Peter snapped. 'We won't leave you.'

'Yer better well do as I say, tosher!' the bogus colonel said, his knuckles gripped the revolver whitening as he applied pressure. 'Cos, it's either you or me . . . and remember, you boys-in-blue,' he added for the benefit of the armed ratings behind him without turning, 'if any of you lot try any tricks, his nibs here gets it first.'

Peter hesitated. It would be a supreme irony, he told himself, if he were shot at Dunkirk by one of his own countrymen. The man was quite capable of doing so, though, he could see that; yet he couldn't allow his ship to be shanghaied like this. Suddenly he was overwhelmed

with an all-consuming rage at this rat who was prepared to sacrifice the lives of others as long as his own miserable, skinny neck were saved.

'I'm going to give you three to drop that revolver,' he said quietly, surprised himself at just how cool and collected his voice sounded. 'And then I'll let you crawl back into the hole from which you came. If you don't drop it, I'm coming for you.'

'You and whose army!' the man sneered.

'*One!*'

The look on the man's ratlike face changed to one of fear.

'I'm warning you!' he threatened, jerking up the pistol.

Around him on the deck, the ratings tensed. Down below the soldiers ceased their moaning. All was silence, save for the boom of the artillery in the far distance.

'*Two!*'

There was a sharp click as the bogus colonel took first pressure.

'*Three!*'

In the same instant that Peter dived at the man with the gun, the latter fired. Peter felt a burning pain in his right calf, and then he was on top of the rat, pounding him with his fists, smashing them into the man's face till he felt them go warm and wet with his blood and the man's body grow limp as he blacked out. Then, and only then, did he stop and sag there, leg now afire with pain, dully looking at his knuckles which were red with blood.

'Sir . . . you're hurt, sir?' half-a-dozen ratings cried in alarm.

'It's all right . . . all right,' Peter snapped irritably and waving them away, levered himself up weakly by the bulkhead. 'Get the line moving again . . . and toss that rat overboard!'

'He's still unconscious, sir,' a rating called, bending down over the soldier, whose face was a bloody pulp from Peter's infuriated blows. 'He . . . might drown.'

'I don't care,' Peter said, 'Get it over with and let's get

on. It'll be light in another thirty minutes.'

A moment later, two brawny ratings grabbed up the unconscious soldier and threw him over the side. He did not come up again. Peter, limping wearily to the bridge, trailing blood behind him as he did so, did not even look. The evacuation continued. . . .

'E-boats, Captain!' the port look-out called out, jumping up on the deck so that he could be seen in the blanket-covered brown sea of soldiers that flooded the place.

'Oh Christ, that's torn it!' Peter cursed as he sat there on a cabin chair on the bridge, one hand gripping the tourniquet wrapped around his thigh to stop the blood from the gaping bullet wound in his calf. He raised his binoculars.

The look-out was correct. Two lean white shapes were racing towards the little convoy, the morning sun gleaming on their woodwork. Almost instantly, their 20mm cannon started to bark and white tracer shells curved towards the convoy, gathering speed by the instant.

Panic broke out among the soldiers, as Peter grabbed his loud-hailer and cried sternly. 'Everyone down! There is no need for panic. Just keep down! Sparks,' he yelled at the waiting operator, 'get on your radio. Give our position. Tell 'em we're being attacked and ask for immediate –' He ducked hastily as a burst of shells punched a line of gleaming steel holes along the front of the bridge. The radio operator flashed below, obviously glad to get out of the firing.

Now the MTB's guns started to answer the E-boats fire, as the two white craft swung the length of the convoy, raking it with their fire. The flak sent the water flying in huge spouts on both sides of them, but the inexperienced gunners simply could not seem to range in, as the yacht owned by the middle-aged stockbroker suddenly burst into flames, with her crew and the soldiers leaping over the sides into the sea.

Behind it, one of the Clydeside tugs lowered speed, as if its captain were preparing to stop and pick up survivors. Angry and frustrated, realizing that there was a tragedy in the making, Peter bellowed through the loudspeaker, 'Leave them, damn you, Captain! Leave them!' And then he looked away hastily, as the tug proceeded on course, ploughing its way through the screaming men in the water all around its sturdy sides.

Now Peter's gunners were at last beginning to range in and the young captain, new hope in his heart, could see that the E-boats seemed to be begging off, as they roared away, throwing up two tremendous white wakes behind them. 'Please God, let them bugger off *now*!' he prayed fervently to himself, knowing that unless his gunners struck lucky in the next few minutes their fate was sealed.

But God apparently was not listening to Lieutenant Peter Harding's prayers on this particular May day. Now the E-boats came roaring in again, their bows cutting the waves like sharp knives, their engines racing full out from port and starboard. Their tactic was obvious. They hoped to fool the gunners. Once one of them had drawn the Tommies' fire, he would veer off, leaving his running-mate to come in for the kill unopposed.

Peter yelled, 'Machine gunners concentrate on the second one to port! Gunners, take the other one!' He sucked in a great chestful of air. 'Be prepared to take on the other Jerry as soon as I give the command!'

A thousand yards . . . eight hundred . . . seven hundred . . . the two E-boats were coming in at a tremendous speed, smacking each wave as if it were solid rock and then skimming over the sea for moments before hitting the next wave . . . *six hundred and fifty . . . six hundred yards* . . . their oerlikons were chattering violently again, spewing deadly white fire at the craft in front of them, scattering wildly in all directions to get out of the line of attack. Peter gripped the rail tense and anxious, the pain in his leg forgotten now, willing his sweating gunners to hit one of the bastards. But he was out of luck.

The gunners' shells consistently missed the racing E-boats.

'*Draw 'em into your fire . . . for Chrissake, draw the sods into it*!' he cried desperately above the din of battle.

One of the tugs faltered to a halt and began to sink by the stern. Again the panic-stricken soldiers sprang over the side into the heaving water, while the skipper wrestled frantically with the wheel which no longer answered. Slowly the blue and white St Andrew's flag, which the Scot favoured over the Red Duster of the Merchant Service, started to disappear beneath the water.

Peter gave up. He closed his eyes, knowing that his raw inexperienced gunners had failed him. In a minute, one of the E-boats would break for clear and come hurtling at the MTB to plant her fish right in his keel. Then, as if by a miracle, there was the roar of new engines and at five hundred yards, their cannon still chattering crazily, the two E-boats had broken off their final run-in and were streaking northwards at top-speed, followed by a barrage of shell-fire. Peter gasped and let the loud-hailer drop out of his nerveless fingers. It was Toby and the rest of the squadron. They had been saved from annihilation at the eleventh hour. Suddenly, for some reason that he was quite unable to comprehend, the deck came up to meet him and he was lying there, the dark clouds of unconsciousness submerging him. . . .

'Well,' the far-away voice said, 'that's the end of Operation Dynamo, thank God!'

Peter's eyes flickered open and closed again. His eyelids seemed tremendously heavy. He tried once again and this time he succeeded. Toby Roxburgh's plump face swam into view.

For what appeared a long time, he attempted to focus his eyes. Finally he managed to do so and now he could see it really was Toby, his beard strangely grey and with dark-blue circles under his eyes. 'It's you,' he gasped

stupidly, now becoming aware of the rows of men in white hospital cots on both sides of him, and the stink of ether. Of course, he had to be in a naval hospital. He had been wounded by that cowardly bastard back there on the ship.

'Who did you think – the Fairy Queen, perhaps?' Toby smiled down at him wearily, the old spirit gone from his fruity voice. 'Just thought I'd pop by and see how you were getting on before I get my old head down and sleep for a couple of million years.' He licked his cracked lips and Peter could see the strain he had been subjected to.

'How did it go?' Peter croaked, still feeling very weak from the drugs.

'Well, we got your little lot home after you flaked out – and another three hundred thousand as well.'

'Three hundred thousand, Toby?' Peter said, not quite understanding.

'Yes, virtually the whole of the BEF has been eva-cuated, though of course most of their heavy equipment has gone for a Burton. The Jerries have run us out of Europe. God knows what's going to happen to the old country now.' He rubbed his blood-shot eyes wearily. 'I've got an awful feeling, Peter, old lad, that we're knackered . . . But forget that.' He forced a smile. 'How are *you* feeling?'

'Not so bad, really. Have you talked to the sawbones, Toby?' The other man nodded. 'What do they say?'

'It's not going to be easy. But you'll survive Peter. You'll have to stay in dock for a while. Now, old boy, that battle-axe of a ward sister tells me you've got to have a pee, before you get another needle stuck in your skinny bum. So I'm off.' He grinned slightly. 'But at least for this one, they won't give you a bloody gong, will they? They don't when you kill yer own side . . . Bye, Peter. Here comes the battle-axe. . . Look after yourself.'

'Bye Toby.'

Then he was gone. Peter never saw him again.

TEN

'How, Big White Chief,' Hartung said with a grin, as the familiar, portly, white-clad figure of Professor Hirschmann appeared at the door of his hospital room.

Hirschmann held up his right hand and said, 'How, Big Red Chief Red Claw.'

'How indeed? I'm feeling exceedingly fit, Prof. Look . . .' He swung himself out of the cot, biting his bottom lip to hold back the little cry of pain as the old agony shot up his right side and along his arm.

'Excellent . . . excellent,' Hirschmann agreed. 'You've made remarkable progress, Hartung, I really must say that. Third degree burns and a bad thigh wound. I doubt very much if those poor chaps who were hit with you on the *Hipper* are doing so well this fine July morning . . . Now, then,' the Professor was businesslike now, 'let's have a look at that red claw of yours.'

Hartung obediently extended his skinny stump of an arm, seared by that terrible flash fire on the *Hipper*, when the Tommy torpedo had struck home, to a hideous lobster pink, and looked away. Even now, after three months, he could not bear to look at it, in spite of the fact that he had christened himself 'Red Claw' on account of it.

Professor Hirschmann made the usual little noises that doctors all over the world make, as he felt the upper arm with his broad capable fingers and then ran them down the length of the withered forearm, occasionally glancing up, as if he were looking for signs of pain in Hartung's drawn white face. Finally, he said, 'Red Claw, let me see you bend the arm.'

Hartung grinned and drew a deep breath. The moment

had come, for which he had been preparing these last three weeks in secret, exercising for hours in the privacy of his own room when the nurses were not about. 'I'll do better than that. Stand back, Big White Chief.'

'Red Claw, he speak with forked tongue,' Hirschmann declared, obviously puzzled. All the same he did as Hartung had requested.

The young blond officer with the drawn, taut face of a man who had suffered a great deal of pain, bent and thrust both arms underneath the cot.

'What in three devils' name are you up to, Hartung?' Hirschmann cried in sudden alarm.

By way of reply, Hartung heaved, the sweat abruptly bursting out all over his face, a pain like fire running up his arm. Slowly but surely he raised the one-hundredweight bed until it was parallel with his shoulders and held it there for a count of thirty seconds before lowering it with a crash, his bottom lip bloody where he had bitten into it to stop himself crying out with the pain.

'Now, oh Big White Chief,' he gasped, wiping the blood away, 'what do you say to that? Am I ready for a return to sea-duty, or not?' He smiled expectantly at the head of *La Charité*'s surgical department.

Professor Hirschmann was impressed but not convinced. 'My God, Hartung, you mustn't do things like that, although I do admire your tremendous courage! Lesser men would have been content with a medical discharge and a pension from the state with your terrible injuries.'

'*Gemeinnutz geht vor Eigennutz**' Hartung said cheerfully, using the old Party slogan. 'All I want is to get back to the service. There's a war to be fought.'

Hirschmann sniffed. 'Let me see you do another weight-lifting trick, Chief Red Claw,' he said and took a match out of his pocket.

Hartung looked at it in bewilderment, as the Professor

---

*Roughly, 'public good is more important than private'.

laid it carefully on the blanket covering the cot. 'What am I supposed to do, Prof?'

'Lift it,' Hirschmann said with a faint smile, becoming aware of the brass band music down below for the first time now.

'*Lift that!*' Hartung exploded. 'What kind of damn-fool trick is that?'

'Just lift it – *above your head*,' Hirschmann said calmly, a knowing look in those dark, smart eyes of his.

'*Himmel, Arsch und Wolkenbruch*, all right, anything you say!' Hartung exploded. He picked up the match and raised it to a spot level with his shoulder. Abruptly pain stabbed his arm. Just in time he caught himself from yelling aloud with it.

'Go on, *Leutnant* Hartung – further!' Hirschmann urged.

Hartung gritted his teeth and raised the matchstick a couple of centimetres. Now his body was wet with sweat and his arm ablaze with sheer agony.

'*Weiter*! . . . further,' Hirschmann commanded, iron in his voice now. '*Weiter!*'

Hartung raised his hand another centimetre. The fiery-red, highly taut skin of his arm cracked ominously. It seemed as if the whole limb would incinerate at any moment. Now his whole body was trembling violently with the effort.

'Further!' The Professor ordered harshly. 'Go on, you hero, show me just how fit you are and I'll certify you ready for active service this very day. *Weiter!*'

Hartung tried. His eyes wild with rage and frustration, great pearls of sweat mingling with the tears that ran down his skinny cheeks, he attempted to lift the matchstick further. But he couldn't, he simply couldn't. The agony was too great.

'I can't . . . I can't, damn you, Great White Chief . . . *I damn well can't*!' He dropped the match and slumped to the bed, his shoulders sunk in defeat, sobs

racking his painfully thin body beneath the blue-and-white hospital pyjamas.

Gently Professor Hirschmann laid his hand on Hartung's heaving shoulder. 'It's all right . . . all right, Horst . . . I just had to show you that you weren't as fit as you think you are. You have done a tremendous job, but it will take time, much time, before you are really well enough for active service.'

Hartung looked up, the red claw lying like a separate part of him on his lap. 'But the *Kriegsmarine* is my life, Prof. I wouldn't know what to do without the sea.' He looked pleadingly at the doctor, his eyes wet with tears of pain.

'I understand . . . I understand. And we'll get you fit in due course. You'll get back to the Navy. But it'll take time, Horst. You must understand – time!'

'But Prof time is what I haven't got! I want to get into the war.'

'War!' Hirschmann echoed. 'Come here – to the window.'

Hartung followed him to the tall window overlooking the gaily decorated street below, with the Hitler Youth in their grey shirts and black shorts standing behind the soldiers waving their little swastika flags furiously.

'Look,' Hirschmann said as the military band swung round the corner, led by a giant of a drum-major swinging his baton effortlessly, as he goose-stepped, to the roars of applause and cheers from the delighted civilians crowding the pavement on both sides. 'It's the *Leibstandarte* returning home from France.' He indicated the young grey-clad soldiers, healthy tanned faces covered in grins, flowers sprouting out of the muzzles of their rifles as they slammed down their heavy jackboots in perfect, hobnailed unison in that old manner which had once gained them the name of 'the flat-foot guards' in their home garrison of Berlin. 'They're all there, the young heroes – Sepp Dietrich, Gert Bremer, young Jochen Peiper. And do you know what will happen to them, Horst?'

Hartung, envious of the healthy young giants stamping by below, shook his head mystified.

'I shall tell you. They'll go back to playing soldier in front of the New Reich Chancellery – those who are regulars that is. The reservists will be demobilized. The *Führer* has already announced he is preparing to demobilize fourteen divisions. Why? I shall tell you.' Carefully he closed the window to muffle the cheers and the silver blare of the band. 'The war's virtually over, Horst. The Tommies will surrender before this summer is out. We Germans are the masters of Western Europe. What else can they do?' He smiled sympathetically. 'Chief Red Claw, I'm afraid to say – and please forgive the cliche – for you the war is over. . . .'

Horst Hartung was not the only one frustrated by the doctors that particular fine July morning. Half a thousand miles away, Peter Harding pushed his way through the excited crowds outside Buckingham Palace and then leaning his stick against the wall, watched by an eagle-eyed sentry from the Grenadier Guards, he removed the D.S.O. from his tunic, stuffed it in the case and put the case inside his pocket almost shame-facedly. Seizing his cane, he limped past the silly excited women in their floral dresses and broad-brimmed hats posing next to embarrassed husbands, displaying their new awards, while the press photographers clicked away.

The skinny, nervous King had been kind. He had even exchanged a few words with Peter in that highly strung, stuttering manner of his, on the dais after he had presented him with the D.S.O. But his words had not cheered Peter up. Not even the fact that he was in London on a forty-eight hour pass from Dover Naval Hosptial could shake him out of his black mood, which was almost akin to despair.

On the previous day, the surgeon-captain in charge of wound cases had adamantly refused to up-grade him from

his present C-3 category to A-1 or A-3. 'It's no use, Harding,' he had said in that thick Scots accent of his, eyeing the young officer facing him and apparently not liking what he saw. 'It's not on. You're simply not fit for sea-duty yet.'

Outside, another salvo of German shells from Calais crashed into Dover as the usual 'morning-hate' worked up to a crescendo and the shrill of ambulance bells indicated that the civilians were beginning to take casualties again.

The surgeon-captain stared at Harding's face, no longer as handsome as it had once been, with the cheeks hollowed out by strain and suffering, hard lines around the mouth. He knew all the signs. He had seen them often enough in these last few terrible weeks. The officer facing him had undergone a lot of pain and a lot of tension. He needed care and rest. 'I'm going to ask you a personal question, Harding' he said, his voice gentler now. 'You don't have to answer it, if you don't want to.'

'It is, sir?' Peter snapped in that new harsh manner of his, as if he were impatient with the whole world.

'When did you last have a . . . woman?'

Peter did not hesitate. 'In Hull, last year, sir. A prostitute to be exact.'

Surprisingly it was the surgeon-captain who blushed, not the young officer, who could have been his son. 'I see,' he said, trying to cover his embarrassment with a severe professional frown. 'Then I recommend you to go out and find one when you go up to London to receive your gong from the King. Somewhere around Shaftesbury Avenue, they tell me, you can find the – er – ladies of the night.'

'No, sir, that's for pansies, sir,' Peter said maliciously. 'But it's not a woman I want, it's a big ship!'

All that Peter had received by way of an answer was another tremendous crash, as once more a salvo from the German heavy guns across the Channel had smashed down on Dover.

Now, Peter Harding, feeling miserable and somehow

an outsider among the happy throng of medal winners'
families, limped slowly across the street, ignoring the
cockney newspaper sellers with their raucous cries and
hastily scrawled blackboards. '*RAF downs another fifty
Jerries*,' they barked. '*Winnie says we're winning
. . . Read all about . . . get yer paper, guv . . .
Winnie says we're winning the Battle o' Britain*. . . .'

Peter halted and let a platoon of the newly formed LDV
march past*: a group of elderly gentlemen in baggy khaki,
their chests ablaze with the ribbons of the old war, pitch-
forks and broompoles instead of rifles across their
shoulders. 'Luck, duck and vanish', the wags were calling
the Local Defence Volunteers; and they looked just like
that, Peter could not help thinking gloomily. What *could*
they do, or for that matter the Regular Army as well,
when the well-trained German troops started landing in
Britain, which was likely any day now?

Thus engrossed in his gloomy thoughts, it took Peter a
few moments to comprehend that he was now accompanied by a female dressed in the unform of the FANYS,
who was smiling encouragingly, almost as if she knew
him. Indeed, he realized with the shock of growing
awareness, her face seemed familiar too. 'Why,' he exclaimed, stopping short and facing her, 'it's the
Hell-Cat . . . *Anna*!'

People turned and stared. An elderly clergyman in
gaiters and carrying his gas-mask in a cardboard-box over
his shoulder tut-tutted. At the corner, a steel-helmeted
special constable looked sharply at the young officer, as if
he expected a cry of rape at any moment.

'Of course, it's Anna,' she said in that delightfully
accented English of hers and before he could stop her she
had reached up and kissed him.

'Shocking!' a woman in a picture hat said sternly. 'The
things young people do in public these days is simply
shocking! And in uniform too!'

---

*The forerunner of the Home Guard.

Anna, as aggressive as ever, stuck her tongue out at the woman and said 'Ba, ba!'

The woman fled.

'But what . . . what are you doing in that uniform, Anna?' Peter stuttered.

'You thought they would have packed me off to Canada or interned me on the Isle-of-Man, eh, Peter, like they've done with the rest of the Germans? After all I am Jewish you know. Come to think of it, there are those here in England who think that is excuse enough to send me there.' She laughed charmingly, though there was a trace of bitterness in her eyes. 'And you, the wounded hero, how are you?'

'You knew?'

'Of course, that's why I am here. I took the afternoon to come and see you. It might be my last chance.'

'Last chance?' Peter queried.

'I'm probably being posted from London soon,' she said quickly and suddenly Peter had a fleeting suspicion that she was lying.

'You're stationed here in London?'

'Yes, I work at the Ministry of Economics . . . courier work and that sort of stuff.' She thrust her arm through his. 'But let us not talk about such boring things. Take me somewhere, give me a drink, let's talk about *us*.' He felt the urging pressure on his arm as the sirens started to sound the alert and the special policeman began to call 'Take cover . . . everybody into the shelters! Come along now, please!'

'Yes,' he said, 'that's a ruddy good idea. Let's get into a pub before they get too packed. . . .'

'*Now this is number one and I've got her on the run . . . Roll me over, lay me down and do it again . . . Roll me over in the clover, lay me down and do it agen. . . .*'

At the piano, the drunken RAF pilots swung into yet

another ditty from their seemingly endless repertoire of mildly dirty songs, while the cockneys in their cloth caps grinned in amusement, stamping their feet in time on the sawdust-covered floor of the pub. Outside the guns thundered and occasionally the whole place shuddered as another German bomb smashed to the ground. But no one seemed concerned. The pub was staying open longer than usual on account of the raid and there was still plenty of beer.

Anna smiled at Peter, who was as entranced as he had been that first day back in Wilhelmshaven in what now seemed another age, and said, 'The English don't appear to take their war very seriously, eh. They laugh and dance and drink, and Hitler has all of Europe in his power.'

'Yes, you're right I suppose,' Peter agreed, as the drunken RAF men launched into '*Now this is number two and he's got it up her flue. . . .*'

'Most of them don't know what the war's all about. They haven't got a clue what combat's like. Do you know I've lost two commanding officers in the last three months. Out there in the Channel it's bloody murder! If it's not the E-boats, then it's the subs and those bloody Stukas of theirs.' He shook his head in anger. 'But they'll learn, they'll learn one day soon!'

'You sound bitter?' Anna queried, searching his face and noting that there was a hardness about the lips which had not been there before. Peter's eyes no longer seemed sensitive, but savage and angry; the brutalization of total war had had its effect upon them.

'Perhaps, I don't really know, Anna. All I know is this – that if we don't wake up soon, we'll lose this war.' He took her hand instinctively and pressed it urgently. 'Anna, my advice to you is to get out while there is still time. You could go to Canada. After all, you are Jewish and you know what they do to Jews.'

She shook her head firmly. 'No, Peter, I am the last person who should run. If I start running now, there will be no stopping.' She laughed, suddenly bitter. 'Then I

really will become that contemptible creature, the Wandering Jew. You know what that woman said during the Spanish Civil War, better to die on your feet, than live on your knees.'

Peter nodded his head. 'I suppose you're right, Anna.'

She squeezed his hand. 'I *know* I am,' she said with conviction. 'Listen . . . the All Clear, come I'll take you to my flat.'

Without waiting for his agreement, she threw her sling bag over her shoulder and walked out followed by wolf-whistles and the envious stares of drunken RAF sergeants.

As they walked in silence down the sunny street, followed by the landlord's tolerant 'Now come along gentlemen, time *please*', Peter knew with sudden certainty exactly what was going to happen this bright July day. . . .

Part Three: 1941

ONE

'Here they come!' the umpire shouted. 'Stand back gentlemen, *please*!'

The group of Army, Air Force and Navy officers gathered on the cliff with the handsome new head of Combined Operations, Lord Louis Mountbatten, quickly stepped back. The rehearsal had commenced.

Down below, the first two landing craft hit the beach and their ramps immediately slapped the damp sand. Swifly, expertly the khaki-clad commandos with their blackened faces and stocking caps doubled to left and right, crunching over the shingle towards the base of the cliff. The bren gunners opened up from both flanks sending white tracer zipping just over their heads.

'Live ammo, gentlemen,' the umpire commented.

'Dangerous isn't it?' Mountbatten asked.

'We can live with it, sir,' the umpire replied, his eyes now on the stop-watch in his right hand.

A minute passed. Now the little groups of commandos crouched down below had assembled their rocket launchers. There was a series of faint plops, followed immediately by bursts of white smoke, through which flew gleaming steel grapnels, trailing their rope-lines behind them.

Clang . . . clang . . . clang! The hooks dug into the chalk surface all along the top of the cliff.

At once the first commandos started shinning up the

hundred foot long rope. At the top of the cliff, soldiers began to drop hand grenades on them, which exploded sending their ropes swinging violently from side to side. The commandos kept coming.

'Thunderflashes, gentlemen,' the umpire explained. 'Frightening, but not lethal this time.'

'Thank you for that particular piece of information.' Mountbatten breathed a sigh of relief.

The first crimson, sweat-lathered face appeared over the edge of the cliff, a commando with a fighting knife clenched in his teeth.

'Melodramatic admittedly,' the umpire said drily, 'but highly useful if a Jerry sentry should happen to be stupid enough to be standing there.'

'I certainly wouldn't like to meet him on a dark night,' Mountbatten commented, to the accompaniment of laughter from the assembled planning-officers.

Now the first skirmish line of commandos doubled forward, running for the triple line of cruel-looking barbed wire which defended the 'enemy post', manned this fine winter's morning by a group of middle-aged soldiers from the Pioneer Corps. The latter looked as scared of the burly figures pelting towards them, weapons at the ready, as any German might well have been.

The commandos hit the wire. Without hesitating, a colour-sergeant threw himself on it, arms outstretched so that he lay spreadeagled on the cruel prongs like Jesus on the cross. Standing just behind Lord Mountbatten, huddled in his greatcoat, Lieutenant-Commander Harding winced. The commandos did not falter. Instantly they began to run across the human bridge to drop on the other side of the wire, while the terrified Pioneer Corps soldiers fired blank cartridges at them, looking as if they might drop their rifles and scuttle for safety at any moment.

There was a clash of steel as the commandos locked bayonets with the Pioneer Corps privates. For a few minutes the two groups swayed back and forth, with the occasional commando sneaking in a swift knee to the

groin when he thought the officers were not looking, and then it was over and the defenders were 'surrendering' everywhere.

The colour-sergeant with the ripped battledress, his face covered with bloody scratches and tears, immediately took over, hustling the 'prisoners' to one side, to make room for the bombers and tommy-gunners. They doubled forward to the line of the sod-covered mounds, which were the enemy radar positions. Legs braced apart like gangsters in some pre-war American thriller, the commandos poured a stream of tracer into the bunkers, while the bombers rained down grenades upon them making a racket that prompted Lord Mountbatten to grimace.

The umpire had seen enough. He clicked home his stop-watch and in the same moment, raising his flare pistol, fired a red very light into the air. It soared upwards, bathing the scene in a ruddy hue which made the 'prisoners' faces glow unnaturally. This was the signal for the end of the 'dress rehearsal'.

'Well?' Mountbatten demanded.

'Six minutes and thirty-three . . . no, thirty-*four* seconds from the time the landing barges hit the beach, sir,' the umpire replied promptly.

'Excellent.' Mountbatten's handsome, sharp-featured face broke into a smile. 'Please tell the soldiers I am exceedingly well satisfied with them. They have done an excellent job.'

'Sir!' The umpire clicked to attention, while beyond the wire, the commandos slumped to the turf and began wiping their sweating, blackened faces.

'See that they get their char and wads, will you,' Mountbatten added, turning to the assembled officers. 'We'll go and do our little critique out of this wind, I think.' He smiled winningly.

'And I expect that a little spot of Nelson's Blood wouldn't do any harm, what?'

The naval officers among them laughed, and then they

were trailing back to the Nissen hut which had been allocated to them by the commando colonel.

Mountbatten cradled his mug of steaming hot tea laced with rum – 'sergeant-major's char', the commandos' mess-sergeant had called it proudly – and looked around at the men who were going to carry out the big raid.

He was obviously pleased with what he saw. They were the best the hard-pressed country could provide this winter of 1941.

'Well gentlemen,' he commenced, 'I don't need to tell you that Britain is in a sorry state. Our only ally is Russia, the Germans dominate Europe, our convoys are being slaughtered – this year we'll be lucky if we can provide the kids with an orange for Christmas – and we haven't had a real victory since the war started. The nation needs something to pick them up, afford them a little cheer at a very gloomy time. That's why Winston is so wild about this raid. We must have a success – the morale of the nation demands it. And gentlemen, this time we're after bigger fish than at Guernsey.'

'Is it the radar sites in Northern France then, sir?' the big bluff squadron-leader whose planes were to cover the operation asked confidently.

'I'm afraid I have misled you a little, Squadron-Leader. Those dummy radar sites out there were to fool the troops. You know careless talk costs lives,' Mountbatten quoted the slogan of the familiar security poster. 'And commandos do tend to boast in the pubs, I'm afraid.'

The tough-looking commando colonel frowned at his muddy boots. 'It's not France at all.'

There was a little gasp of surprise from the assembled officers. Mountbatten seemed pleased with the success of his deception. He took a careful sip of his steaming hot tea. 'It's the Lofoten Islands. And in case some of you brown jobs,' he used the navy's phrase for the soldiers, 'don't know where they are, they are off the coast of

Norway – here.' He touched the spot on the map with his elegantly gloved hand.

'We've been there before, sir,' someone said, but Mountbatten didn't seem to hear.

Peter Harding frowned. His new MTBs would make it that far without difficulty; the 1941 model had a range of over seven hundred miles. But they would need refuelling on the way back and if the *Luftwaffe* were after them . . . He did not complete the thought as he remembered that it was precisely while refuelling in the Channel that poor old Toby had bought it in the summer of 1940.

'Our aims in the Island are threefold,' Mountbatten continued. 'We want to destroy the enemy oil refineries located there. We want to encourage Norwegian resistance against the Quisling government in Oslo and the Germans, and we want to take back as many prisoners and anyone of the local populace willing to come with us. They are urgently needed by our Intelligence.' Mountbatten's face hardened. 'But the most important thing of all, and I must emphasize this once again, gentlemen, *we must have a victory* . . .'

He let the words sink in before saying to his aide, 'All right, Jenkins, let them have the individual task sheets and other information.'

Obediently the young officer opened the big buff envelope marked in red 'top secret' and started passing out the typewritten sheets to the officers, making each one sign for his personal copy.

Mountbatten crooked a finger at a waiting Peter. 'Commander Harding, could I have a word, please?'

'Sir.'

Mountbatten guided Peter out of earshot of the others, and said 'I presume you've heard of the Fifteenth Flotilla, Commander?'

'The cloak-and-dagger boys?'

'Yes.' Mountbatten sniffed. 'I didn't realize their security was that bad. What do you know of them, Commander?'

'Not *that* much, sir. I know they have their own mother-ship and they don't seem to be engaged on the same kind of ops as my own chaps. I know they're always practising surf landings in the Dartmouth area, so I guess they can only be employed carrying out clandestine landings.' Peter shrugged, 'I suppose in France.' He looked directly at the Head of Combined Operations in that new challenging manner of his as if to check whether he was right. He was.

'Yes, you've guessed right,' Mountbatten said. 'The Fifteenth Flotilla is specially employed for running agents of the SOE, SIS and the Franco-Belgian resistance movements, in and out of France. Highly dangerous work as you can probably guess.'

Peter grunted and waited for Mountbatten to tell him what this had to do with him and the planned operation against the Lofoten Islands.

Mountbatten took his time, as was the prerogative of the hero of *HMS Kelly* and a member of the Royal Family, sizing up this young lieutenant-commander with the hard eyes and even harder face. Finally he explained, 'Now, Harding, you can guess you will be playing a very important role in covering the commandos' landing craft from the moment they leave the mother ships until they hit the shore?'

'Yessir, I guessed that would be the role of my squadron.' He laughed hollowly, but the hard eyes did not light up. 'After all, MTBs are cheaper to lose than destroyers.'

'You're a cynic, Harding.'

'No sir, just a realist. When it comes to balancing the books, their Lordships prefer to see us on the debit side and not their precious destroyers.'

The former destroyer captain smiled now. 'Perhaps you're right, Harding. Well, to continue, DDODI*, which runs the Fifteenth Flotilla, have just been given a top-level, number-one priority assignment. They've been

* Deputy Director Operations Division, Irregular.

ordered by the PM personally to run an agent into France to cover the enemy-held ports in Brittany peninsula. Why? I shall tell you. The *Gneisenau* and the *Scharnhorst*, as you know, have been on a rampage in the North Atlantic ever since the *Ramillies* lost them last week. So far they've sunk two hundred thousand tons of our merchant shipping and the PM wants it stopped – and stopped soon!'

For a moment Peter thought of those long sinister grey shapes he had seen sliding out of the fogbanks off the Norwegian coast the year before. How powerful and impregnable they had seemed then; now they were obviously proving just how dangerous they were.

'Our guess is that they'll soon be forced to return to port. They can't steam the high seas for ever without supplies and oil. So where will they run? The Denmark Strait is out of the question. The Home Fleet and the Fleet Air Arm have got that all sealed up. Intelligence's guess is that they'll head for Brest and that's why we must have an agent over there when they do, so that the RAF can get accurate, up-to-date information on the two of them.'

'But what has all this got to do with me, sir?' Peter asked. 'I mean we'll be bound for Norway soon.'

'Exactly. Now the Germans are constantly watching our movements out of Dartmouth for obvious reasons. So they'll see our own flotilla move out – they know all about you according to Intelligence who have discovered you on their intercepts.'

'Fame at last.' Peter said.

'Notoriety is closer to it, Harding. You are regarded by them as particularly aggressive, hard-hitting *englischer Schweinhund*.' He grinned at Peter. 'So when they find you have moved out and are heading for France, they'll conclude you are on one of your usual fighting sweeps. Our hope is that they'll send out the E-boats to fight you. Strangely enough, this time the English pig-dog will not make a fight, but will disappear northwards, back on the course which will eventually take him to Norway –

though they won't know anything about that.'

'And?'

'In the general confusion, the cloak-and-dagger chaps from the Fifteenth will slip away and deposit this agent on the beach at Anse Cochat in Brittany. That, at least, is the plan.' Mountbatten waited for a moment and then said, 'Well?'

'All right with me, sir. Two birds with one stone – fair enough.'

'Well done, Harding . . . Right, we'd better get back to the others and start arranging the syndicates.' Gently he began to steer Peter back to the little groups of chatting officers.

Just before they reached them, Peter said apropos of nothing, 'Must be a brave sort of chap to do it, sir, don't you think?'

'What?' Mountbatten asked, his mind obviously now on the Lofoten raid again.

'The agent who's going to find the *Gneisenau* and *Scharnhorst*, sir. If the Germans catch him, I suppose it will mean his neck, sir.'

Mountbatten flashed him a quick smile. 'But the Joey – that's what the Fifteenth call their passengers – isn't a man. The Joey's a woman and she has a remarkably pretty neck, I can you tell that, remarkably pretty. . . .'

TWO

Above them the white signal lamp of the big, four-engined Sunderland flying-boat from Coastal Command commenced flickering off and on. On the bridge of the leading MTB, Peter Harding snapped, 'Bunts, read it!'

Swiftly the signaller began jotting down the letters on his pad, while the white-painted Sunderland swept across the Flotilla in a slow, lazy curve. Then, satisfied that the little ships below had got its message, the Sunderland's pilot wiggled his wings, the engines started to roar, and it flew away, its mission completed for this day. 'Back to bacon-and-eggs and the local popsies,' Drewer, Peter's second-in-command, said a little enviously. 'Jammy buggers!'

Peter grinned momentarily. Sometimes one would think the RAF was the enemy, not the Germans, he told himself. Most matelots had nothing but scorn, tinged with envy, for the young eagles of the RAF. 'Alright, Bunts, let's have it.'

The signaller cleared his throat, as if he were going to make a public speech. 'Spotted E-boats – six in all – leaving Brest zero fourteen hundred hours. Proceeding on a north-westerly course. Estimated speed is thirty knots. Good luck. Your winged friends.'

'Your winged friends!' Drewer snorted at Peter's side. 'Those Brylcreem boys are no friends of mine!'

Peter ignored him, his mind busy with a quick calculation. If the E-boats were after him – and he was sure that German radar in Brittany must have picked up their presence by now – they would probably be here just before dusk. He flashed a quick glance at the winter sky, the dark clouds of night already beginning to roll in from the

east across a sullen green sea. In an hour it would be pitch black. The conditions would be ideal for the lone gunboat from the Fifteenth Flotilla to drop its passenger at the Anse Cochat, while the Germans were concentrating on the MTBs off their coast.

'Bunts,' he commanded once again.

'Sir?'

'Get ready to send a signal to the gunboat from the Fifteenth.' The signaller sprang to the Aldis lamp and waited attentively. 'All right, begin: "E-boats advised. We're now to resume our normal course for Scapa, trailing our coat at them. You're on your own. Happy landings."'

Five hundred yards away the signal lamp of the gunboat started to flash, its superstructure camouflaged in the German fashion and with no White Ensign at its stern so that it might well have been taken for an enemy E-boat. Impatiently, wanting to get underway now his mission off Brittany was completed, Peter tensed on the bridge while Bunts took it down. He nudged Drewer, 'All right, Number One, let's get our digit out of the orifice. Just in case Old Jerry is looking for us with aircraft too.'

'Ay, ay, sir.' Drewer sprang to the controls.

'Here we are, sir,' Bunts said, holding up his pad, and clearing his throat once again.

'Unaccustomed as I am to public speaking,' Peter said sarcastically.

But sarcasm was wasted on the owl-faced signaller, who Peter knew was a methodist lay preacher off-duty in one of the Portsmouth chapels. He took his time. 'It reads, sir: "Thank you for company, big friends."'

Peter shook his head. How stereotyped these naval signals always were with their 'friends' and their 'good lucks'! Where were the bold, original signals he had read about in the history books at Dartmouth?

'Make new heading immediately: "Our Joey says all the best, *Hoellenkatze*."'

The rating blinked at Peter, whose face had suddenly

gone a deathly white. 'Did I misread that, sir?' he asked plaintively. He looked down at his pad again. 'Our Joey says all the best, Hoellenkatze . . . Can't make head nor tail of it.'

'Oh my Christ!' Peter howled, his face contorted with a dozen conflicting emotions. It was Anna. *Anna was the Joey, the agent!* He roughly elbowed the bewildered lay-preacher to one side, yelling over his shoulder at an equally bewildered Drewer: 'Half-speed . . . *for God's sake, half-speed Number One!*'

He lifted his glasses. The white blurs of the faces of those standing on the bridge of the departing gunboat leapt into the bright circle of glass. With trembling fingers he adjusted them and the blurs were suddenly distinguishable. There was the skipper, cap set rakishly. Next to him his number one, a fresh-faced sub-lieutenant, intent on the course. A rating in a big blue duffel coat. *And Anna!* There was no mistaking that face, though her fine blonde hair was covered with the kind of bonnet favoured by French women of the lower classes in the mid-thirties.

'*Anna!*' he croaked, while the signaller and Drewer looked at their captain, as if he had suddenly gone mad. '*Anna!*' There was something almost animal about that cry of despair, as the gunboat put on speed and began to disappear into the growing dusk, taking her away from him for good. . . .

'Why can't I see you again?' He had asked when she had told him her decision, pulling on her stockings and looking at his shocked face in the flyblown mirror of her little battered dressing-table. 'It was that damned Fleming, wasn't it?' he added angrily. 'He got you into this business, whatever it is.'

She had said nothing, but had stood up and straightened her skirt, turning to face him, her features composed with no trace of that passionate woman who had loved him with such tremendous fervour only half an hour be-

fore. He sat up in bed and tried to control his emotions. 'But why, Anna?' he asked softly. 'You bring me here from the palace and let me make love to you, as if it were the most natural thing in the world. Then you say I must not attempt to see you again. *Why*?'

'I'm being posted,' she had said, her voice devoid of any feeling. 'It will be difficult for you to get to the place where they are sending me.' There was an air of finality about her words, but Peter was determined not to give up just like that. He knew her feelings for Horst had always been greater than those for him – they still were, he suspected – but this chance meeting had once again kindled the love he had always had for her since that day in Wilhelmshaven, when he had first seen her hitting the fascist with the umbrella, her beautiful face flushed with anger.

'But what is your job and *where* are they posting you?' he had persisted. 'Besides, don't you get leave like any other service-woman? Now come on Hell-Cat be reasonable,' and he had forced a tense smile at her as she stood there in her smart, khaki-uniform, looking down at him, as if she were trying to imprint his every feature, down to the ugly purple scar on his calf, in her mind's eye.

'Peter,' she had replied. 'I can't tell you my job. Nor can I tell you where I am being posted. And we don't get leave.'

'Who's we?'

She ignored his question. Instead she had returned his smile with one of her own, revealing those beautiful white teeth of hers. 'And don't ever expect a cat to be reasonable – especially not a Hell-Cat like me. Cats just take what they want without as much as by-your-leave.' She touched his thin face with her hand tenderly, and Peter felt a shudder of desire surge through his body. He almost pulled her down on top of him, uniform and all. But that wasn't to be. She retreated hastily. 'You were this parti-cular Hell-Cat's prey for this afternoon. I hope you liked it. *I did*! Now hurry up, you'll miss that last train to Dover,

and I wouldn't like a budding lieutenant-commander to get into trouble.'

She had come to the station with him, and they had waited there for his train to arrive, holding hands without warmth, each one of them preoccupied with his own thoughts, as streams of sailors shuffled by, blue kitbags slung over their shoulders, watched by the hard-eyed Redcaps on the lookout for deserters. She even bought a platform-ticket to accompany him onto the platform itself, while the hollow boom of the loudspeakers drowned the words of what could be the couple's parting. Up ahead, the locomotive gave snorts of steam, as if impatient to be off, away from the silly emotionalism of the scene.

'Look after yourself, Peter!' she had cried as the wheels clattered and the heavily-laden train, packed with servicemen returning to Dover, creaked and began to move.

'I'll write!' he had cried desperately above the rattle of the wheels on the steel rails, as the train started to gather speed. 'Anna, I'll write!'

Her beautiful face set and suddenly weary, Anna had shaken her head and said something, but he had been unable to catch her last words. Then she had been wreathed in steam and the train had swung round the curve, out of the station and into the night. . . .

Now, as the gunboat of the Fifteenth Flotilla vanished for good, he realized why she had been unable, or perhaps unwilling, to write. She had been a 'Joey' all the time, probably in training at some remote location in Scotland, where they trained the agents in lonely country houses. And he had been the one who had unwittingly led to her recruitment by that sardonic swine Fleming that day on Slapton Beach.

Of course, Anna was ideal material. She was brave and bold. She hated the Nazis for what they had done to her

and her family, and she knew the *Kriegsmarine*, having been brought up at Wilhelmshaven. She would be perfectly at home in Brest and, with her looks, it would not be too long before she started picking up unwary German sailors who would give her the information Intelligence required.

A tortured Peter had a sudden vision of Anna, naked on a bed, writhing with pleasure, her hair in disarray, her face filmed with greasy sweat, as she enjoyed it in that uninhibited animal manner of hers. He winced visibly and at his side, Bunts said, 'Anything wrong, sir?' Peter swung round on him, his eyes blazing. The signaller swallowed hard and retreated to the side of the bridge. 'Sorry, sir,' he gasped fearfully.

Peter ignored him, willing himself to forget that terrible vision, which had filled him with almost unbearable sexual desire and jealousy. 'Number One,' he barked. 'What the devil are we hanging about here for?'

'But sir –'

'No buts!' Peter interrupted savagely, his thin face flushed with rage, 'Let's get this show on the road before the E-boats find us. Full ahead – both engines!'

Confused, and not a little embarrassed, the young officer, whose respect in this skipper whom he idolized was badly shaken, thrust home the twin throttles. The MTB shot forward with a great bound and roar of engines, that sent the other two careering against the bridge side.

When the German attack came, it was from a completely unexpected quarter. Of course the look-outs saw the Heinkel immediately, in spite of the poor light. There it flew, a long pencil-thin shape, flying in wide circles and keeping well out of the instant barrage which peppered the dusk-sky with black cottonwool puffs of fire.

For a while, the watching MTB skippers who were following its strange course with their glasses, thought it was simply a spotter, radioing back their position to the

hurrying E-boats somewhere beyond the horizon, and telling themselves that by the time they made their appearance, night would have fallen and they would be safe. But that wasn't to be.

After ten minutes of these strange tactics, which had some wag on the deck of Peter's craft singing in his best four-ales bar tenor, '*I'll walk beside you through the growing years*', the Heinkel III set a course straight for the little flotilla below. Instantly, the men firing the Chicago Pianos – the multiple pom-poms – concentrated their fire on the German plane.

Everywhere the alarm bells shrilled their urgent warning, while the Heinkel raced through the crazy patchwork of flak like a vulture pouncing on its prey. Then, when it seemed to a tense, watching Harding that the Heinkel couldn't survive a moment longer, the sinister black plane broke to port. But from its wings the strange object that he had become aware of at the very last moment, kept on diving straight for the MTBs. The last Intelligence briefing flashed into Harding's mind. The officer from Room 39 had made quite a thing of the new secret weapons the Germans were intending to employ against the convoys. This was one of them.

'Take evasive action,' he cried in sudden alarm and sprang to the wheel himself. '*Glider bomb!*'

Too late. The strange, silent object came hurtling in directly towards his own ship. Instinctively Peter closed his eyes like a suddenly frightened child, knowing with the clarity of a vision that they weren't going to get away with this one. The MTB gave a violent shudder. A tremor ran through the whole craft. She staggered like a stumbling horse and lurched to a sudden stop, as the whole bow was shattered by a great, stupefying explosion, that sent Peter smashing against the bridge and numbing his arm from shoulder to wrist. In a flash the MTB started to sink.

Peter struggled upright and became aware of the vicious hiss of escaping steam drowning the eerie gargling sounds coming from the men drowning below or trapped

in the scalding agony of the tiny engine room. 'Abandon ship!' he cried in a cracked voice. 'Abandon ship, Number . . .' He stopped short.

The young officer lay sprawled in the corner, apparently cradling the signaller in his arms. But the lay-preacher was minus his head and there was a steady dribble of scarlet blood from the Drewer's ravaged ribcage. Peter recoiled in horror. Both of them were dead!

He staggered down the twisted ladder. The MTB was settling rapidly, her deck rearing up at an impossible angle. Everywhere there was noise and confusion, with signal rockets sailing into the air from the rest of the MTB, like angry red hornets. Below, there was a series of thunderous bangs, mingling with the ghastly shrieks of those who were trapped, as the bows started to tilt ever higher.

Dazed, head still ringing with the crash of the exploding glider bomb, Peter pushed a sailor over the side and then another, crying in sudden fury. 'Over the side, you silly sod! Over the side!' He aimed a wild kick at another panicked rating and missed. The man went over the side in a fast, shallow dive.

Now the survivors were jumping into the water on all sides. Peter staggered through the chaos of the sloping deck, hunched forward as if he were climbing a mountain, satisfying himself that there was no one trapped in the superstructure – he knew there was little he could do for those below – halting now and again to catch his breath, feeling sick and helpless.

Then there was a strange howling noise which he couldn't quite identify. The deck lurched violently and he hastily grabbed a grotesquely twisted stanchion. To no avail! He was slithering helplessly across the deck, his world turned through ninety degrees. There was a gurgling sound, obscene and stomach-churning, like the sound of some enormous bath-tub being drained. Abruptly he was in the freezing water, going down and down, his ears popping, little bubbles exploding around his mouth.

Everything became hazy. He supposed he was drowning, but the thought didn't seem to worry him. He felt as if he were drunk, relaxed like he always was after a liquid wardroom party. He closed his eyes and let it happen. What did it matter after all?

That was not to be. Lt Commander Peter Harding was to be allowed to live a little longer.

Suddenly the hazy feeling of careless indifference was replaced by one of sharp stabbing pain, as the pressure of the depth to which he had sunk started to crush him. He screamed – or tried to. His mouth filled with salt water. He gurgled and spat, and then he was heading for the surface, carried upwards by his life-belt, feeling his ears roaring and scarlet lights exploding in front his his eyes.

Moments later he was in the midst of bobbing heads everywhere and there was the put-put of an outboard motor and a cheerful broad Cornish voice was saying, over and over again, 'Hang on, me darlings, we'll have you out right tiddley . . . hang on. . . .'

THREE

General Haydon, the guardsman in charge of the attack force, looked around the faces of the officers assembled in the wardrobe of the cruiser *HMS Kenya*, which would be his headquarters for the big raid, and said: 'Gentlemen, we have sailed, so I can tell you our true destination.' His eyes twinkled. 'It is *not* the Lofoten Islands as Lord Louis told you at the critique.'

Peter, grouped in the centre of his own officers, most of them pale-faced and hung-over from the previous evening's Christmas Party, where the rum and pink-gin had run very freely indeed, showed mild interest. At the back of his mind that new cynical little voice, that accompanied him everywhere these days since he had learnt about Anna, said carelessly, 'So what? What does it matter?'

'The Lofoten Island ploy was to fool the soldiers and allow us draw Arctic gear,' the Irish Guards officer continued. 'We are going to Norway, but our objectives are to destroy certain military and economic targets in the Norwegian town of South Vaagso and the nearby island of Maaloy, and to capture or sink any enemy shipping found in the Ulvesund – the strip of water which divides the port of Vaagso from the island of Maaloy. Happy Boxing Day, chaps.'

There were several raspberries from the younger officers; they had been fooled again.

The brigadier took it in good part. 'Nothing's fair in love or war, chaps,' he said. 'Now the Jerries have fortified the southern end of the Ulvesund and have established coastal defences on the island of Maaloy itself, as well as in and around the town of South Vaagso. On

Maaloy, there is a battery of field guns with some anti-aircraft and machine guns. Four miles to the south, there is a battery of fairly heavy guns on the island of Rugsundo – God, these Norwegian names floor me!' he said. There was a murmur of sympathy from his listeners. 'So, there's plenty of opposition, especially for you chaps of the little boats,' the Brigadier looked at Harding and his officers, 'who are going in to cover the commandos. Of course, you'll get the covering barrage from *HMS Kenya* – at the start at least.'

Harding nodded, but not with approval, just confirmation. He knew that if the cruiser's six-inch guns didn't knock out the German batteries, his MTBs would get the full blast of their guns.

'So this is the way we'll do it. We'll approach both the town and island up the Vaags Fjord. Its entrance is marked by two small lighthouses at Hovdenoes and Bergsholmene. On reaching the small bay behind Halnoevik Point, south of the little village of Hollevik, a little way off South Vaagso, we'll lower both the commandos' landing craft and the MTBs. The landing itself will be made under the cover of a naval bombardment and smoke laid by aircraft.' He nodded at the squadron-leader, who was the RAF's ground liaison-officer. The guardsman's voice hardened. 'Once ashore, gentlemen, the island of Maaloy and the town of South Vaago are to be captured and anything of value to the enemy is to be destroyed.' He swung his gaze around the wardroom. 'May I say this, Lord Louis wants no failures. Either we give the country a victory, or we better not come back.' His voice rose. 'Gentlemen, reveille is at zero four hundred hours. I suggest you turn in straight away. December 27th, 1941 is, I imagine, going to be a long day. . . .'

Peter was already awake when the marine bugler sounded reveille over the cruiser's tannoy system. Instantly he got out of his hammock and slipped into clean underpants and

vest to minimize the risk of infection in case he was wounded. Buckling on a forty-five, he stepped out and walked down to the wardroom, past the line of sleepy commandos and sailors lining up for their bangers and bacon. The steward was only mildly surprised when he asked for a brandy to go with his coffee and no bacon and eggs; obviously he knew the effect of high-speeds on the stomachs of MTB officers.

Outside on the deck of the cruiser, everything was still quiet, although there was something eerie in the silence as the *Kenya* steamed slowly into the fiord. Here and there Peter could see lights burning in little huts perched precariously on the mountainsides, their roofs heavy with new snow. The scene seemed very unwarlike. He sighed and wondered how long this remote fiord would remain so peaceful.

Five minutes later, the sailors started to lower the MTBs into the water, their crews already on board, with above them the commandos beginning to assemble ready to embark on their landing craft which would follow. But despite the imminence of violent action, Peter could not seem to shake himself out of his lethargic mood. Instead, he gazed at those little lights from the huts, now astern of the cruiser, with a kind of ill defined nostalgia. He stood on the bridge of the motionless MTB and started his personal countdown. The big cruiser sailed on deeper into the still silent fiord, the landing craft chugging behind it like ugly black beetles. As soon as the *Kenya* opened up with its six-inch guns, he would order engines to be started.

At precisely 8:48 am, with the winter sun tipping the craggy horizon a pale yellow, making the snow peaks gleam and sparkle, a lone star shell hissed into the sky above the island of Maaloy. It was the marker for the naval gunners and the squadron of Hampden bombers that were due in at any moment, now the Arctic dawn was beginning to break.

All hesitation forgotten, his strange lethargy vanished

now in the urgency of the moment, Peter cried, 'Start engines!'

The great Thorneycrofts burst into life, making the whole craft vibrate and quiver under his feet, like a racing dog eagerly waiting to cast off its lead. All around, the MTBs' motors came to life with an ear-splitting roar. Suddenly the clear sea air was full of stink of petrol fumes, which abruptly coloured the sky a light blue.

'Full ahead!' Peter ordered in the same instant that the *Kenya*'s B-turret opened up, and the twin-engined Hampdens came winging in at mast-height to drop their deadly eggs on the island. The big raid had started, and it looked to Peter Harding riding the waves as the MTB sped forward at thirty knots an hour, his eyes narrowed to slits against the sudden vicious wind, that the British had for once achieved complete surprise.

December 27th, 1941 had begun on the island of Maaloy in the same way it had for the last five hundred odd days of the German occupation: slow and boring. In the wooden huts grouped around the tiny harbour, the field-greys were shaving and washing, prior to facing another icy Arctic day, whispering details of their latest conquests among the Norwegian girls, or if they had been celebrating the second day of Christmas too unwisely, dousing their heads repeatedly in the icy water.

At Commanding Officer Butzinger's quarters, his batman, who also manned the telephone connecting HQ with the look-out posts further down the coast, was busily engaged cleaning Major Butzinger's riding boots. The major was a stickler for correct and immaculate boots, although no one ever noticed in this godforsaken hole, and the batman laboured mightily; he didn't want the major, whose temper was uncertain at the best of times, sending him off to Russia.

Thus it was, engaged in his task, he did not pick up the telephone when it started to shrill on the kitchen table at

his side. It was an unfortunate oversight, for it ensured that not only did *he* get sent to the Russian front to die miserably at Stalingrad in 1942, but also the innocent Major Butzinger.

The German batteries on the island received no warning of the Tommies' approach. But the navy did. High on the hilltop above the German-occupied village, a naval signaller received the message that British ships were sailing down the fiord. He abandoned his post at once, leapt into the nearest boat he could find and, as if the devil himself were after him, rowed as fast as he could to the headquarters of the German naval commandant on the main island of Vaagso.

Breathless, his skinny chest heaving with the effort, his face purple with the morning cold, he gasped out his warning.

'Did you warn the army gunners on the island that the Tommies are coming?' the commandant demanded urgently, as the alarm sirens started to howl and down below on the cobbled street there was the clatter of heavy boots as the soldiers doubled to their duty stations.

'Oh no sir,' the naval signaller replied. 'It's an army battery and this is a naval signal.'

The commandant clapped his hand to his head with a groan of dismay. '*Gott in Himmel!*' he cried. 'Man, don't you know the only reason you've got a head is so that you don't have to carry your straw in yer paws. . . Out of my way!' Impatiently he thrust by the rating and flung open his door, already aware now of the faint rumble of heavy guns in the distance. 'Thomsen!' he bellowed down the corridor. '*Leutnant Thomsen . . .* at the double, man!'

Ex-*Obermaat* Thomsen, who had been promoted and beached in 1940, ran awkwardly down the corridor in his heavy sea-boots, his face heavy and bejowelled, the result of too much rich Norwegian food and strong German *Korn*. 'Sir?' he cried.

'Alert the HQ defence platoon, Thomsen!' the commandant snapped, as the roar of the guns up the fiord

grew ever louder. 'The Tommies are on the way and we're in for trouble. Take up your defensive position. '*Los, Mensch*!'

The overweight *Landratte**, as the beached former-seagoing personnel contemptuously called themselves, hurried away to carry out his chief's orders, telling himself as he did so that everything was going wrong. The commandant was paying the price of nearly two years of neglect and slackness. Now the shit had really hit the fan and it was the *Landratten* who were going to suffer as a result.

Now the *Kenya* had stopped firing. For a few minutes there was no sound save the chug-chug of the landing-barge motors and the steady hum of the MTBs accompanying them at quarter speed. Here and there a machine gun on land flashed, but the tracer they fired seemed harmless, a series of beautiful, multicoloured dots and dashes.

The sun was now touching the peaks, covering the mountainsides in a violent, vivid mauve which was rapidly spreading to the still depths of the fiord, making it glow a deep indigo. Everything was surprisingly beautiful and peaceful.

Harding, flashing his glasses from left to right as the fiord grew ever narrower, shook his head as Norwegian patriots lined the banks, brought out of their houses by the firing, and waved white handkerchiefs happily. They might have been the crowds which had welcomed the Royal Navy vessels at Pompey and Plymouth before the war.

'Trouble, sir!' his Number One broke in his thoughts.

'Where?' he swung round, hastily focusing his glasses as the first burst of machine gun fire came zipping towards the MTBs from what looked like an armed trawler an-

*Land Rat.

chored next to a merchantman flying the Dutch flag.

'Brave buggers,' Peter snapped, unable to conceal his admiration for the little ship taking on a whole flotilla of the latest MTBs. 'All right Number One, let her have a salvo of fire from the three-inchers and then we'll board her with an armed party. I'll command.'

The young officer stopped in his tracks. 'You, sir?' he said, eyes wide with surprise. He hadn't much wartime experience, but enough to know that lieutenant-commanders in charge of flotillas didn't normally take on such tasks; they were far too dangerous for them.

'You heard me, Number One,' Harding said harshly, reaching for his steel helmet which hung by its strap from a stanchion on the bridge.

'Ay ay, sir.' He doubled away.

The MTB's guns thundered. There was the clearly audible sound of metal being torn apart and flame flashed high into the air. Immediately the trawler began to burn. But still her machine guns continued to fire and now, as the MTB came ever closer to the stricken German ship, Peter could see the dark figures scurrying to take cover in the superstructure, obviously prepared to take on the boarders lining up on the British ship's deck.

Peter pelted down the deck, gasping at the acrid stench of burnt cordite from the three-inch guns. The men were ready to go, armed to the teeth, with the CPO in charge even carrying an old-style cutlass. In spite of his despondent mood, one that he had not been able to fling off ever since he had learnt who the Joey was, he grinned. 'All right, Nelson, are we ready to go?'

The CPO's leathery face cracked into a smile. 'Better be prepared for every eventuality, sir. I rather fancy myself in the Errol Flynn bit.'

'Come on, Captain Blood, off we go!'

With a great yell the ratings sprang over the gap of gleaming water below as the two ships bumped close. Almost immediately, the Germans hidden above around the bridge took on the new challenge. Next to Peter, a

rating yelped in agony and clapped his hand to his shoulder, fingers suddenly stained a bright scarlet. Peter flung up his big Colt and fired at the sniper. The weapon erupted in his fist and the bullet went well clear of its target. The CPO rushed by him, crying, 'Fanny's drawers, sir! You got Fanny's drawers!' A German scuttled out of an open hatch and the CPO cut him down with a tremendous side-swipe that nearly severed the man's arm. Next moment, the old petty officer hit the deck, a slug neatly planted in his forehead. He was dead before he reached the ground.

Peter held the big American pistol with both hands to steady it and fired again. His bullet smashed into the sniper who had killed the CPO. He screamed in absolute agony and fell headlong from his perch behind the bridge, crumpling to the blood-stained deck like a bundle of abandoned rags.

Now the heart started to go out of the defenders, with the boarding party relentlessly pushing them back. Peter thrust his way by a small group of German and British sailors swaying back and forth in wild, confused hand-to-hand combat, cursing crazily as they did so. He scrambled up the gangway. A German, bleeding from a bad wound in one arm, weakly tried to stop him. Peter clubbed his pistol in the man's pale face. He reeled back, spitting teeth out, blood streaming from a shattered nose.

Peter flung open the door of the captain's little cabin, the obligatory portrait of Hitler holding pride of place on the wall behind his desk. But at that moment Peter had no eyes for the Fuhrer. His gaze was reserved for the middle-aged officer knelt at the safe, hauling out the trawler's confidential books. '*Hände hoch*!' he cried in his best German, knowing that the books were vital; Intelligence maintained that such things were worth their weight in gold. '*Hoch*!' he jerked the big pistol upwards to make his meaning quite clear.

The German cursed, but did not react in the way that Peter had anticipated. The document sack, leaded for

security reasons, flew through the air. He was caught completely by surprise and went crashing against the wall. Next instant, the German captain had drawn his tiny Walther. As Peter lay sprawled there, the man put the muzzle to his forehead and cried, '*Heil Hitler*!' The bullet exploded inside his skull. Before Peter's horrified eyes the German's head bulged outwards and suddenly erupted blood-red gore, flecked here and there by brilliant white bone splinters. The German slumped to the floor, his features shattered beyond recognition.

It was thus that the triumphant boarders found their skipper crouched in the corner, a Colt held in nerveless fingers, staring hypnotically at the almost headless figure in the far corner of the cabin. Lt Commander Peter Harding had almost reached the end of his tether.

Now there was a pause in the battle for Naval HQ, filled with a strange, eerie stillness. Outside the houses blazed fiercely and there was a hideous stench coming from the burning fish-oil factory.

Thomsen sobbed with rage, frustration and pain, as he tried to stop the flow of blood coming from the suppurating pit which had once contained his left eye. He knew there was no hope for him. He was alone in the battle-littered front office. The rest of his defence platoon were dead or had surrendered. Soon it would be his turn. Already he could smell the stink of petrol as the Tommies below swamped the bottom floor of the HQ with fuel. Then in would sail the incendiary grenade and that would be that: either he surrenderd or he would be burnt alive.

But his pain and frustration as he waited there, revolver in his one good hand, overcame his fears and turned into an ever-growing anger. Why should he die thus, so ignobly and without meaning or significance? When they had sailed out of Wilhelmshaven so proudly all those years before to attack the Tommies in Hull, he had never

imagined he would die in this mean manner, with his torn, stained trousers full of the evacuation of his own bowels, one eye gone, his left arm shattered, the blood draining from the severed artery in sharp, scarlet jets. 'It's wrong, *all wrong*!' he said aloud, half-crazed by pain. 'Those shits in HQ were too busy with the girls and the booze to know what was coming. . . .'

Down below the Tommies tossed away the jerricans with a loud metallic clatter. He could hear someone bellowing an order in English. It wouldn't be long now. Suddenly, through the red shimmering haze that threatened to overcome him at any moment, he saw the telephone on the table behind which he crouched ready to make his last fight. Numbed by pain as his senses were, the dying officer recognized it. It was the top-secret scrambler that had direct access to Admiral Raeder's HQ at Murwik near Flensburg.

Flensburg! The name shot through him. He felt a pang of emotional pain. It was his home town and he would never see it again, hear the nasal sing-song of his local dialect, eye the long-legged blonde Danish girls down for the day, easy meat for an old hand with a handsome, confident face. Now his face was hideous, he knew it. *Flensburg*. . . .

For what may have been a long time, his confused mind wandered through the past, his pain forgotten, everything obliterated by the red wavering haze. Then the rage surged through his dying, pain-racked body. He'd tell them. He'd tell the Grand Admiral himself. They would know that had happened in this remote arse-hole of the world; the whole of Germany would know just how it had been let down by these base stallion shits who had never fired a shot in anger in their whole military careers.

He seized the phone with his good hand, letting his pistol drop carelessly – he couldn't see to aim it properly anyway. The line buzzed. The Tommies hadn't managed to get this one. Far away in Oslo, the precise clear voice of

the 'grey mouse'* operator asked, if he had scrambled. He ignored the request. 'Get me Murwik . . . the HQ of the *Grossadmiral*. . . .' As an afterthought he added, trying not to slur his words, 'Senior Captain Hansen here. It's an emergency, priority one . . . *hurry!*'

'Yessir,' the suddenly flustered female operator said. Perhaps she, too, could now hear the renewed artillery fire outside and the snap-and-crackle of a small arms battle in the street.

'*Marineleitung – Kapitänleutnant Hartung am Apparat,*' the voice came through remote, yet clear and precise.

The dying officer gasped. 'Thomsen – *Leutnant zur See.*'

'What is it? Why the call, Lieutenant?' the staff officer far away in Flensburgh asked.

To Thomsen the voice seemed vaguely familiar, but he was too far gone to attempt to search his memory for where he had once heard that clipped voice. 'The Tommies . . . they're attacking in force . . . Everything's gone wrong . . .' Thomsen's phrases came out in harsh little breathless gasps. 'We weren't prepared . . . we weren't prepared. . . .'

'What is this, Lieutenant,' the voice demanded. 'Report as per regulation, Lieutenant. Do you hear, report in the regulation naval fashion. . . .'

Thomsen heard the grenade explode below quite distinctly. The petrol ignited at once in a fierce whoosh. Immediately the stairwell started to blaze fiercely. Dully he took it all in, while that far away voice snapped in sudden alarm. 'Why don't you reply, man? What is the matter up there? *Hello, can you hear me?*'

Numbly Thomsen sat there, with the flames roaring ever closer, the phone in his hand, accepting his fate like some humble, beaten animal.

---

*Nickname for the German Army's female auxiliaries.

Now it was time for withdrawal. The raid had been a complete success. Every objective had been taken and the German military had been totally defeated. Yet an anxious Number One, who was covering the pull-back of the triumphant commandos in their landing barges, could feel no sense of triumph, in spite of the messages of congratulations flashing back and forth among the ships; he was too worried about the captain.

Lt Commander Harding stood at the bridge, apathetically watching the busy scene, as boat after boat pulled away from the burning town over which hung a black pall of smoke, as if he might be viewing a particularly boring newsreel, which had nothing to do with him personally. Even the sight of their own wounded, piled high in one of the landing barges their faces sunk and ashen with shock didn't seem to move him.

The young officer was too inexperienced to recognize that Lt Commander Harding was already virtually a broken man. In these last terrible years he had seen and suffered too much. Outwardly he was healthy; a typical, bold young naval officer of the time. Inwardly he was a hollow man.

It was with a sigh of relief that the Number One saw the last landing-barge leave the burning waterfront to the cheers of those Norwegian patriots who were forced to stay behind; and Harding left the bridge to go below, eyes blank, ears deaf to the hoots of the ships' whistles signalling victory, as the convoy got underway, bound for Britain once more.

Outside it was snowing gently, the flakes drifting down slowly, almost sadly in the fading light as dusk swept across the mountain peaks. Here and there, in the great houses which surrounded the *Berghof*, the candles flickered on the Christmas trees placed in the windows and on the carved wooden balconies. But soon they would be doused, on account of the blackout regulations; then it would be night.

But inside the Berghof, Hitler's personal retreat in the Bavarian mountains that marked the old boundary between the Third Reich and Austria, there was no letting up of the hectic activity, as orderlies, resplendent in immaculate uniforms, hurried back and forth, and behind closed doors typewriters rattled and telephones rang. In five minutes the Fuhrer would be finished with his afternoon tea – peppermint, of course and plenty of cream cakes in spite of total war – and then the usual round of evening briefings would get under way. Indeed, less important officers and officials had been known to wait for a chance to speak with the Fuhrer at such briefings for days in advance, camping out in the guest houses in the valley below or, if they were lucky, in the select mountain community's one hotel.

Kapitänleutnant Hartung, standing next to his chief, Admiral Raeder, in the midst of the nervous crowd of Party officials and officers from every branch of the service, was not worried that they wouldn't be received this evening by Hitler. Their presence had been specially requested and due to the appalling weather they had made the long train journey from Flensburg to Obersalzburg in

the Fuhrer's own special train. It was a sign of the importance of their summons.

If Hartung was not nervous, the elderly Admiral for whom he had been working as a personal adjutant ever since he had been finally discharged from the *Charité*, his arm permanently crippled into an ugly claw, was terrified. Hartung knew why. Raeder's days were numbered. He was not ruthless enough for Hitler and his caution, especially with his precious capital·ships, irritated the Fuhrer. Everyone in the *Kriegsmarine* knew that Doenitz was the man of the moment. His submarines had virtually brought England to its knees. If all accounts were true and not the Poison Dwarf's* usual propaganda, the English were about starving. Now this bad business in Norway in which poor old Thomsen had been killed – Hartung had soon found out that the strange telephone call had come from his former *Obermaat* – had soured Hitler even more. This evening there would be tantrums, accusations and counter-accusations and the chain-smoking Admiral Raeder knew it.

Hartung smiled a little grimly and stared out at the tremendous view over the snow-covered Alps. Did *Otto Normalverbraucher*†, the little man, out there somewhere realize what his masters were really like? How vain, how selfish, how self-seeking, how basically scared they were? Always attempting to maintain their privileged position or enlarge it? He frowned, and looked down at the red claw which carried the Admiral's briefcase; he carried it in that crippled hand deliberately, almost like challenging anyone to mention the matter, although the hand was as weak as that of a two-year old child's. God, how he wished he could get away from these vain, pomaded officers and officials, back to the cleaner life of the sea! Drink hadn't helped. Women hadn't either, and he had made himself seduce girl after girl, just

*Nickname for Minister of Propaganda Goebbels.
†Roughly: Mr Smith.

to prove that the red claw did not frighten them off. Some of them even confessed, with a shudder, that the sight of that obscene, burnt hand on their naked breasts excited them. He had had the so-called *Prominenz* of the Third Reich. Give him the rough, but honest cameraderie of the sea.

'*Meine Herren, der Führer!*' the self-important voice broke into his gloomy reverie.

Hartung spun round and looked by the gigantic flunky in his black SS uniform who had made the announcement. The doors to the tea-room had been opened and there was Hitler, kissing the hands of the women who were filing out, even those of his secretaries. Hartung flashed a look at Raeder's face and noted with satisfaction the look of disapproval there. A gentleman did not kiss the hand of a common secretary.

The ritual finished, Hitler turned to stare at the assembled officers and officials in the ante-room, all of them at attention and gripping their bulging briefcases in nervous anticipation, wondering if this time the mightiest man in Europe would have time for them.

Hitler swept back the dyed lock of black hair hanging across his forehead in the usual dramatic manner, then his face set in a scowl, as if all he saw depressed him greatly. He began to stride through the lane opening up for him with over-long strides, making his hangers-on scuttle after him like short-legged children. Without a word, even to the brown-shirted Party officials who had served with him in the 'battle-time' – the period prior to 1933 – he strode into the conference-room. The great doors closed behind him and his entourage, leaving the assembly shuffling their feet nervously, and coughing delicately behind upraised hands.

Hartung was amused. One or two of the fat Party officials were even sweating in apprehension. 'Let them, the fat bastards,' he told himself maliciously. They waited. Here and there someone bolder than the rest looked at his wristwatch impatiently and then flashed a

look at the gigantic SS adjutants guarding the door to the conference room. Superciliously the SS officers returned the look. They had seen it all before. They were not impressed. They waited.

Finally, when Hitler had decided they had waited long enough, he sent out his senior adjutant, blond and bemedalled, to let the assembly know who had been favoured this particular December evening.

'*Grossadmiral Raeder,*' the adjutant barked, '*Der Führer lässt bitten.*' Like a waiter in a third-class restaurant, he gave a slight bow and swept out his right hand.

There was a sigh of disappointment from the others; another evening wasted! Raeder smirked and, followed by Hartung carrying the briefcase, he marched into the room where Hitler and his staff waited, their faces set in imitation of the Fuhrer's well-known brooding gaze.

Hitler took Raeder's hand, using only one of his and not the double-handed hold, the normal token of his esteem. Standing directly behind Raeder, Hartung told himself that there was going to be trouble. The Old Man was for it this evening. Sparks would fly.

Hitler got down to business at once. 'The Doenitz paper,' he snapped without looking around, hand outstretched, while he fumbled for his nickel-rimmed spectacles with the other. Hastily the orderly placed it in his hands. 'Vice-Admiral Doenitz forwarded me this last week, Raeder.'

Raeder frowned at the mention of the name; he knew as well as anyone else at the Navy HQ at Murwik, that the ambitious Doenitz was after his job. But he contented himself with a laconic, '*Ja, mein Führer?*'

Hitler's gaze flew across the single sheet of paper. 'Doenitz maintains that dockyard labour should be restricted to projects of construction or repair that are – and I quote – "absolutely necessary to the war effort".'

Hartung flashed a look at his chief and saw that Raeder had been caught completely off guard. He had expected an angry outburst on account of the raid on the Nor-

wegian island. Instead he had been confronted with some of Doenitz's machinations, and it confused him.

'Now Admiral, Doenitz maintains further that the days of your heavy ships are over. The Atlantic forays carried out by them have been highly courageous, he states, but they have outlived their usefulness. Instead of being able to attack, they are invariably obliged to withdraw in the face of the enemy's superiority in capital vessels. I will quote again, "The C-in-C U-boats therefore wishes clearly to contradict the view that our battleships and cruisers are indispensable to the Atlantic campaign. . . From that follows the logical conclusion that these ships no longer play a vital role in the present war and consequently should no longer have a call on repair facilities urgently needed by the U-boat Arm."' Hitler looked up. 'What do you say to that, *Herr Grossadmiral*?' There was no overlooking the sneer in that '*Herr Grossadmiral*'.

Raeder flushed an ugly red. 'We can afford to be indulgent to a younger officer pleading the cause of his own special branch of the service, *mein Führer*,' he said weakly.

Hitler's dark eyes blazed. 'My dear Raeder, this is not peacetime and we are not playing promotion games.' Raeder looked down at his boots unhappily. 'Admiral, this last month Doenitz's U-boats have sunk 600,000 tons of British shipping. Now I ask you this simple question, what is tonnage sunk by your capital ships? Well. . .?' Hitler's jaw jutted out aggressively, and Hartung could see his staff tense. Soon the expected outburst would come.

'My ships are all confined to port. Damage, weather, the British blockade have all contributed to making December a bad month for them, *mein Führer*.'

'So,' Hitler sneered, little flecks of spittle in the corners of his mouth. 'Nearly three hundred thousand tons of expensive warships are bottled up in the ports, doing nothing, with your Lords – I believe that is what your sailors aptly call themselves – getting fat, living like the

King in France, while Doenitz's submariners do the hard and risky work.'

'*Mein Führer, mein Führer*,' Raeder said a little desperately. 'I beg you to understand! By February next year, a mere two months from now, my heavy ships at Brest – the *Gneisenau*, the *Scharnhorst*, the *Prinz Eugen* – should be ready for action again in the Atlantic. However, after a long period of inaction down there in Brest they need training and under the constant threat of British bombing they can't get it there. Only here, in the Homeland, can we give them the facilities they –'

He broke off suddenly. Hitler was holding up his right hand, the signal for silence, his eyes sparkling. 'Admiral,' he said urgently, 'is it possible to bring the ships home to Germany by a surprise break-back through the English Channel?'

Raeder was caught off guard. 'The *Prinz Eugen*, yes,' he stuttered, obviously appalled by the query. 'The two battleships at this moment, no.'

'Why?'

'The training problem, *mein Führer*. The navigation problems. The threat presented by the enemy light naval and air forces . . . mines. . . .' Raeder shrugged angrily, as if he could hardly bring himself to explain the difficulties of naval warfare to this land-lubber, who had even become seasick when visiting the fleet in Kiel Bay.

'I need those ships, Raeder,' Hitler countered. 'All the indications are – as we have seen in that unfortunate affair a day or so ago – that the English are preparing to invade Norway soon to help the Russians. We'll need every surface vessel we can find when they do so.' His voice sank almost to a whisper. 'I could naturally decommission them, you know, and release their crews for Doenitz's U-boats.'

Raeder gasped and staggered back as if Hitler had struck him a physical blow.

At that moment Hartung felt for him. Ever since the

Imperial German Fleet had scuttled itself in Scapa Flow
after the Old War, Raeder had worked single-handedly to
build a new German navy. He had fought for every ship
against a Hitler who had no understanding of seapower.
The thought that his capital ships might be sent to the
yards for good was a shock he could hardly bear. For a
second, Hartung thought the Old Man might faint, but
just in time he caught himself and said in a weak voice.
'*Mein Führer*, you couldn't do that. . . Why, their crews
would need re-training for the submarine service!'

Hitler grinned, showing his poor dingy teeth, and
farted. It was yet another of his bad habits, the product of
his vegetarian diet and the sixty pills he swallowed a day.
'All right, then I shall send their crews and their guns to
Norway where they will be very useful when the British
come. . . Don't you think, Admiral, the best method is a
completely surprise break through the Channel *without*
any earlier movements for training purposes. These
would only cause the British to step up their attacks.' Now
Hitler began one of those monologues which had bored
Hartung terribly in the past. 'You see, in view of past
experience, I do not believe the British are capable of
making and carrying out lightning decisions. I do not
believe that they will be as swift as the Naval Staff and
Vice-Admiral Ciliax down there in Brest believe. Picture
what would happen if the situation were reversed; imagine that a surprise report came announcing that British
battleships had appeared in the Thames estuary and were
heading for the Straits of Dover. Even we would hardly be
able to bring up fighters and bombers swiftly and metho-
dically. The situation of the Brest Group is like that of a
patient with cancer who is doomed unless he submits to an
operation. An operation, on the other hand, even though
it may have to be drastic, will at least offer some hope that
the patient's life may yet be saved. . . . The passage of
our ships through the Channel is such an operation.'
Hitler gasped for breath, iron in his voice now. 'The
passage of our ships through the Channel is such an

operation. It must therefore be attempted. . . .'

Raeder's shoulders slumped in defeat.

Gently Hartung thrust the glass of cognac under the Admiral's nose, as the train raced through the blacked-out, snowbound countryside on its way back to Murwik. He felt sorry for the Old Man. But at the same time, he knew Hitler was right and Raeder was wrong. Whatever he did now, the Old Man's days were numbered, Hitler had seen through him. It wouldn't be long before Doenitz replaced him as head of the Navy.

'Thank you, Hartung,' Raeder said softly and raised the glass, '*Prost*!'

'*Prost, Herr Admiral*,' Hartung replied equally softly.

'Of course, Hartung, you realize, that any attempt to do as the Fuhrer says will mean severe damage, perhaps even total loss of our ships. I can't really feel any deep conviction about this operation.'

'I understand, sir. But you will do it?'

'Yes. As we have always obeyed the Fuhrer's orders these last years.' His eyes fell on Hartung's crippled hand. 'We old ones won't suffer naturally. It's the young officers like you who have to pay for our failures.' He sighed and stared at the tiny blue light which was the compartment's only illumination. 'Always the young.'

'I expect it has always been that way, sir, ever since Prussia founded our first navy.'

Raeder nodded. 'You will go to Brest as my personal representative, Hartung. I trust you as, I must admit, I don't altogether trust Vice-Admiral Ciliax. I want you to give me a full and frank report of the ships and their crews, their morale and their state of training. You will have every authority and you will report to me personally.'

Hartung's heart leapt with excitement. Temporarily at least he would be going to a fighting front, getting away from the stifling atmosphere of Naval HQ. Who knows,

he might somehow manage to wangle an active command, once he was out of Raeder's jurisdiction. The possibilities were boundless. 'Thank you, sir. I promise you, I shall do my best.'

'I know you will, Horst.' The old Admiral leant forward across the little table and pressed his ruined hand gently with a surprising show of affection for such an unemotional man. 'I know. You are like your father . . . He was in my crew at the Academy as a midshipman. A fine sailor, but he too was sacrificed by the politicians, as we will all be sacrificed . . . Take care, Horst, I pray you. There are black times ahead for us all in Germany.'

But Horst Hartung was no longer listening to the Old Man's gloomy ramblings. His mind was too full of the new opportunities that had just been opened to him this December evening, with outside the stars burning a hard silver and giving a magic to the snowbound Bavarian landscape. He was going to Brest . . . and adventure. . . .

Part Four: 1942

ONE

On the dockside the fishermen were busy gutting the fish, while the gulls hurtled down in screams to beak and claw at the glittering mounds of cleaned cod and herring. Peter Harding stood and watched, as the nets dropped another wash of sliding, threshing spill of scale and fin on the quay. Of late, he found he was often fascinated by such things which in the past had never interested him. How often had he passed fishermen at work in ports all over Europe, but they had never made him stop for an instant! Now farmers tilling the land, welders working on a damaged stanchion, even street-cleaners, elderly men in slouched hats who plied their trade in Harwich like displaced Australians, they could all cause him to stop and stare, as if he had all the time in the world. Perhaps if he asked himself seriously why such commonplace things intrigued him, he could come up with an answer. But on this cold bright January day, he preferred not to ask himself that particular question. Instead he stood on the docks, a too thin old-young officer in faded blue, whose eyes seemed washed out and empty of all feelings; as if he had felt too much and did not want to feel anymore.

Below, beyond the mud flats, lay his flotilla, anchored in a neat line next to the destroyer squadron, which made up Harwich's main naval strength. But he had no eyes for the grey-painted shapes of the Royal Navy vessels; his gaze remained fixed on the red, greasy fingers of the

fishermen, working at the new catch. The thumb and index-finger into the gills, the knife stabbed into the corner of the gill, the quick slice down the length of the shining body and the red-grey guts erupting out of the sliced-open stomach to be scooped out and dropped to the concrete as offal for the screaming, greedy gulls. A moment later, the body was hurtling towards the nearest pile, to remain twitching, headless and eviscertated for a few more moments before all life fled.

'They're the lucky ones,' the sudden voice at his side startled him. 'Not many deckies can get a job ashore like that. Before this lot there was no work for a retired fisherman.'

Harding turned and snapped to attention.

Captain Drake, the senior destroyer officer, half-raised his big hand, the knuckles lumpy with rheumatism. 'Relax, Harding. The days of playing soldier are past.'

'Thank you, sir,' Harding said, being forced to look at the destroyer officer who towered above him. He liked the man. His eyes, set in a seamed, no-nonsense, typically Senior Service face of the old school, were kind and good-humoured, for all Captain Drake's bluff manner.

'Suppose you are going to this thing for the Yank officers, what, Harding.'

'Good grief, sir, I'd totally forgot! Of course, Admiral Ramsay's briefing on the exchange officers.'

'Mustn't forget things like that, Harding,' Drake said heartily, moving off at a brisk pace, followed by the young officer. 'Not with Admiral Ramsay at the helm. Hate to think what your promotion sheet would look like if you did.'

'Quite frankly, that's the least of *my* concerns, sir.' Harding answered as they started along the dingy road which led to the dull-grey concrete bunker which was Naval HQ Harwich.

'Don't say things like that, Harding,' Drake rapped. 'All career officers *must* be interested in promotion in every situation and at all times. That's what war's about –

to ensure somebody senior to us can get bumped off so that we get promoted.' He beamed at Harding. But Peter did not return his smile. 'What's the matter with you, Harding? Your gal let you down? Hangover from last night's wardroom binge, eh?'

'I don't know, sir,' Peter answered. 'I feel very tired, somehow exhausted, though I sleep like a log when I'm off-duty. Ten, twelve hours a night. Blame it on the war, I suppose.'

Drake shot him a searching glance. 'Hm. You might be right. The war's to blame for a darn lot of things.' Before them a pretty Wren had started to hurry towards the HQ, as if she might be late for duty. 'Now look at that, Harding,' Drake said, taking in her shapely legs clad in black stockings and plump, but trim behind in the tight short dark-blue skirt. 'After promotion, that's what you should be interested in, all young officers should – not to mention older ones too.' He lowered his voice and held his hand in front of his mouth. 'Take it from old dog, Harding, C . . . U . . . N . . . T is the answer to all our problems.'

Peter laughed and told himself, if only it were. But he didn't tell Captain Drake that.

The American officers were grouped in a loose square at the far end of the big conference room, making no secret of their curiosity, while the British officers present threw them secret glances. They looked bigger, fatter and younger than their British counterparts. To Peter, the Americans seemed to have more teeth than they did, and there was something annoying about their easy, self-confident manner. They were innocent, too damned innocent, he told himself and decided there and then that he didn't like them.

Admiral Ramsay, commander of the area between Harwich and Dover, got down to business without formalities.

'Gentlemen, I was once told this about making a speech – stand up, speak up and shut up,' he said. 'I'm going to do just that. Since December 7th and Pearl Harbour, the United States of America has been our ally, for which we are very grateful. I remember Winnie – Winston Churchill,' he added hastily for the benefit of the Americans, 'once saying that there is only one thing worse than allies, that is, *not* having them.' There was a ripple of laughter from the Americans and Ramsay beamed, obviously pleased that his little joke had gone down so well. 'So now we're allies, each of us with his particular cross to bear. Now I know it won't be easy. Both nations have their pecularities, but remember this,' he raised his forefinger in warning. 'The main thing is that we fight the Germans and not each other.'

There was a rumble of hear-hears from the British officers, in which Peter did not join. He was bored by the whole business. After two years of going it alone, he could understand the nation's delight at having America as an ally, but he was slightly nauseated by the abandoned way that the nation had thrown itself into the arms of the new 'Yank' lover. The Germans were winning the war and it would be a long time before the Americans made their impact felt.

Almost as if he had read Peter's gloomy thoughts at that moment, Ramsay said: 'Now let us not fool ourselves, we can still lose this war, both of us, America and Britain. On land and at sea, our position is very bad, if not desperate. You Americans are going to have to learn the hard way and the fees you will be forced to pay are going to be in blood.'

The smiles remained glued on the Americans' faces, Peter noted, as if the words meant nothing. He shrugged. What did it matter to him?

'Right gentlemen, end of homily. Now I'll leave you to get acquainted. The destroyer men with each other and you chaps from . . . what do you call them in American?'

'PT boats, Admiral,' a tall American with a blaze of

cropped red hair supplied the missing word.

'That's it. Well, you get together with the chaps from the MTBs over there,' he indicated Peter. 'All right, steward,' he bellowed for the benefit of the wardroom steward waiting somewhere beyond the door, 'bring on the booze.'

As if by magic, white-coated waiters started to file in, silver trays piled high with pink gins and gins-and-tonic. The get-together could start.

'Lieutenant, junior grade Kelly, Commander,' the young American with red crewcut introduced himself, glass of pink gin still untouched in his hand.

Peter, who had already tossed down three of them, frowned at the big young American, who had the shoulders of a wrestler and the lean clever face of an intellectual. 'Yes?'

The American thrust out his big hand. 'I've been assigned to you, sir. I'm the PT officer,' he added when he saw the look of bewilderment in the Englishman's eyes. 'You're to train me and then I guess I go back to Melville, Rhode Island.'

'Melville, Rhode Island?' Peter echoed, signalling the wardroom steward for another drink.

'Yessir. That's where we train our own people – Motor Torpedo Boat Squadrons Training Centre – though I'm hoping for an active command of my own soon.'

'Of course,' Peter agreed, and took another slug of pink gin. The American seemed a very likeable young man, but somehow he wasn't interested. At this moment, the only thing that interested him was the gin and its effects, and when he could escape this boring get-together.

'With a name like mine you can guess I'm of Irish descent,' Kelly was saying. 'From Boston to be exact in the first generation and the second, Cork. My old man was Fenian. In my home you never said British. It was always the goddam British.' He flashed a whitetoothed

smile. 'There was only one person in my home street who wasn't Irish – and he was a Jew. I . . .'

'Spare me your childhood memories,' Peter said brutally. 'You've been assigned to me?'

The smile vanished from Kelly's face. 'Yessir.' He looked hurt.

'Good. Then you can act as my number one for the time you are with us, Kelly.'

'Number One, sir?' Kelly queried, obviously puzzled.

'Yessir! My God, don't you speak English? Jimmy the One . . . the Dogsbody . . . my second-in-command.'

A light dawned on Kelly's handsome face. 'You mean your Exec?'

'Do I?' Peter snapped. 'Well, if I do, you're it.'

'Thank you, sir,' Kelly blurted out.

'Don't thank me – *yet*,' Peter said cruelly and tossed back the rest of his drink. 'Let's get out of this place and get some work done.'

Thus Desmond Kelly entered into the final chapter of Peter Harding's short, very short, life.

TWO

Admiral Otto Ciliax stared around the assembled officers from the *Kriegsmarine* and *Luftwaffe*, while outside the compressed air-drills hammered away, clearing away the foundations for Brest's new submarine pens. '*Meine Herren*,' he announced somewhat pompously, 'that sound is the music of the future. We must go to make room for Doenitz's U-boats.'

Hartung smiled a little to himself. Vice-Admiral Ciliax was very much in the Raeder tradition: a big-ship man. But unlike Raeder he was determined to fight for his position; he would obey Hitler and go ahead with the daring plan. Ciliax's next words confirmed what Hartung had confidentially reported to Raeder the previous day. 'Although I feel the Fuhrer does not completely understand our position here in Brest,' he said, 'his general assumption is correct. The big ships must make the attempt.'

There was a murmur of approval from the junior officers present, though Hartung, standing at the edge of the group, noted that Ciliax's senior captains remained stony-faced and non-committal.

'An excellent decision, *Herr Admiral*, if I may be permitted to say so,' *Kapitänleutnant* Jensen said in his somewhat affected Northern voice. 'We of the E-boats welcome it greatly.'

Ciliax frowned at Jensen's too handsome, almost pretty face, but said nothing. In spite of his fine combat record, which had already gained for him the coveted Knight's Cross, nobody liked Jensen. There was something about his overly smart uniforms, his rakishly tilted cap and the

manicured, tinted nails that he affected, which rubbed his comrades up the wrong way. Hartung, who had been with him on the same gunnery course as a midshipman before the war thought he knew why. Jensen had seemed to favour the company of the kind of handsome young men who always hung around naval stations, and there was a rumour now that the E-boat flotilla commander was currently keeping a French boy-friend somewhere in the suburbs of the rambling Breton port.

'So we go, gentlemen,' Ciliax continued, 'and we go at night. With the favourable tides expected next month, we should be able to make an average speed of some twenty-six knots for most of the way. Now,' he tapped the wall map with his pointer, 'we shall hug the coast for the length of Brittany, up here by Belgium and Holland, making full use of our own naval and air force bases, preceded by mine sweepers to clear the channel in case the British have dropped mines we are not informed about . . . As protection for the capital ships, we shall use as escort the five destroyers presently in Brest.' He nodded at Rear-Admiral Erich Bey, the destroyer leader. 'And in addition, the 6th Torpedo-Boat Flotilla under the command of – er – *Kapitänleutnant* Jensen.'

Jensen preened himself and toyed with the medal hanging from his neck, as if he wished everyone present to be aware of his honour.

Hartung frowned. 'Pansy bastard,' he told himself, reflecting the next minute that he was darned envious of his former shipmate.

'Jensen's E-boats,' Ciliax continued, 'will have the task of ranging deeper into the Channel. In case our aircraft fail to detect any English reaction, it will be their job to report to us what the Tommies are up to and,' he paused momentarily and frowned hard at Jensen, still playing with his Knight's Cross, 'stop them at all costs, even if it means the destruction of the whole flotilla. You understand, Jensen?'

Jensen hesitated merely for a fraction of a second be-

fore replying in an even voice. '*Verstanden, Herr Admiral.*'

'Good. Now we can assume that the British will be slow to react, as our Fuhrer Adolf Hitler has predicted, but we must be completely honest with ourselves. In the end they *will* discover our presence in the Channel. So where will the trouble start?' Ciliax answered his own question. 'My guess is here,' he tapped the map, 'at Dover, where they've got destroyers and heavy coastal batteries. And here at Harwich where we know from aerial reconnaissance, the Tommies have both motor torpedo boats and destroyers. Up to that time, my belief is that our main danger will come from their bombers, for which I think we are amply prepared. What say you Colonel Galland?'

The dark-haired, un-German Colonel Galland, the *Luftwaffe*'s reigning fighting ace, nodded his agreement. 'I think we'll be able to protect your ships there, Admiral. I have some two hundred and eighty fighters under my command, mostly Me-109s and FW-190s, based in fields around Le Touquet, with smaller concentrations near Caen and Amsterdam. I am confident that we shall be able to keep a minimum of sixteen and a maximum of thirty-two fighters over your ships the whole voyage, with a considerable stepping-up of our effort once the capital ships have entered the Straits of Dover, closer to our Le Touquet fields.'

He stopped speaking and there was a murmur of approval from his listeners; even the stern-faced senior captains relaxed a little. The *Luftwaffe* was doing them proud and they knew it. Never before had the *Kriegsmarine* been provided with such an air umbrella.

Ciliax took over again. 'Now, there are two further things I should like to tell you, gentlemen. Both are interlinked. Let us remember we are in a foreign port, already buzzing with rumours as it is. Hence we must make one hundred per cent sure that the date of sailing does not get outside this room. For that reason I want all

of you, high and low, to have no further dealings with French civilians.'

He let his words sink in and Hartung could have sworn that Jensen blushed, as if he felt the order was addressed to him personally.

'Already we have started jamming British radar – for over three weeks now – so that the extensive jamming planned to coincide with the breakout will arouse no suspicion there. But we must keep an absolutely water-tight check on security within the port itself.' Admiral Ciliax forced a smile. 'So all that remains now, gentle-men, is to tell you when. Met forecasts low cloud and poor visibility in the Channel for the second week of February.' He shrugged almost carelessly. 'So that's it, gentlemen, the night of February 11/12th, 1942. Thank you.'

And with that he was gone.

Jensen smirked at Hartung. 'Well, you land-rat, now that we're going into the nunnery for a few days, what about a few drinks before the misery starts, eh?'

Hartung shook his head. 'No thanks, Egon. I've got other things to do.'

'I see you've got religion since you became a land-rat,' Jensen said and pulling on his elegant grey gloves and setting his cap at a suitably rakish angle for a day on the town, swaggered out after the rest.

'Arse with ears!' Hartung cursed under his breath, knowing that it had been sheer envy that had made him turn Jensen down, and followed. . . .

Less than a kilometre from where that fateful meeting had just taken place in the rundown little *pension* opposite Brest's dirty, white-stuccoed station, Anne Restignac, as she now called herself, lay on her back in the violently squeaking iron bed, gaze fixed on the dirty, flaking ceiling and let the young gasping sailor enjoy himself, as he pumped his muscular naked body up and down on top of her. She was dying for a cigarette and wished he would get

it over with so that she could reach over for the packet on the stained bedside table.

Outside, the cobbled little street was busy with the chug-chug of the wood-burning taxis and the harsh sound of hobnailed jackboots – obviously more reinforcements coming in from the station. The Germans were building up their garrison in Brest rapidly, it seemed. Jo-Jo, the ex-pimp who ran the *pension*, would be happy. It would mean more trade for the girls who used the place by the hour.

'*Ach, Sch-eisse*!' the young sweating sailor screamed in ecstasy and collapsed on top of her, mouth open and gasping like a stranded fish, eyes suddenly blank of emotion. Routinely Anne patted him on his damp back and said in accented German, 'Is good, cherie . . . good, *hein*?'

The sailor nodded his head, unable to speak for a moment. Gently Anne eased herself from underneath him and going over to the *bidet* squatted on it and cleaned herself, while the sailor stared at her stupidly, his long blond hair hanging down over his glistening brow.

'How much did you say?' he said finally, as she began to pull up her black pants once more.

She feigned a laugh and said, 'For you, sailor, *nothing*!'

'*Nothing*?' he echoed astonished.

'You heard, cherie,' she said, going into the old, old routine she had used so often in these last months.

The sailor sat up. 'But you're in the business, aren't you? Pavement-pounder and all that. Why don't you want the Marie?'

Outside the reinforcements were singing the usual song they did when they arrived in Brest, '*Wir fahren gegen Eng-land**.' The words of the old chant reminded her of her purpose here.

'Don't you know, my little sailor, that when you can please a girl like me, it's for free.' She smiled at fake

---

. *We sail against England.

passion. 'And there aren't many men in this world who can do that, I can tell you, cherie. Besides,' she simpered, 'who knows where you might be tomorrow. A brave fellow like you might . . .' she puffed out her lips in the Gallic fashion. 'It is a dangerous life you sailors from the er . . .' she deliberately mispronounced the name . . . '*Scharnhorst* lead.'

'*Gneisenau*' he corrected her, looking under the sagging bed for his socks.

Her heart leapt and she was glad the young German couldn't see the look in her eyes at that moment. She had guessed right. Her latest pick-up was from one of the heavy ships anchored outside in the shipping lane.

'*Gneisenau* then,' she laughed, fastening up her stockings. 'All of them are dangerous, yes?'

The sailor shrugged modestly. 'Well, yes and no,' he answered, sitting up on the bed to pull on his socks. 'Not these last months since we've been in harbour it hasn't been dangerous, except for the raids.'

She stretched out her right leg to give him a better view of it and keep talking without thinking.

His eyes gleamed. 'Of course there is a buzz that things are going to change,' he continued.

'A buzz?'

'A rumour.'

'*Ah oui*,' she said quickly, still displaying her leg, her pulse racing now with barely suppressed excitement.

'It might not be anything, naturally,' he said. 'But you can't tell me we've been loading ammo – I'm a gunner's mate, you see – for the last two days for nothing.'

'You think you might be leaving me, darling,' She crossed and stroked the side of his face lovingly. 'Don't tell me you'll be leaving?'

'Now I've not said that,' he said hastily, hands grasping for her buttocks. 'In the *Kriegsmarine* you can get into serious trouble for spreading rumours. I mean it's just my guess that's all.'

She let him fondle her buttocks for a few moments, not

wanting to press her luck too far, before she said. 'But you *do* think you're going?'

He nodded, his lips nuzzling her erect nipples through the thin artificial silk of her blouse.

'When?' The word came out strangely. She knew that one false move now and everything could be jeopardized.

But the blond young sailor was too busy with her breasts. 'Don't know,' he said thickly. 'But soon . . . very soon.' And with that Anne Rastignac had to be satisfied.

THREE

'The skipper sez would you come up on the bridge, sir,' the grizzled petty officer said.

Lt Kelly frowned and put down the wire he had been holding prior to casting off. What had he done wrong now, he asked himself. For the last week, ever since he had joined the MTB squadron, Lt Commander Harding, who could only be a couple of years older than himself, had been finding fault with him. 'Number One,' it had been, 'your wake is like a dog's hind-leg, steer closer, will you!' . . . 'Number One,' had been the acid comment from the captain when he had ventured to talk about the way the Russians were holding the Germans at Moscow, 'in the Royal Navy, we do not talk shop in the wardroom'. It almost seemed as if Lt Commander Harding had a special grudge against him, though he couldn't imagine why. Miserably he hurried down the busy deck to the bridge.

'Sir,' he reported.

Harding spun round. 'Number One, you seem to be in some doubt about which wires should be used down there, eh?'

Kelly swallowed hard and felt his face flushing as red as his thatch. 'A bit, sir,' he admitted unhappily. 'You see I was on cruisers before I asked for a transfer to the PT boats and there –'

Harding cut him short with a wave of his hand. 'Don't apologize, Number One. An officer should never apologize. But remember this. These boats have a hull as thin as egg-shell. One wrong move and you're in trouble, serious trouble.'

'I understand, sir,' Kelly said miserably, his brashness of a week ago totally vanished now.

Harding relented. 'Listen Number One,' he said, his voice softer now. 'I've been in this business for nearly three years now. All my predecessors were killed within a matter of months. Somehow or other, I have managed to last longer than they did. But it'll come to me, undoubtedly it will. I know it.'

Kelly stared at him open-mouthed. How could a man discuss his own death so calmly, almost as if he looked forward to the event, he asked himself, shocked.

'When that eventuality occurs, Number One, I want a second-in-command who will be able to take over firmly and efficiently, knowing that the lives of several score seamen depend upon his ability. Do you understand that, Number One?'

'Yessir.'

Harding gave him a little smile, but his faded tired eyes did not light up. 'Now off you go and sort out those bloody wires, then double back up here to watch me take her out!'

'*Yessir!*' Kelly said with new energy, almost falling over the side in his haste to carry out the skipper's orders.

That afternoon Peter enjoyed a rest, while Kelly had the con, taking in his favourite view of the MTB, feeling anew the efficiency and deadly strength of her superstructure from where he lounged on the bridge, as the flotilla of little boats ploughed steadily through the rolling grey-green waste of the North Sea. For late January the sea was remarkably calm, but visibility was spoiled by a thin fog that rolled across the water in low, wavering banks, so that Peter thought it would be hardly likely they'd be able to spot one of the enemy's coastal convoys that often used this route northwards heading for the Dutch ports, before they themselves were spotted so that the enemy ships would be able to escape to the nearest Belgian harbour. It

was his own guess that the sortie would prove as un-eventful as all the others they had carried out this week. It was almost as if the enemy had been swept from the Channel and North Sea for good.

Drake's destroyer's had proved equally unlucky of late too, as well as the destroyers and MTBs stationed down at Dover. 'E-boat Alley', as their sector of the Channel was known in the popular press, was strangely devoid of that particular craft, although God knows the Germans still had plenty of them available. And despite the improvements made in the British ships since 1939, the German E-boats were still their superior in speed, armament and sea-worthiness. So where had the Germans gone?

Peter sucked his bottom teeth thoughtfully. Of course, there was a buzz going the rounds of the pubs and ward-rooms back in Harwich that the Germans were planning some big scheme. Nowadays, when they got back from a sortie, the wallahs from Naval Intelligence pestered them for hours about what they had seen of the enemy, so obviously the bright boys in Room 39 thought that something was going on as well. But what? That was the damned question.

'Sir!' an urgent voice said.

Harding dropped the problem worrying him at once. He could tell from the tone of the bare headed rating's voice that something had happened. 'What is it, Jones?' he asked swiftly.

'Picking up confused sound on the hydrophone, sir. Could be old Jerry.'

'Can you give me a reading . . . and how far roughly?'

Hastily the rating supplied the information and added, 'My guess, they're about a mile off our present position.'

'Thank you. All right, back to your instruments.' Harding raised his voice. 'Bunts!'

Swiftly he supplied the new course and speed to the signaller to pass on to the other MTBs and turned to Kelly, whose face had turned a little white. Now there was an anxious, perhaps even apprehensive, look in his eyes.

Harding smiled slightly. 'Don't worry, Number One. It'll all happen so quickly, you won't have time to be scared. Besides,' he added, smile vanishing as swiftly as it had come, 'they've always said the Irish love a good scrap. . . .'

The disembodied voice said, 'Bridge!'

'Yes?' Peter answered immediately.

'Surface contact bearing green eight-five,' the operator answered.

'Large contact, sir . . . several vessels.'

'Starboard twenty-five,' Peter sang out. 'Full ahead together!'

The MTB surged forward. Its sharp prow tilted upwards. Suddenly they were racing towards the enemy, still hidden by the grey mist, at thirty knots an hour, spray shooting up behind them at mast height, smacking into each wave with a solid thud. To left and right the other MTBs of the flotilla picked up speed too, forming a fast V, alarm bells jingling, crews rushing to their posts on the wildly heaving decks, gunners throwing off the tarpaulins from their weapons, the mates ripping the clips from the ammunition racks, ready for action. Now all was controlled, tense speed, the look-outs' eyes narrowed to slits as they peered through the rolling fog to catch the first glimpse of the enemy.

'B-gun stand by for action!' Kelly cried, as if he had been giving such orders all his life. 'Local control!'

Effortlessly the turret swung round on its electric motor, as the first dim shape appeared on the horizon and Kelly rapped out the directions. 'Range one thousand. Bearing green one-oh!'

'Range one thousand . . . Bearing green one-oh!' the gun-layer sang back, as he lined up his piece on the dimly perceived shapes of what looked like a couple of trawlers. Next to him, his loading number bunched his shoulders and heaved. The bright gleaming shell clattered into the

breech. Deftly he closed the breech. The loading handle shot upwards metallicly. The gun was ready to fire.

On the crazily vibrating bridge, the wipers going all out to clear the flying spume away, both Kelly and Peter focused their glasses on the three objects to their immediate fore, desperately trying to identify them as the range between the MTBs and them diminished by the second. Behind the silent gun, the layer waited, his heaving cross-wires dead centre on the leading vessel's bridge.

The crooked cross banner flashed into the gleaming circle of glass that was Peter's binoculars. 'German!' he yelled. '*They're German!*'

Next instant Kelly confirmed his identification with a wild shout. The gun-layer waited no longer. He jerked back the firing bar. The three-inch gun erupted. Peter jerked up his glasses again. A burst of white water shot up some fifty feet to the leading barge's bows.

'Up fifty feet!' Peter yelled.

The layer waited impatiently.

'Range set!' the cry came.

He pressed the bar once more.

A gout of scarlet flame shot up from the vessel's bridge, through which Peter could just see the wireless mast come tumbling down before a sudden mushroom of thick black smoke obscured his vision. 'Check . . . check!' he yelled exuberantly.

The gunner ceased firing immediately. He had had his victory. The trawler, for that was what it was, was now burning fiercely and sinking rapidly by the stern. Now the other MTBs had to be given a chance to score. Captain Harding was very strict about the division of spoils among the little boats. He sat back on his haunches and allowed his back to be struck by the men crowding around him, as the other boats went speeding in.

Dewey, in the lead boat, slid round in a slick bow turn, heeling dangerously. Something long and lethal leapt from the MTB's knife-like prow at the last moment.

'Torpedo?' Kelly queried, his voice tense with excitement.

'Yes. He's been wanting to use his fish for a month of Sundays now!' Peter yelled back, focusing his glasses on the trail of white bubbles racing for the second trawler in a straight, arrow-headed line. On the enemy ship the captain, a dim silhouette in the box-like wheel-house, fought crazily to bring his ship round in time.

Peter and Kelly tensed. Suddenly there was a slamming thud against the enemy ship's plates. She seemed to jump out of the water. To her rear the water appeared to be racing backwards. Abruptly the grey light was rent by an intense white burst of flame. The water heaved up, swelled into a hillock and then a mountain, before flinging itself apart in huge heaving columns of boiling spray and spume, in a great thunderous explosion that sent vicious chunks of metal flying high into the burning air. Next moment, the ship broke in half, with crazy men throwing themselves into the sea everwhere.

On the deck of Peter's MTB the crew broke into a ragged cheer, as the MTBs converged on the last remaining vessel, which was now trying to make smoke. In vain! The MTBs, heaving and weaving at thirty knots an hour, each skipper fighting for position, trying to keep out of the wake of his neighbour which would slow him down, came in firing as they did so. Even at that distance and in spite of the racket made by the tortured engines of the MTBs the two men on the bridge could hear the tearing, wrenching sound of metal being torn apart, as shell after shell struck the helpless victim.

'Oh, my Holy Christ!' Kelly whispered in awe, as the concentrated barrage at such close range ripped the superstructure of the enemy ship apart, stanchions and masts falling everywhere like metallic leaves. 'The poor bastard hasn't got a chance!'

'It's war,' Peter said, as now more and more shells rent the stricken vessel's length into a shredded mess of holed, twisted steel. 'And there'll be worse to come yet.'

'What can be worse than this?' Kelly moaned.
'You'll see, Number One, you'll see. . . .'

'Stand by to pick up survivors!' Peter ordered as the boat
heaved to within a safe distance of the burning third
trawler, the flames throwing a blood-red hue on the water
filled with bobbing heads, 'Hurry it up there
now . . . And look-outs, keep yer eyes skinned!'

Now the ratings lined the deck, their boathooks at the
ready, as the MTB drifted closer to where the survivors
swam or floated among the dead and debris, crying out
piteously '*Sanitäter . . . bitte helfen Sie mir . . . Sani
. . .*' Waving one hand so that they would not be over-
looked.

Kelly gulped with horror. Directly below him in the
water, a dead German bobbed up and down, his skull split
open by a splinter as if cleaved by a giant axe, what looked
like thick red jelly oozing out of the gaping wound. At his
side Peter nodded grimly. 'Didn't I say there was worse to
come, Number One?'

Kelly could not answer this – his mouth was full of hot
vomit.

Now they started to fish the Germans out of the water,
the air full of the sickening, cloying stench of diesel oil.
All of them dripped the dark-brown goo, their bodies
shivering and slippery, so that it took the rescuers all their
strength to keep hold of them as they were pulled up and
deposited onto the deck, coughing and vomiting the oil
which now burnt away their lungs and guts. Kelly could do
nothing. He was rooted to the bridge, unable to move,
shocked into petrified immobility by the sight below.

He had never imagined war at sea could be like this: the
blackened wretches spewing chunks of diesel, the stokers
burnt a gleaming bright pink by scalding steam, the sailor
who lay unconscious on the deck, the obscene grey-purple
length of his gut, bulging out of his ripped-open stomach,
pulsating hectically with every sharp, shallow gasp he

took and the dead being trundled over the side again. Indeed he had never seen a dead man before in all his twenty-three years. Not once.

Now there were dead, dying, and horribly wounded men everywhere, moaning piteously on the deck, slumped like bundles of abandoned rags in corners, floating back and forth in the lee of the stationary MTB like logs among the debris.

'Not pretty is it, Number One?' Harding said, wiping a mixture of blood and oil from his hands with a piece of rag waste and tossing it over the side to land on the upturned face of a German sailor.

'It's horrible,' Kelly breathed in revulsion. His eyes fell on Harding's blood-stained wrists where he had succeeded in wiping off the stuff. 'You've got blood . . . blood on your hands, Captain!'

Harding looked at him hard. 'Number One, I've had blood on my hands these three long years now. It will never come off, if I cleaned them from now to doomsday.' He turned and walked away to supervize the removal of the wounded down below, leaving Kelly staring at his back, sick with horror at this terrible new world to which he had been consigned. . . .

FOUR

Lt Commander Fleming lounged against the great white mantelpiece of Room 39 and waited till the creaking old porter had built up the coal fire and limped out before he spoke. 'Admiral, you have seen the report about yesterday's action by the MTBs off the Dutch coast?'

Admiral Godfrey, the broad-faced Head of Naval Intelligence, took his gaze off the barrage balloon tethered above Horse Guards Parade like a sluggish, silver elephant. 'Yes, I saw it, Ian. So?'

'Well, sir, we sink three Boche vessels right under their noses with Zeebrugge and Dunkirk, full of Boche *Schnellboote*, and nothing happens. They just accept it!'

Godfrey smiled. Ian liked to air his knowledge of German at every available opportunity. Anyone else on his staff would have said E-boats, even the German linguists; but not Ian Fleming. Again he said, 'So?'

'Well, sir, that kind of thing has been happening for the last fortnight now. We have the run of the Channel and the North Sea.' Fleming raised his shoulders in that unEnglish gesture of his, which added to his habitual self-dramatization that made him so successful with women older than himself and such a failure with the conventional senior officer at the Admiralty. 'Where have all the E-boats gone?'

'Where the flies go in the winter, I suppose,' Godfrey said trying to get a rise out of the other man.

Fleming ignored the flippancy. 'Sir, I have a theory.'

'You always have.'

In the City the sirens had begun to wail yet again. In the corridor outside the porter was creaking by, calling in a suitable low voice for that august place, 'Gentlemen, the

warning is being sounded. Would you please repair to the shelters. Gentlemen, the warning is being sounded. Would. . . .' Both men ignored the *sotto voce* appeal. Only lower grade ratings and Wrens went down to the shelters these days. To the east and along the Thames the Bofors began to thunder.

'Several things are beginning to fall into place, sir,' Fleming persisted. 'First the absence of E-boats from E-boat Alley. Then this persistent jamming of our radar and now finally the reports from our Joeys in France.

For the first time Godfrey really took interest. 'You mean the Daisy Chain *Riseau*?' he asked sharply.

Fleming nodded and grinned at the memory of the little Free French homosexual, who had first suggested the spy ring and had given it its name. 'You mean to say, Ian,' Godfrey had exploded that summer when it had all started, 'that you are going to allow this little Frog pervert to spy for us?'

'Naturally, sir,' Fleming had replied, as if it were the most obvious thing in the world. 'Where there are sailors, there are nancy-boys. Always have been. Did Old Winnie himself not say that the Royal Navy in the old days was famous for the lash, rum and buggery?' He had shrugged. 'So, we use him to pump the jolly old Boche boys in blue. After all, sir, who would suspect a homosexual of being a spy, what? Far too soft for that kind of thing.'

Thus the Daisy Chain Ring had come into existence, an espionage network based on the French ports using men and women voluntary prostitutes to obtain the information Room 39 sought.

'Well, what do your precious agents have to say?' Godfrey asked, as the rumble of anti-aircraft fire grew closer. The German bombers were obviously heading for the City again.

Ian Fleming frowned. 'There are lots of little bits and pieces, sir, which could mean something of significance, and then again they could mean nothing. Just matelots' rumours and boastings.'

'Well, come on Ian,' Godfrey urged. 'We are paid in Naval Intelligence, to do just that – put the jigsaw together. I know you. You have come up with something.'

'Alain, the little French nancy-boy, has apparently a high-ranking German officer as his current lover,' Fleming began hesitantly. 'According to Alain, his boy-friend is highly chuffed about some new mission he is going on. This man is an E-boat man by the way and a *Kapitänleutnant* – lieutenant-commander, sir,' he added by way of explanation.

'I know what *Kapitänleutnant* is!' Godfrey snorted. 'I'm not totally ignorant, you know. So one queer Boche lieutenant-commander boasts that he is going on a mission. That's pretty thin, Ian. You'll have to do better than that to convince their Lordships, my boy.'

'Yessir. But another one of the ring – code-named Anne – has also reported that one of her – er – clients, maintains that something is on,' Fleming paused in that melodramatic manner of his, while outside a lone Junkers 88 came winging in, miraculously dodging the cables stretched between the barrage balloons, the sky peppered with brown puffs of smoke all around it. Godfrey shook his head in admiration. The Boche pilot was a brave bastard. Perhaps, he told himself, they should have gone to the shelters after all.

'But the give-away, sir, is this. The Boche sailor was from the *Gneisenau*!'

'What did you say?'

Fleming smiled, pleased with himself. His statement had had its effect. He repeated the ship's name and hurried on, as the German dropped his bombs not more than a hundred yards away and the building trembled under their impact. 'So put the pieces together – the absence of E-boats, the radar-jamming, this talk of some important mission being scheduled and what do you get . . .'

Godfrey beat him to it. 'The *Scharnhorst* and *Gneisenau* at Brest are going to make a run for it!'

'Exactly, sir!'

Godfrey bit his bottom lip, his broad face serious, his brow furrowed. At the mantelpiece, Fleming lit one of his special, handmade cigarettes and waited, quietly enjoying his little triumph, mentally recording the picture this January day; the chaos outside and the controlled calm here inside Room 39, with the old clock inexorably ticking away the minutes on the wall, as the middle-aged Admiral made his decision. Still-life, 1942. It would come in useful later, after the war.

Finally the Admiral broke his silence. 'All right, Ian, this is what I am going to suggest to their Lordships. Increased surveillance of Brest, as follows. A stopper patrol of one submarine and Coastal Command aircraft on permanent duty at the bottleneck that forms the entrance to Brest harbour. Alerting Ramsay's Dover Command for immediate action. Two-hour state of readiness for Bomber Command. I know old Harris* won't like it. It'll mean that his precious bombers will have to stop all training and all ops, except the bombing of Brest itself. But still, he'll have to lump it. Finally Joubert's† Coastal Command's Beauforts, they're torpedo-bombers, you know?' Ian nodded his understanding. 'There are three squadrons of them. Well, Joubert will have to have them concentrated in the south. At present they're scattered all over the show, even as far north as Leuchars in Scotland. We want them down around Thorney Island off Pompey, so that they can get first strike at the Boche.' Godfrey frowned. 'Ian, you realize, it is going to be a tremendous operation, and I doubt if their Lordships are going to be able to make a decision on this alone. It will have to go to the War Cabinet and I can imagine that in the end it will be Winnie who'll make the decision. After all, it not only affects the Navy, but also Bomber and Coastal Commands.'

'I understand that, sir,' Fleming said, suddenly alarmed

*Air Marshal Harris, Chief of Bomber Command.
†Head of Coastal Command.

by the fact that his little intelligence games were escalating into something very big and beyond his control. What if he had been a little too smart, he asked himself fearfully. He couldn't hope for a better and more interesting job than that of Godfrey's personal aide. What if he had made a mistake? God, they could send him up to the Orkneys, away from his clubs and his women! What a fate that would be. He bit his bottom lip.

Godfrey laughed softly. 'Don't worry, Ian. Your name won't even be mentioned. From now onwards it will be all committees and panels and brasshats. They won't even know of your humble existence.'

Fleming smiled with relief, though at the same time he was a little annoyed that his effort would go unnoticed.

'Now,' Godfrey said, as the thin wail of the all clear started up somewhere in the City, 'I need more information and I need it fast. Ian, those agents of yours in Brest, that nancy-boy and his whores, they've got to give us more information. We want to know the day of sailing and the *direction*! Are the Boche capital ships heading out into the Atlantic again, or are they going to run the gauntlet of the Channel? If they are, then we've got them.' He squeezed his big right hand into a fist, as if squashing a fly. 'But I've got to know!'

'It'll be dangerous, sir, highly dangerous – for the agents I mean,' Fleming warned.

'You can't make an omelette without cracking eggs, Ian. After all,' he added carelessly, walking over to the stand to reach for his gold-braided cap. 'What do the lives of pansies and prostitutes matter, eh, Ian, compared with those of our chaps?' He put his cap on firmly and said with a note of finality in his voice, thickened by thirty years of command, '*Nothing!*'

But Lt Commander Ian Fleming was to receive no more information from the Daisy-Chain Ring. Three hours before that decisive meeting between Vice-Admiral

Godfrey and his aide, which set the whole cumbersome machinery of obtaining a decision in wartime in motion, a civilian truck had driven up to one of the shabbier streets off the port of Brest. It remained there parked for some time, while the sabot-shod French workmen, cigarettes glued to their lips, cloth-caps pulled down over their foreheads, cycled by in their hundreds, reporting for another day at the German-occupied dockyard.

At the stroke of seven, a long black Horch, filled with middle-aged, beefy men, clad in long leather overcoats, the broad brims of their felt hats hiding their eyes, braked to a stop behind the stationary truck. Instinctively the French workers on their cycles parted to let the Horch by. They knew who the occupants of that car were; indeed they wore their hats and creaking leather coats like an unofficial uniform. '*Flics*,' they whispered fearfully to each other and kept their eyes on the dirty *pavé*, '*Gestapo!*'

Again nothing happened.

Over at the corner bistro, the *Café de la Paix*, the one-eyed owner busy pouring out glasses of morning *rhum* for his morning customers, took the stub of *Gauloise* out of his dingy teeth and growled, 'They're after their own kind – Boche. Deserters, perhaps?'

One of his customers grinned. 'You didn't think you were important enough for a raid, Jacques, just because you serve alcohol on a "day without"?'*

The bar owner raised his shoulders in an eloquent shrug. 'What do I care about the Boche – or the English either! Let them get on fighting their silly war and leave our poor people in peace.'

At seven-thirty precisely, as the sirens began to shrill their summons to a new day of work at the dockyard, the big Gestapo man standing next to the Horch whipped out a whistle and blew three sharp blasts on it. Immediately

---

*In Occupied France, no alcohol was supposed to be served on alternative days.

the back-tarpaulin of the truck was flung back and French gendarmes, some of them armed with sub-machine guns, began to drop to the cobbles and run to the flop-house almost immediately opposite the *Café de la Paix*. The middle-aged, beefy Gestapo men were slower off the mark. They clattered across the cobbles to the front door, while the gendarmes slipped to left and right, capes flying, to surround the house. Their leader, a heavy-set man with gold teeth and a clipped, Hitler-type moustache, nodded to his companion. 'All right, Sour, hit it!'

Next to the door the *flic* raised his eyes upwards as if appealing to God. Why didn't the Boche check to see whether the doors were opened first?

Sour smashed his shoulder against the door. It flew open. From within there came a sudden cry of alarm. 'In you go, my lucky lads!' the Gestapo chief yelled, slapping each man as he went in.

At the door of the dingy stairwell, a knife of yellow light slid into the gloom. 'There they are!' Sour cried and went puffing up the stairs, drawing his pistol as he did so.

A fat woman tried to hold the door. Again his shoulder smashed into it. The woman flew to the floor, her skirt slipping back to reveal that she wore no underclothing. Sour jumped over her grinning. 'You're showing the flag, old woman!' he cried, running down the corridor. 'And it's black!'

'*Sales cons*!' the *madame* cursed as Gestapo men started to fling open the doors of both sides of the gloomy corridor to cries of fear and rage from within, as the occupants sat up startled in the rumpled sweaty beds to find themselves staring into the business end of a Gestapo-man's pistol.

In five minutes it was all over, and Sour, leading a flushed, unhappy naked man in front of him, who carried what appeared to be a German naval officer's uniform over his arm, made his triumphant report to his superior. 'Twelve deserters, fourteen pavement-pounders, one of them male,' he jerked his pistol at the undersized skinny

Frenchman standing pressed up against the wall, trembling in every limb, hands stretched high above his head,' and this gentleman from the *Kriegsmarine*.' He leaned forward and whispered something urgently to his superior, while the naked German looked miserably at his toes.

Sarcastically the Gestapo chief clicked to attention. 'May I introduce myself, *Herr Kapitänleutnant*, *Oberkommissar* Grau of the *Gemeine Staatspolizei**, known to his associates as "Sweet".' He wagged a big, tobacco-stained finger under the sailor's nose, 'But not for the same reason you might think,' he said jovially and winked at his subordinate. 'What Sour?'

'Definitely not, *Oberkommissar*,' Sour said, enjoying their little private joke.

'In three devils' name,' the naval officer snapped, finding his tongue at last. 'Can't we stop this farce? You know who I am and I know the penalty for my . . . crime. I am an officer and a gentleman, let me take the honourable way out.' He swallowed hard. '*Please!*'

'That would be the easy way,' Sour taunted him. 'Wouldn't it? That would be just like you fine gents with yer fancy manners and fancy perversions,' he sneered. 'No, my dear *Kapitänleutnant*, it's not going to be as easy as that for you. Swine like you will have –'

'He's got the Knight's Cross,' Sweet interrupted his subordinate, using their old technique, the one which had given them their name within the inner circles of the Gestapo. 'I mean, Sour, he must have been a brave chap once.'

'You've got too soft a heart, Sweet,' Sour said aggressively. 'I don't care if he's got a whole cupboard full of tin. He's a pervert-swine who only thinks about sticking his perverted salami into perverted little frogs like that.' He flung the Frenchman pressed against the wall a murderous glance. 'Frogs who belong to the *Résistance*.'

The sailor groaned. 'Oh no, not that too!'

*Gestapo

'I'm afraid so, sir,' Sweet said affably. 'Information we have received has led us to believe that there is a whole network of pimps and prostitutes – female and male –' he added delicately, lowering his gaze as if he could not bear to see the naked officer any more, 'pumping our Lords for information.'

The sailor threw a glance at the trembling Frenchman, and flung up his clapsed hands in the classic gesture of supplication. 'I beg you gentlemen, *please* . . . let me have a pistol and put a finish to it all! Think of my family. The Service! Oh, the disgrace, the utter disgrace!' Suddenly his shoulders slumped and he started to sob, his whole body racked with sorrow, great tears streaming down his ashen face, while his lover, the Frenchman stared at him, his expression a mixture of contempt and sympathy.

'*Um Himmelswillen!*' Sour sneered. 'Try to act like a man, even if you aren't one . . . Snivelling like a –'

He never finished his outburst. In that same moment, the sailor gave him a sudden push. Sour was caught off balance and staggered into his chief, sending him reeling. Next instant all was cries, chaos and confusion, with the naked sailor, dropping his clothes as he ran, pelting down the corridor into the gloom and the Gestapo chief yelling urgently, '*Nicht schiessen* . . . For God's sake, don't shoot, men! *Nicht schiessen.* . . .'

The naked sailor crashed through the glass door in the gloom and screamed as the shreds ripped open his flesh in a dozen pieces. Jetting blood from a deep gash in his wrist he staggered. He had to get to the roof. *The roof* . . . it had to be the roof! He flung open another door. A woman, ashen-faced with fear, her pendulous breasts hanging almost to her fat waist, looked up at him from beneath a sagging bed. 'Have they gone?' she gasped in French and then stiffled a scream, as she saw the state of the blood-stained sailor.

He ignored her. Springing onto the bed, which creaked alarmingly under his weight, listening to the clatter of

heavy boots down the corridor outside, he heaved with all his strength. The skylight squeaked open. With the agility that had once made him one of the best gymnasts at the cadet school, he hauled himself up and stood there, outlined on the slate roof against the grey winter morning. Below, a score of white faces turned up to see him, as he balanced there like a circus trapeze artist about to commence his act.

'*Ne pas tirez*!' Sweet yelled desperately in his confused French out of a window. '*Nix tirez . . . il est allemand* . . . Don't shoot . . . he's a German officer!'

Staring open-mouthed out of the fly-blown window of the *Café de la Paix*, the owner saw how one of the gendarmes raised his machine pistol and winked at his grinning companion. He was just close enough to catch the *flic*'s words. They were, 'I've always wanted to croak a *Boche*.' Next moment, he started as the cop pressed his trigger.

High above, the naked man flung up his arms, spreading them outwards crosslike, a sudden line of bright scarlet stitched across his white chest. For what seemed an age, he remained thus and then, with a great echoing cry that appeared to go on for ever, he plunged to the cobbles far below.

Contemptuously, Sour turned over the naked body with the toe of his boot, as it lay there sprawled out in a star of bright blood, which would stain the cobbles long after the Germans had vanished from Brest.

Sweet looked at him enquiringly.

Sour turned down his thumbs.

Sweet nodded. 'The little banana-sucker then?' he said.

'Guess so, *Chef*.' Sweet grinned and there was nothing pleasant about his grin now, in spite of his nickname. 'You know what, Sour, I think we're gonna enjoy this one.'

'Well, you know what they say about us behind our

backs, *Chef*,' Sour said, as the French police started to bring out the heavily chained prisoners to the truck, in the lead the little mincing homosexual Alain. 'The two of us could get a mummy to talk.'

Sweet chuckled. 'That you can say again, Sour . . .'

FIVE

'Have you heard the news, Horst?' the chubby little MO asked as Horst walked into the *Kasino*'s dining-room to take a late breakfast, now that all the other officers, save the doctor, had gone to their daily duties.

'No,' Hartung lowered the *Völkischer Beobachter*, its headlines screaming out the details of yet another tremendous victory in Russia. 'Has Churchill finally succumbed to too much whisky eh?'

'Comedian!' the MO said. He was the base VD officer and led a very gloomy life examining sailors' genitals for six hours a day. There was a rumour in the mess that he was a secret drinker and Horst told himself that he would be too, if he had a job like that. 'No, it's your friend, our handsome hero *Kapitänleutnant* Jensen.'

'Oh,' Horst said mildly interested, helping himself to a cup of acorn coffee from the urn. 'And what has he been up to?'

'Nothing much – except he's gone and killed himself.'

Horst heard the cup rattle in his hand and the chubby little doctor smiled, pleased with himself. 'Yes, took a nose-dive off a roof this very morning. Naked as the day he was born too. Not a pleasant sight my colleagues at the hospital told me.'

Hartung put his cup down suddenly. 'But why, Doc? What was his problem?'

The MO looked left and right, as if he thought the Gestapo might be listening to him. 'Well, you know the problems for you Navy chaps? You're at sea too long and there aren't enough women to go round when you get back to port.'

'Go on,' Hartung said mystified.

'Must I draw you a picture? Well, what do you boys in blue do on your long nights?' The MO answered his own question with a knowing smirk. 'It's either the one-handed widow.' He made an explicit gesture so that a puzzled Hartung could not fail to understand him, 'or it's some willing young fellow among your own ranks. Now do you get it?'

A sudden light dawned on Hartung's face. 'So you mean –'

'Of course, it's only a buzz, but that's the way it looks. My colleagues at the Naval Hospital are presently chopping him up. Undoubtedly they'll finally have the evidence the authorities need to prove it.'

Hartung shook his head grimly, his appetite for breakfast abruptly gone. 'Poor bastard,' he said softly, remembering that it was just that which he had always suspected of Jensen even back in their old days of training together. Still to be forced to die in order to satisfy that urgent itch between the legs; it seemed too high a penalty to pay.

'How was he found out, Doc?' he asked finally.

Eagerly the little medic began to explain the details of Jensen's suicide, but suddenly Hartung found himself not listening as it began to dawn on him that now the E-boat Flotilla would be without a commander for the great breakout operation.

'So then apparently,' the MO was saying, 'he pushed by the Gestapo chap and started to run down the corridor in order to get onto the roof . . . hey, Hartung, where are you going?' he cried suddenly, as Hartung swung round and started to hurry towards the door, as if he had just remembered a very important appointment.

'To see an admiral,' Hartung flung back over his shoulder and then he was gone, leaving the chubby MO to reflect on the fact that soon he would have to start on the morning's boring routine of shortarm inspections. 'God,' he whispered to himself mournfully, 'why do those sailors

have to go and stick it into anything with hair around it? Why indeed . . .?'

But there was nobody there to answer that particularly overwhelming question. . . .

'*Herr Admiral.*'

'Hartung. You wish to see me?'

'Yessir, please.'

Admiral Ciliax looked up from his paper-littered desk and sighed wearily, as if he were very tired although it was only ten o'clock in the morning. 'Where's the fire then, Hartung?' he asked, noticing the young officer's flushed excited face and smiling a little.

'It's about *Kapitänleutnant* Jensen, sir.'

'You've heard about it then?'

Hartung nodded.

'A bad business, a very bad business, Hartung. I'm afraid we won't be able to sweep this one under the carpet. There will have to be an enquiry. Himmler will get on to it and he hates the Navy. There'll be trouble.'

'Not if Operation Cerberus succeeds, sir,' Hartung said eagerly. 'I can imagine the Fuhrer will hold his protective hand over our service if we can get the heavy ships back safely to the Reich.'

'*If*,' Ciliax said. 'A little word with a large meaning. You know that Jensen was involved in some sort of spy-ring. Apparently the Gestapo is presently occupied in finding out the details from some of the French nationals they have rounded up down in the port. But I can tell you now what the gentlemen of the Gestapo will discover – namely that the spies were working for the Tommies trying to ferret out what they can about our plan.'

'Possibly, sir,' Hartung said, not allowing his inner excitement to be dampened by the Admiral's words. 'But when Admiral Raeder met the Fuhrer last December to discuss the breakout, the Fuhrer made the point that

whatever happens, the British will react too slowly, so that the advantage of virtually any set of circumstances will be on our side.'

Admiral Ciliax was not convinced. He rose heavily to his feet. 'Come here, Hartung,' he commanded and adjusted the powerful telescope, which he always kept looking out of the window of his office when he was ashore; as if he wished to keep the atmosphere of being at sea with him all the time. 'Take a look through this . . . say, at sixty degrees.'

Obediently Hartung swung the long telescope to the left. The narrow entrance to Brest harbour leapt into the gleaming circle of glass, with the surf breaking about it, a boiling white confusion of angry water.

'Up a little bit, Hartung,' the Admiral urged.

Hartung did as he was told. A white-painted shape swept slowly into the glass and he could just make out the red-white-and-blue circle of the RAF on its plump side. He turned and looked enquiringly at the Admiral, who stood there stony-faced, hands dug deep into his pockets, as if he were trying to restrain his anger.

'An RAF Hudson,' the Admiral answered his unspoken enquiry. 'I should imagine you know my little quirk with the telescope? I like to have a quick look through it every half hour or so, when I can. It takes my mind off this damned paperwork and reminds me I'm still a sailor. Well, thirty minutes ago I took a quick glance and what I did see – I saw that.' He sniffed. 'And do you know what it means, Hartung?'

'Not exactly, sir.'

'It means that the Tommies have smelt a rat. I think that plane out there is on permanent patrol because they *know* that's the way we are coming out.' He frowned and dismissed the matter. 'Well young Hartung, now what is your problem?'

'Sir, I'd like to take over Jensen's flotilla for the break-out.'

The Admiral's eye fell on Hartung's red withered claw

of a hand and Hartung felt himself flushing. 'You, Hartung?'

'Yessir. I am the most experienced E-boat commander in Brest and I am the senior man. I have already contacted Admiral Raeder,' he lied glibly, 'and he has given *his* approval. Now it's up to you, sir, and if, as you say, the Tommies are on to us, you'll need a skilled man out there on the flank with the E-boat flotilla.' He paused and looked expectantly at the Admiral, his chest heaving slightly with the effort of so much rapid talking.

Admiral Ciliax looked at Hartung's hard, enthusiastic young face and knew that he was the man he needed, but still he hesitated, as he considered whether or not Hartung was physically fit for the mission. 'Your hand, do you think you can manage, Hartung? Now be realistic about this.'

'I can do it, sir. Kaese, the second-in-command of the flotilla is an excellent officer. I know I can rely on him one hundred per cent.'

'All right,' Ciliax decided, 'you've got the job, Hartung.'

'Thank you, sir!' Hartung cried.

'Don't thank me, young Hartung,' the Admiral said, his face sombre. 'Remember, if the Tommies *are* waiting for us out there, your mission could well be a one-way trip.'

But Horst Hartung was no longer listening – he was going to sea again!

SIX

Now everything was frenzied activity at Brest, as the fleet made its last minute preparations for the big breakout. Everywhere the supply trucks and horse-drawn carts rattled along the cobbled quays. Ammunition barges chugged in and out of the crowded shipping lanes, hauling the shells of every calibre that Admiral Ciliax hoped his ships would never have to use. Mountains of canned food disappeared into the holds of the capital ships to feed their crews on the great dash north and the sweating ratings loading them could not restrain their wonder as they saw the labels on the cans. They were not the usual *Alter Mann* – cans of meat reputedly made from dead old men collected from Berlin's many warehouses – but fine French delicacies, both meat and cheese, the like of which they had not seen these many years. There was even real bean-coffee instead of the usual *ersatz*. Hartung, hurrying about his many duties that day, heard one young rating exclaim in awe, 'Holy strawsack, they'll be giving us caviare next!' To which a sour-faced *Maat* replied, 'They might at that, laddie. They always fatten us before the kill – like animals before they slaughter them!'

Hartung had laughed, but there had been a slightly hollow ring about that laugh.

In those last days of the first week of February 1942, Hartung's major concern, however, was not to add weight to his E-boats by loading them with more supplies, but to decrease weight in order to heighten their speed. His crews didn't like the fact that they were not going to enjoy the delicacies being handed out so liberally to the men manning the bigger ships; and they did not conceal their outrage. In the end, after Kaese – known being his back

as 'Cheesehead' on account of his name* and large moon-like face which did resemble a pale Emmentaler cheese – had told Hartung that the men were moaning about having to off-load their spirit and beer rations, he paraded his crews on the wind-swept quayside. Maliciously de-lighting in the fact that a thin cold rain was now adding to their discomfort.

'Now,' he barked above the noise of the port and the howl of the wind, which rippled their bell-bottoms around the sailors' skinny legs and had their cap ribbons stream-ing upwards, 'I know you've all heard the buzz that we're leaving Brest – and the buzz is right. But by God and all His triangles, I'll have the eggs of any lord here who says I told you so!'

There was a ripple of laughter from the seamen at their CO's salty language intermingled with many 'I told you so's'.

'Lieutenant Kaese here tells me that you are complain-ing because you're not getting the same goodies as the crews of the other vessels. You're right. You aren't and you have reason to complain. A sailor's life is a hard lot, as my friend Doctor Pox tells me.' Again his men laughed and Hartung knew he was winning them over. It was time to make his point. 'But there is a reason for it, men. We're going to need every bit of speed we can get out of boats before this business is over.' Hartung's face hardened and swept his eyes along the blue-uniformed ranks, as if trying to fix a picture of every man in his mind. Here and there a sailor shuddered involtunarily at the cold ruthlessness of their new CO's gaze. 'Because our lives might well de-pend on our ability to make an extra knot. Never forget that – *our lives depend on speed*!'

He let the words sink in, while the gulls above their heads wheeled and dived into the wind, crying like long-lost children.

'All right, so you don't get your goodies on board.'

Kaese is German for cheese.

Hartung's hard face relaxed. 'But there is nothing to say that you shouldn't have them *before* we sail, is there? At zero six hundred hours today, I'm going to stand you down, *everybody*! If the Admiral wants us, we won't be there. Do you know why? I'll tell you. Because this flotilla is going to have the biggest *Kameradschaftsabend** ever known in Brest. There'll be a bottle of corn-gin per man and two bottles of French champus, plus as much roast pork and sauerkraut as anyone wants. I think even *Obermaat* Heinze won't even complain this time.' He indicated a long thin drooping petty officer, with a dewdrop at the end of his beak of a red nose, who was notorious throughout the flotilla for the amount of food he could tuck away. 'Comrades, back to work. Tonight E-boat Flotilla Six gets blind drunk!'

His command 'dismiss' was drowned in a wave of excited cheers and hurrahs. . . .

The *Kameradschaftsabend* had degenerated into a drunken orgy. The noise was tremendous, with drunken sailors bawling away off-key, while others shouted filthy jokes at the top of their voice, trying to make themselves heard over the racket. Unconscious sailors lay everywhere; on benches, slumped across tables, on the floor – there was even one suspended by his collar from the hat stand, placed there by unkind comrades, who now snored peacefully unaware of his position.

Hartung grinned at Kaese through the noisy, smoke-filled atmosphere, across a table littered with empty champagne bottles, and said, his words slurred a little, 'Cheesehead, old house, I think it is about time the officers retired.'

'Why?' Lieutenant Kaese enquired, draining the last of his champagne from the bottle and tossing the 'dead soldier' carelessly to the glass-littered floor.

---

*Roughly a 'company smoker'.

A group of four sailors, swaying dangerously, passed by carrying an unconscious comrade on a trestle table, his hands arranged as if in prayer, cap placed reverently on his chest. 'Eyes . . . *eyes, right!*' the leading rating commanded and four pairs of eyes clicked in the direction of the officer's table. 'Beer corpse, sir,' the man who had given the command said solemnly, 'gonna bury him properly – *in the latrines!*'

Grinning, Hartung touched his hand to his blond head in salute, and giggling wildly, the 'burial party' passed on its way.

Hartung looked at his watch. 'Doctor Pox's girls are due in five minutes,' he said. 'Don't want the boys' style to be cramped by the presence of the officers.'

'I wouldn't mind my style being cramped,' Kaese grumbled. 'It's been a whole week since I managed to find time to get to the officer's brothel.'

Hartung laughed. 'Wait till we get back to Kiel as heroes, Cheesehead. You'll have to fight them off.'

'*If* we get back,' his second-in-command grumbled, but he got to his feet willingly enough and said. 'All right, you young officers, let's make steam. The girls are due now.'

'Girls!' they exclaimed, rising to their feet drunkenly. 'Did you say girls?'

'Yes, I did. What's the matter with you? Have you been eating big beans or something and gone deaf? Anyway, you lot wouldn't know what to do with one anyway, especially the kind Doctor Pox is supplying, all with their yellow card signed, sealed and right bang up-to-date.'

Hartung nodded to *Obermaat* Heinze, still stuffing cold *sauerkraut* into his mouth, the only sober NCO in the place. 'Heinze, let them in! Come on, you lot, let's get out of here before there is an accident.'

Grumbling good-humouredly, his officers began to trail after him through the shambles, while *Obermaat* Heinze, chewing on an abandoned pork-chop, went to the door. He opened it and bellowed, '*Allez vite . . . Matelot allemand wollen ficki-ficki . . . Allez!*'

There were squeals of delight from outside and everywhere the drunken, bleary-eyed sailors sat up on their benches as the whores, carefully selected as healthy by the chubby little VD Doctor, came running in, all shaking bosoms, eager faces, and wooden heels clattering on the stone floor.

Hartung grinned at Heinze. 'Well done, *Obermaat*, we'll make you the *maître de plaisir* for this night. See that all the boys get home afterwards.'

'Don't hold with this sort of carry-on,' Heinze said gloomily. 'Not right, it ain't. Look at them,' he exclaimed as the girls ran between the rows of suddenly delighted and surprised sailors, who were reaching out for them everywhere. 'They'll be fornicating in half a minute. I know they will!'

'Did you say *fornicate*?' Hartung cried above the shrieks and yells. 'A petty officer using a word like –'

The sentence died on his lips as he saw the big blonde French girl, who was entwining her arms around the neck of a young seaman, who was fumbling drunkenly for her breasts.

Obermaat Heinze followed the direction of his CO's gaze and then looked back at the officer, whose face had abruptly gone ashen. 'Anything . . . anything the matter, sir?'

Hartung didn't reply; he couldn't.

There was no mistaking her. She was older, of course, and in appearance she looked no different from the rest of Doctor Pox's selected whores: the skirt too short, the heels too high, the scarlet mouth set open in that look of professional concupiscence, which he had seen on the faces of whores all over the world. But it was Anna. Of that there was no doubt. It was Anna Hurwitz, the 'Hell-Cat' of those days that seemed so long ago now, and instinctively with the clarity of a sudden vision, Horst Hartung knew why she was here – a Jewess in the middle of a room full of German sailors in Occupied France. *Anna Hurwitz was a spy!*

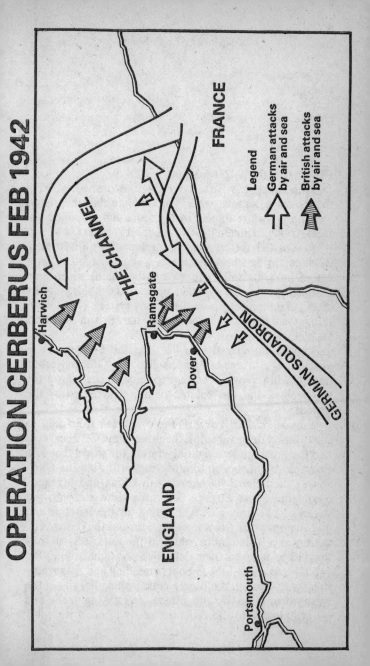

SEVEN

February 11th, 1942! Midnight.

Over Brest, the British Wellingtons droned, seeking their elusive targets, while the German flak thundered and the icy-white fingers of the searchlights probed the skies, trying to box in the two-engined bombers.

'*Leinen los!*' the cry rang out in ship after ship. Bosuns' whistles shrilled and the alarm gongs clanged. Everywhere hurrying sailors threw off the chains which held their ships. Anchors rattled up into the holds. Orders crackled metallically over the tannoy system. Now everything was hectic activity, while the British bombers searched and hunted.

Engines thundered into life. On the bridges of the armada, the bridge-telegraphs clanged. Officers jerked back the brass levers. Urgent commands sped down the voice pipes and the volume of noise increased by the instant.

'*Alle Maschinen voraus!*' the order ran from ship to ship. Slowly the giant ships, the pride of the German Navy and the most modern fighting craft in the world that cold February night, began to move forward. First the *Gneisenau*, then the *Scharnhorst* with Ciliax and his staff, finally the *Prinz Eugen*. The three ships slid into the darkness like grey ghosts, heading for the harbour exit and the open sea. Now it was the turn of the destroyers, their wakes a luminous white in the darkness, as they hurried to take up their defensive positions around the capital ships. Then the E-boats threading and zig-zagging their way through the bigger craft, rolling heavily in the wash thrown up by the others, overtaking them and hurrying out into the Atlantic, ready to meet whatever

challenge lay awaiting there on its heaving green infinity.

The great escape had commenced. The actors were in their positions; the drama could begin. . . .

Now it was quarter to eleven. Ramsay slumped in his big leather armchair, collar ripped open, glass of whisky almost untouched next to him on the wardroom table, looking at the aide who had just come through the door.

The lieutenant shook his head. 'Stopper One,' he said, referring to the Hudson covering the exit to Brest, 'reports nothing. Its radar is blank.'

'Thank you, Jenkins,' Ramsay said and yawned. 'You can turn in now, if you wish.'

Jenkins hesitated. Ramsay had been glued to his desk all day waiting for any news of the German ships at Brest. For the last three days, everyone at Dover Naval HQ had been on tenterhooks, waiting nervously for the Germans to make their move; for Met had forecast these would be the only days in February when the conditions in the Channel would be most favourable for a breakout. The Old Man looked exhausted. 'What about *you* turning in sir? You look pretty tired, if you don't mind my saying so? I can stay on here till the duty officer comes on at midnight.'

Ramsay smiled his thanks. 'No, I'll wait till Stopper Two reports in. If it's negative, I'll get my head down then.'

'All right. Good-night, sir.'

'Good-night, Jenkins.'

Now all was silent in Dover Castle, perched high above the harbour, though Ramsay knew that all over the south coast of England right up to Harwich, there were men and planes and ships waiting, just as he was waiting, for the order to go. Ramsay was not a romantic individual, but at that moment he could not help thinking that this is how it must have been in England in 1588, when the country awaited the Spanish Armada.

He smiled at his own fancy and took a tiny sip of his whisky-and-soda, wondering idly whether Drake really had played bowls on Plymouth Hoe to wile away the time. At his side the telephone rang suddenly, startling him. He grabbed it and barked, 'Ramsay!'

'Admiral,' the disembodied voice said. 'Thorney Island, here.' It was the call he had been waiting for from Coastal Command.'

'Yes?' he said eagerly.

'Negative, sir. Stopper Two's radar picked up nothing and nothing has been sighted.' The unknown speaker hesitated. 'What do you say, sir?'

'Send up Stopper Three. Give him the sector off the Sussex coast, though it looks as if we've drawn a blank this night. Old Jerry has put it off for another day, it seems.'

'It does that, sir,' the RAF officer agreed. 'Well good-night, sir – and pleasant dreams.'

'Good-night.' Ramsay put down the phone, telling himself that the remark was typically RAF; the fly-boys had absolutely no respect for rank. All the same the youngster had been right. It was bed and hopefully pleasant dreams for him. He yawned and drained the last of his whisky before looking at the old-fashioned Ministry of Works clock on the wall.

It was midnight. High time to hit the hay. Stiffly he rose and went to his bedroom. Outside there was no sound now save the soft hush of the waves and the crunch of the sentry's hobnails on the gravel. . . .

As dawn slowly began to break, as if reluctant to light up another grey day of death and destruction, the German fleet was steaming at top speed off Barfleur due south of the Isle of Wight.

The Admiral on the *Scharnhorst*, which led the fleet, its ensigns streaming proudly in the cold wind, had unlike Ramsay not slept at all. All night long he had waited anxiously as report after report came flooding in, each

one of them making him sigh with relief when it turned out to be negative. So far, his fleet had sailed for nearly two hundred sea-miles without having been spotted. It was a miracle, but one which, the Admiral knew, would not last for ever.

'Aircraft off the port bow!' the look-out on the deck below sang out suddenly. 'Bearing green. . . .'

At once a dozen pair of binoculars swung in the direction indicated, not even waiting for the sailor's bearing, as their owners focused them anxiously on the dark specks rapidly approaching from the east.

Ciliax waited tensely for the first identification. Down below the alarm gongs started to beat. Was this the RAF at last?

'*Messerschmidts*! a young officer on his staff cried. '*Messerschmidts 109, Admiral!*'

Ciliax mopped his damp brow with his white linen handkerchief, noting that as he did so his hand trembled slightly. They would be Galland's air cover. 'Signal welcome,' he ordered, his voice shaky with tension. 'And add – it's good to see that the *Luftwaffe* can also manage to get up early in the morning too.'

There was a rumble of hearty laughter from the assembled staff and the signals officer departed to carry out the Admiral's instruction. Slowly Ciliax and his staff crossed over to the great chart of the Channel, attached to the rear wall of the battle-cruiser's bridge.

'At our present speed, gentlemen,' he announced, 'we should be reaching Beachy Head at approximately zero eleven hundred hours. From there it's into the Straits of Dover and I don't need to tell you that those Straits are going to be the most dangerous part of this whole business. Our friends the Tommies have always regarded those waters as their own private duck pond.'

There was laughter from the staff at the Admiral's description. 'If they spot us there, we will be in for one hell of a fight. They'll defend those Straits with all their strength. As far as I can recall, only one foreign sailor has

ever managed to break through there in wartime in the last five hundred years – that was Admiral van Tromp in the seventeenth century. He was so proud of himself that he attached a broom to his masthead to indicate that he had swept the English from the sea. Well, gentlemen,' Ciliax tugged the end of his sharp nose and grinned in spite of his inner tension. 'If we can pull it off this year of 1942 and in view of the Tommies' overwhelming naval strength, I think we deserve a whole truckload of brooms, eh?'

There was a chorus of agreement and the *Scharnhorst*'s captain, an old shipmate of Ciliax, said loudly, 'Here's to the second van Tromp!'

Ciliax's grin vanished as quickly as it had appeared. 'Old friend,' he said sombrely, 'let us keep that particular title until we are through the Straits. . . .'

To Hartung, standing on the bridge of the leading E-boat, it looked the same as a hundred and one other dawns he had experienced at sea. The sea was its normal grey-green, heaving self and there was the usual chill dawn breeze blowing that always made him shiver in spite of his thick leather sea-coat, and from down below there was the same old welcome smell of the dawn 'nigger-sweat', as the sailors called their coffee.

This dawn should have been drenched in drama and excitement. Were they not taking part in the greatest and boldest operation ever carried out in the history of the *Kriegsmarine*? Yet everything seemed grey, flat, normal. Hartung felt drained of all emotion and he sensed the crew was experiencing the same feelings. The boat was strangely silent and down below the crew members on the wet heaving deck seemed to be conversing almost furtively, like men might do in a church.

Hartung thought he knew why and was glad of the solitude the bridge offered him this February dawn with the horizon still a sickly white, as if it would never grow light this particular day. Only here could he think clearly,

sort everything out, divorced from the deadweight of worries and responsibilities of normal duty for a little while at least.

It was Anna of course. Nothing else. The sight of her dying on the wet cobbles of the quayside in the yellow square of light that escaped from the open door had shocked the most drunken of his men into sobriety. They had recoiled from him. Even now he could recollect the burning intensity of their horrified stares, as they had moved away from his as if he were a leper, as he stood there, smoking pistol in his hand.

'Sir!' the look-out's cry broke into his morbid reverie.

He jerked his head up. 'What is it?' he demanded.

The rating did not look directly at him. None of them did now. It was as if he had some terrible stigma attached to him that they could not bear to gaze upon. Keeping his eyes averted, he answered. 'Aircraft, sir . . . I think they're . . . Tommy!'

Hartung flung up his glasses and focused them rapidly. There were nine slow black dots in the grey sky to the west – and west meant England. Impatiently he waited. They seemed terribly slow. Gradually their outlines started to become clearer in the glasses. They were bi-planes. The look-out could be right. The German forces possessed no biplanes. But the Italian Air Force had them. Were they spaghetti-eaters? It seemed hardly likely out here.

Then the first round blaze of colour swept into his sights. It was not the black-and-white of Germany, nor the green-red-and-white of Fascist Italy. It was the red-white-and-blue of the British. 'Sound the alarms!' he cried urgently, as the gun crews dropped their steaming mugs of coffee and pelted for their flak cannon. '*It's the Tommies . . . We've been spotted. . . .*'

Lt Commander Eugene Esmonde, commander the Swordfish squadron, ignored the flak coming up from the

E-boats below, although their fire was damned accurate and was coming dangerously close to the biplanes cruising over them at a steady 87 mph, laden down as they were by the two thousand pound torpedo tugged between the wheels of the undercarriage. Now he knew that he had struck gold. Somewhere ahead, there had to be the German capital ships; the presence of a whole flotilla of E-boats down there in the drink proved that.

Everything had gone wrong since Manston Field had been alerted that the Germans were making a dash through the Channel after all. The five squadrons of Spitfires which were to escort the slow-moving torpedo-bombers had failed to turn up and now he had to be content with exactly eleven fighters, flying somewhere above him in the clouds to ward off the enemy counter-attacks, which they could expect. Neither had the MTBs from Dover, which had been scheduled to put in a diversionary attack on the outer German screen, while the Swordfish slipped in for the big blow on the capital ships. Now he would have to go it virtually alone and the naval airman knew that their chances were slim. The Swordfish had been obsolete back in the early thirties; they were no match for the Messerschmidts and the Focke-Wulfes and even if they did manage to break through the expected German fighter screen, they could expect a flak barrage from the German fleet as intense as that of London itself. Smiling grimly, the young officer pressed the switch of his radio and said, 'I know I'll have to put myself on a fizzer, chaps, for breaking radio silence like this. But,' he paused and looking down saw the first long grey shapes coming into view, 'it's not every day you see the pride of the Hun navy sailing into your sights. Off we go then, chaps. Good hunting . . . *tally ho!*'

'*Alert . . . alert!*' the voice shrilled over the Tannoy system, as the alarm gongs started to sound and the petty officers blew furious blasts on their whistles, sending the

gunners tumbling into their seats at the pom-poms and multiple 20mm flak-cannon. '*Enemy torpedo bombers coming in for the attack . . . alert . . . ALERT!*'

Admiral Ciliax grasped the edge of the bridge with white-knuckled hands, as the slow ungainly British planes came in low across the waves six abreast, while the German fighters zoomed high into the sky to get out of the way of their own barrage, as the flak opened up throughout the fleet. 'Brave fellows . . . my God, what bravery!' he gasped.

Now the slow biplanes started to spread out, obviously preparing to attack from abeam and astern, heading straight for the *Scharnhorst* in what could only be mass suicide; and somehow at that moment, the awed Admiral knew that the Tommies knew they must die.

All around the *Scharnhorst*, her guns slammed into action in one great cataphonic roar. In a flash, the sky was a mass of bursting flame, peppered everywhere with brown puffballs of smoke. Tracer zipped viciously in every direction, so that it appeared the great ship was surrounded by a wall of exploding steel.

The first *Swordfish* was hit. A transfixed Ciliax could quite clearly see the pilot standing up in the open cockpit as thick white glycol fumes began to pour from the shattered radial engine. Was he going to jump? No. He was trying to fire his torpedo! The stricken plane came lower and lower, little tongues of evil purple flame licking about the fuselage now. '*Jump, man . . . For God's sake, jump!*' Ciliax cried, unable to conceal his pent-up feelings any longer.

Suddenly it happened. The Swordfish fell from the sky, its torpedo still unfired. It hit the sea in a great burst of water. Next moment, it disappeared, as if it had never existed. There were no survivors.

A second Swordfish came skimming in desperately weaving to and fro fifty metres above the water, the white blurs of the pilot's and navigator's faces clearly visible, as they concentrated on their task. The whole length of the

Scharnhorst erupted in stabs of violent scarlet flame as the gunners took up the challenge. Ciliax, watching the duel, could hardly believe that any plane could survive that tremendous barrage. But it did. The pilot seemed to bear a charmed life, flying out of clouds of angry smoke time and time, unscathed, getting ever closer to the battle-cruiser. Eight hundred metres . . . seven hundred . . . six hundred and fifty metres . . . six hundred. . . .

Ciliax tensed. If the Tommy was not knocked out of the sky the very next instant, he would fire his fish and at that range he couldn't miss. That was why the unknown pilot was taking such suicidal risks. He was determined to hit his target.

But that wasn't to be. Abruptly one wing was torn off the Swordfish and went whirling to the sea like a metal leaf. It went into nose dive at once, screaming towards the water. There was a flurry of white as the navigator attempted to inflate his parachute. But at that height, he hadn't a chance. Next instant, the plane slammed into the water, the impact crumpling up its fuselage like a banana-skin. For a moment the wrecked craft lay there on the surface of the water, but only for a moment; then it too disappeared beneath the waves. Again there were no survivors.

Still the rest came on. Now Ciliax could see the white splashes as they began to launch their torpedoes. Crazily, the captains of the destroyer screen wrenched their wheels round, as the evil arrowheads of impending doom sped towards them. Ciliax held his breath. Would they do it?

Z 25 sped brilliantly through three torpedoes, miraculously surviving what was a death trap. The captain of the *Paul Jacobi* gave his ship maximum rudder so that the destroyer heeled over violently, seeming momentarily to touch the boiling water, while a torpedo hissed by his stern, a boat's length away. And then they were all through and Rear-Admiral Bey, the destroyer-leader, was signalling triumphantly. *'Now how's that for hand-*

ling, big brother?'

Meyer of the fleet-tanker *Cuxhaven* was not so lucky. A first torpedo struck the vessel with the hollow, reverberating echo of metal striking metal. Ciliax groaned and waited for the inevitable. A moment later a second British torpedo hit the *Cuxhaven* amidships. From deep down within the vessel there was a muffled explosion followed by the ear-splitting screech of high-pressure steam escaping from the shattered engine-room.

Suddenly the oil exploded. Like a blow torch the flame gushed fifty metres or more into the burning sky. For too long, it illuminated all around it with the searing clarity of a photographer's flash. Ciliax turned away sickened, as the survivors, burning fiercely and screaming soundlessly, started to fling themselves into the heaving, tormented sea that itself was aflame, to thrash there in helpless unspeakable agony until the fire finally consumed them.

Five minutes later there was not one enemy plane in the sky and, as one by one the flak guns started to cease fire, Ciliax eyed the burning sky, telling himself that their attackers had fought and died in the best tradition of the British Navy; but they had died in vain. Not one of his warships had been damaged, but before them lay the Straits and somewhere out there in the gloom to the west was Dover, the heart of the British defences. Now they were really going to have to run the gauntlet. The second phase of the great escape had commenced.

Now the whole of southern England was alerted. Everywhere the planes were warming up and the ships steaming out to do battle. From St Eval in Cornwall to Coltishall in Norfolk, the bombers were preparing to take on the bold Germans who had dared to enter the English Channel, ready to brave the terrible weather which might make it impossible for them to aim their bombs, that needed to

fall at least 7,000 feet to their targets, to be effective.

Now the Germans were reported off Ramsgate, speed reduced to ten knots as they entered the heavily mined area, the air above them packed with hundreds of German fighters, ready to meet the British challenge.

It came first from the bombers. Fighting the cloud which virtually obscured the tiny grey shapes far below, the twin-engined bombers, nearly two hundred and fifty of them, started to run in for the bombing attack. Droves of Messerschmidts rose to meet them, flying boldly through their own flak, with Colonel Galland at their head.

He had been fighting the British for two years now. He knew their tactics, their strengths and their weaknesses. Their Spitfires were slower than the 109s, but they could perform steeper and tighter turns. As usual he would not give them a chance to shake off pursuit by a half-roll or a half-roll on top of a loop; he would got straight at them, guns blazing, his throttle wide-open, and eyes bulging out of their sockets. Once they had dealt with fighter cover, the ponderous two-engined Wellingtons would be easy meat. A squadron of Spitfires appeared suddenly from out of the cloud. He felt the usual empty sensation of suspense in the pit of his stomach as he went barrelling in at 500 kilometres an hour, the Spitfires looming up at an alarming rate. Just at the very last moment, when it seemed the Messerschmidt must crash into the leading Spitfire, Galland kicked his rudder to the left to get him at right angles and let the enemy fighter have a four second burst with full deflection. Through his sights, the colonel could see the tracer from eight blazing machine guns thud home, ripping along the metal fabric, tearing off little pieces of aluminium, as the Spitfire hung there, seemingly motionless for an instant. Abruptly scarlet flame jetted the length of its shattered fuselage and the Spitfire fell out of the sky screaming down to the sea far below.

Now the radios were full of shouts, oaths, cries of pain, exhortations and terse savage commands as the two air

fleets clashed above the ships. Now it was every man for himself. Single out an opponent. Jockey for position. Check all clear behind. Press the fire-button. Feel the phallic sensation of eight machine guns pumping thousands of slugs a minute. Tracer sparkling wickedly from behind the cockpit. Enemy on the tail! Tight turn. The remorseless, cruel 'G' thrusting the pilot against the back of his seat, pinning him there, flat-faced, gasping for air, lungs threatening to burst; and then zooming upwards again, guns crackling, blood as thick as molten lead.

Galland ripped through the cluttered mess of dog-fights, heading straight for the formation of Wellingtons, peeling off into a power-dive. Frantically the rear gunner spun his Brownings round to meet the attacker. Galland didn't give him a chance. He pressed the firing button. The dying gunner, his chest torn open, disappeared behind a crazy spider's web of cracked gleaming perspex. The bomber was his.

He took his time. A burst to the port engine. It feathered immediately. Another burst to starboard. The propeller sailed away and the bomber, crippled hopelessly now, seemed momentarily to hang in mid-air. A dark figure tumbled from its belly and another. Galland nodded his head in approval, as the first figure flew past his cockpit at a tremendous speed, whirling round and round crazily, as the flier fumbled for the parachute release-harness.

Then he was gone and Galland was weaving violently out of the way of the dying bomber, guns blazing a vicious purple as he headed for his next victim.

The stricken plane materialized suddenly out of nothingness and came streaming towards the flotilla of E-boats like an ever enlarging tear-drop. Hartung watched it, powerless to move, with a hypnotic, limb-freezing fascination. It never occurred to him to duck. Open-mouthed and rooted to the bridge, he watched the bomber, both its

engines shattered, its pilot slumped dead over the ruined controls, heading straight for them, while the skippers of the leading boats frantically tried to get out of its way.

But there was no escape. With a tremendous crash of rending metal and fabric, it slammed straight into *S-3*. The E-boat hadn't a chance. It broke in half at once, its stern going under immediately, while its bow swung straight into the air, allowing the smashed plane to slither from it into the heaving water, its red underplates standing out stark and gruesome, colouring the faces of the sailors around him that same bloody hue, before it too sank below the surface of the sea.

'Oh, my sweet Jesus!' a sailor said crossing himself, as great bubbles of trapped air started to surface where the boat had been exactly one moment before and burst in a series of obscene pops.

'Stand by to pick up survivors,' Hartung heard himself say.

'There'll be no survivors!' the sailor who had crossed himself snarled, tears streaming down his pale young face now. 'Not in this flotilla . . . We're jinxed,' his voice rose hysterically as he swung round to face the captain, his wet eyes blazing with crazy rage. '*Wir sind verhext!*'

Instinctively Hartung's hand dropped to his pistol and the sailor recoiled. 'Yes . . . Like you did with the girl –'

His words ended with a yelp of pain as Kaese slapped him across the face and snapped harshly. 'Take a grip on yourself, Deschner, or I'll have you put in chains! It could happen to anyone . . . *Now stand by to pick up survivors*!'

But there were no survivors and Hartung, watching his boats swing back into formation once more with a sense of detachment, as if they were no concern of his, felt a chill sense of disaster at the loss and the premonition of further calamities ahead. The hysterical sailor had been right. The flotilla was jinxed and it was because of what he had done to Anna. They were doomed, he knew it. Not one of them would see Germany again. . . .

'Horst!' she exclaimed, as he had pulled her off the sailor's knee and a sudden tense silence had fallen over the party, all eyes upon the two of them now. She had made no attempt to lie. Instead she had returned his gaze, no fear in her beautiful eyes, her ravaged face set and controlled, as if she had already accepted what her fate *had* to be.

For what seemed an age, he had not known what to do with her, his mind racing and confused, filled with thoughts of the past, mingled with that overwhelming knowledge that she was a spy in the pay of the British, employed to see him and his crews go to their deaths violently.

'Well?' she had broken that tense silence, a little knowing smile on her lips. 'What are you going to do?'

There were gasps of surprise from the sailors crowding in all sides and puzzled stares from the suddenly subdued whores at the blonde woman's perfect German. 'Why, she's . . . one of us,' Kaese stuttered.

Anna shook her head, the smile still on her lips. 'No, I am not. I am not one of you . . . I am a –'

'Anna, shut up!' Hartung had snapped, finding his tongue at last, knowing she was taking an irrevocable step. 'For God's sake, don't –'

But already it was too late.

'A Jewess,' Anna completed her sentence defiantly.

'But you're blonde!' Kaese said unbelievingly, echoing Peter's words of so long before. 'I'm sorry.' And like Peter at that first meeting in that back street, he flushed a violent red.

Hartung had known that now the issue was out in the open. He had to report her. If he didn't, one of the crew-members would surely let the information slip sooner or later. '*Why, you could have shat in my palm, but this whore turned out to be a Yid and funny enough – she spoke perfect German as well!*' In the end the Gestapo would find out and that would be that. His career would be ruined, his life endangered perhaps for

having harboured a foreign spy.

'Well, Horst Hartung,' she had said almost mockingly as if she could read the thoughts racing through his mind, 'what *are* you going to do – let me go . . . or,' she hesitated only the merest fraction of a second, 'hand me over to the Gestapo?'

There was another gasp from the assembled sailors. All eyes turned on Hartung as he stood there pale-faced and tense, a vein at his left temple ticking visibly with the strain of his decision.

She gave a little laugh: a strange sound at that moment. 'Come Horst, you were never this slow in the old days. Piss or get off the pot!' she said crudely. 'That's what your sailor-boys say, isn't it?'

The crudity had filled him with sudden rage. 'It's the Gestapo,' he said thickly. 'There is no way. I must turn you in.' He reached out his hand to grab her arm.

There was a murmur of protest from the others, which increased when the awed sailors saw how the girl's brave façade crumpled now, her beautiful eyes abruptly filled with fear at the thought of being handed over to the dreaded secret police.

'Let her go, Horst,' Kaese urged *sotto voce*, as if he didn't want the other officers to hear. 'What does it matter if she's a Yid? She's a pretty one at least.'

Hartung's hand stopped in mid-air, as if he might have changed his mind. A petty-officer said, 'That's the stuff, sir. We ain't heard anything.'

Suddenly Anna jerked back her elbow with the same energy she had once shown that day when she had attacked the Storm Trooper with her umbrella. The sailor standing directly behind her doubled up with a groan, grabbing for his stomach, and next instant Anna was running for the door, zig-zagging wildly like an American footballer carrying the ball through an opposing team for a touch-down.

Hartung awoke to the danger. 'Stop her!' he cried, 'stop that woman!'

The whores fled screaming for cover, as he fumbled with his pistol holster, trying to open the stiff flap.

Anna pulled back the door. The night air streamed in, cold, damp and salty. Hartung dashed forward after her, still tugging at the holster. Outside she was running down the cobbled quayside, obviously heading for the cover of some eighteenth-century warehouses to the right. Once she reached them she could disappear into the maze of blacked-out alleys which led off into the port itself. He would not have a hope in hell of finding her there.

'*Anna*!' he yelled, finally freeing his pistol. 'Stop or I'll shoot!'

She continued running, her high heels making a rapid clacking noise on the damp cobbles glistening in the yellow light that streamed out from the open door into the blackout.

'In three devils' name, Hartung!' Kaese cried. 'You can't shoot an unarmed woman – *in the back*!'

'Anna!' he bellowed desperately. Now she was only a matter of metres away from the warehouse. 'Stop, I say . . . *STOP*!'

'*Hartung*!' Kaese's forlorn cry seemed to be light years away, as Hartung raised the pistol, feeling himself complete detached from what he was doing, as if he were watching someone else, taking part in a little drama that had absolutely nothing to do with him. Almost without knowing it, in complete control of himself, perfectly calm as if he were standing on some peacetime firing range, he took first and second pressure on the trigger and then squeezed it the rest of the way.

The pistol barked and jerked upwards. Anna faltered, took another step, and then flung her hands up in frantic claws, as if she were climbing the rungs of an invisible ladder. She staggered weakly, one hand held out like a blind woman trying to find her way, and then with startling finality she dropped to the cobbles.

Five minutes later she had been dead and Hartung had known that from now onwards he was a doomed man,

who would sooner or later have to pay the penalty for the monstrous crime he had committed against the woman he had once loved. Then and now he had known it, as if it had been ordained by some god on high. There would be no escape. . . .

Now, as the German fleet passed through the narrow channel of the Ruytingen Sandbags, Admiral Ramsay at Dover took up the challenge. Although the men manning his heavy gun batteries could not see the fleeing enemy, he ordered them to open fire, while at the same time his MTBs based at Dover were commanded to attempt to break through the screen of E-boats and destroyers protecting the capital ships and torpedo them.

The MTBs located the Germans at 12:30 pm. Emerging from the black smoke screen laid by the Germans, they found themselves confronted with the main enemy destroyer screen. Almost immediately, the little boats were engaged by Galland's fighters, who came screaming down machine guns blazing. Desperately, frantically, the British ships weaved forward in crazy zig-zags, their gunners flinging up a furious barrage at the Messerschmidts and Focke-Wulfes which were everywhere now, trying to get into position to torpedo the long grey shapes some three or four sea miles away.

But luck was not on their side. The German planes were too many and the destroyer screen was too strong. Boat after boat launched its torpedo and fled, pursued by the fighters, but not one of them managed to get within less than two miles of the capital ships to do so.

By one o'clock, a despondent Ramsay knew that his attack from Dover had failed. Now it was up to Drake and young Harding in Harwich. If they failed, the Germans would have won and Britain would have suffered its most ignominious defeat of the whole war at sea. Reluctantly Ramsay picked up the phone, knowing that by doing so he was sentencing many good men to their deaths; for

Drake's destroyers had been scheduled for a night attack, when they might have some chance against the overwhelming German strength. In order to reach the German ships now they would have to cross a British minefield not clearly marked on Drake's chart. He was gambling with men's lives and he knew it, but it was a desperate gamble he had to play for the sake of Britain.

'Operator,' he said, his voice heavy with despair, 'get me Harwich, urgently. . . .'

EIGHT

Drake looked hard at Peter and put down the phone. 'The black dog,' he announced solemnly to the roomful of destroyer and MTB officers, 'we've got it!'

His announcement was met by cheers, intermingled with moans and curses. 'Bloody hell,' someone said at Peter's back. 'The Old Man really is the limit!'

Drake held up his hand for silence. 'All right, gentlemen, that's enough. Let me give you the facts. The Huns are obviously heading for the Baltic, probably Kiel is my guess. Now according to present estimates of their speed, they'll be in our area within two hours. There are the three capital ships in all, plus an estimated six destroyers and what seems to be a flotilla of E-boats.' He looked significantly at Peter.

The latter nodded his understanding, but said nothing. Obviously Drake had already mentally consigned him to tackling the German E-boats.

'In other words, gentlemen,' Drake continued. 'A bloody big dose of salts to be swallowed by ourselves – six destroyers and a handful of MTBs.'

The officers grinned at Captain Drake's words, but he did not return the grin; he was worried, very worried, Peter could see that.

'And if that weren't bad enough, we've got that damned mine-field out there to contend with. Well, no matter, it's got to be done and this is how well do. Harding.'

'Sir?'

'You'll follow the destroyers out. Your draught is not worth mentioning, so the mines will be no problem for your craft, unless you bump right into one. So, if we go

through first and run into trouble,' he shrugged, and didn't complete his sentence. But Peter knew what he meant. The destroyers might be sacrificed but they'd be able to get through. 'Once we're through the ruddy things, we'll have to go like the devil to catch up with the Huns. Then it's through the destroyer screen, formation broken, with each ship making an individual torpedo run. You MTB chaps stand the best chance of course because you don't offer the kind of target for the Hun gunners that a destroyer does . . .' He paused. 'Gentlemen, I'm not going to attempt to soft-soap you. The situation is very serious and I don't think we of the destroyers have much of a chance of surviving, even if we do manage to penetrate the defensive screen. After all, those Hun battle-cruisers pack one hell of a wallop. But Ramsay has given us our orders and by God we will attempt to carry them out!' He fixed them with a stern look from underneath those grizzled bushy eyebrows of his, as if daring anyone of them to make what he always called, 'a damned Noel Coward kind of remark', his favourite description of what he considered bogus patriotism; then grabbed his cap with the tarnished gold braid on the brim. 'Gentlemen, I think it is time we went.'

They went. Peter Harding would never see Captain Drake again.

As the little blue one and half hundredweight truck carried the MTB officers back to their craft, Peter hurriedly detailed his tactics to the young men craning their heads forward to catch his words above the noise of the engine.

'When and if we hit the German destroyer screen, I want us to go through at top speed and in a tight formation. I'm hoping that might confuse their gunners. As soon as we're through, spread out immediately and operate individually, just as Captain Drake has suggested. Just like the good Captain, I'm not going to appeal to your patriotism or anything like that. But it is vital that

we attempt to knock their capital ships out. You know the havoc they played with our convoys in the North Atlantic last year. They can well do it again. Understood? Maximum effort, that's what I require from you.'

Their young faces grim, the officers nodded their understanding.

'Kelly,' Peter addressed the young American. 'I know you haven't been with us long but with Sub-Lieutenant Hawkins sick, you'll take his boat. All right?'

'*Yessir!*' Kelly said enthusiastically, his face wreathed in a broad grin.

'You'll be our Tail-End Charlie.'

Now it was the turn of the other officers to grin. Tail-End Charlie was the rearmost boat, which had the task of protecting the flotilla's back from any attack from that direction. Not only did Tail-End Charlie rarely see any action, it also took the tremendous buffeting that resulted from being hit by the wakes of the other craft travelling at thirty knots an hour. Officers and crews on Tail-End Charlies had been known to be still vomiting green bile hours after the boat had docked after a sortie.

Peter smiled at the changed look on Kelly's face. 'Don't worry Kelly, I'll lend you some of my Carter's Little Liver Pills before we sail.'

The others crowded in the back of the truck laughed and Sub-Lieutenant Gibbs started to sing in a barroom tenor, '*We are poor little lambs that have been led astray . . .*'

'*Ba, ba, ba,*' the others joined in the chorus, while Kelly grinned, red with embarrassment, all the same.

'*Gentlemen songsters out on a spree . . . doomed from here to eternity . . . Lord have mercy on. . .*'

Thus they went to their little ships, on their way to their date with destiny, trailing the words of that sad ditty behind them.

'*Ba . . . ba . . . ba. . . .*'

HMS Worcester, Drake's lead destroyer, was a blazing shambles, her superstructure wrecked, great gaping holes in her sides where the German battle-cruiser's shells had struck her.

Peter, watching through his binoculars, started as the destroyer took another salvo from the German fleet hidden by the smoke-screen being spread by their destroyers, hurrying forward to do battle with the rest of Drake's flotilla. He could well imagine the slaughter being wreaked on the *Worcester*, as she pushed home her lone attack.

Then he forgot the *Worcester*, as yet another flight of aircraft came winging in and the alarm bells started to shrill their dire warning, in the same moment that the MTB's guns opened up.

'Stukas!' a rating cried identifying the ugly, fixed-undercarriage German bombers.

'Thank God for that!' Harding said to himself, as instinctively the petty officer at the wheel started to furiously zig-zag. They were already obsolete; the MTBs could fight them off with a bit of luck. He flashed a swift glance around his boats. They were all aping their commander, zig-zagging in furious bursts of angry white water, making the most difficult target possible for the planes now hovering directly above them. He glanced to his rear. Tail-End Charlie, commanded by Kelly, was doing the same. The American was learning fast.

'Here they come!' the look-out yelled above the chatter of the machine guns and the steady thump-thump of the Oerlikons.

Suddenly a Stuka threw itself out of the grey sky and came hurtling downwards, sirens howling hideously. Immediately all guns converged their fire on the dive-bomber. Black puffballs of smoke erupted all around it. Red and white tracer hissed angrily at the falling shape.

Peter gripped the stanchion in white-knuckled tension as the bridge heeled violently. 'Hit the bugger!' he cried to no one in particular. '*Hit* . . .' Instinctively he ducked as

just when it seemed the pilot had to plunge nose-first into the sea, he pulled it out of its tremendous nose-dive and a myriad ugly black eggs started to tumble from its blue-painted belly.

Founts of whirling white water rose on all sides as the bombs exploded. A wave splashed the bridge's bullet-proof glass window and obscured a horrified Peter's vision for a moment, but when it drained away again, he saw to his heart-felt relief that every one of his boats had survived the first attack.

But now the Stukas were coming down in a steady conveyor belt of diving aircraft. The afternoon was hideous with the shriek of their sirens and shrill whistle of falling bombs. A Stuka was hit by a burst of Oerlikon shells. It shattered in mid-air, snuffed out like a candle, the pieces raining down to the heaving sea. But still the dead pilot's comrades came on, braving the tremendous barrage thrown up at them by the MTBs' gunners.

A bomb landed only twenty-five yards away from Peter's vessel. The shock wave sent it reeling back and forth crazily, its masts almost touching the water. Behind Peter, the sailor manning the twin Brownings howled with pain, sank to the deck and clapped a horny hand to his wounded shoulder, the thick scarlet blood already oozing through his tightly clenched fingers. Beside himself with rage, Peter sprang over his moaning body and grabbed the guns himself. Screaming incoherently, he fired a vicious burst at the retreating Stuka. The stream of slugs caught the dive-bomber in its ugly blue belly. Quite distinctly, Peter could see the series of little explosions, the flurries of angry blue sparks, as he shot away the Stuka's electric apparatus. The plane faltered. Its engine gave a number of thick coughs, like an ancient asthmatic trying to clear his lungs. Then it stopped altogether. Peter had a quick vision of the pilot flinging himself out of the cockpit without a parachute and then the Stuka was plunging, out of control and pilotless, straight at Gibbs' MTB. Horrified Peter took his hand off the Brownings' trigger. 'For

Chrissake,' he cried, as if Gibbs might be able to hear him at that distance, 'take evasive action, Gibbsie! Come –'

The words died on his lips as the Stuka descended upon the MTB like some evil metal gull, ripping the length of its deck, taking bridge and superstructure with it in a sudden searing burst of blue flame. A moment later, the flame had gone and with it the plane. Behind it, the Stuka had left a sinking MTB, its shattered deck littered with dead and dying sailors, and a headless Sub-Lieutenant Gibbs crouched on his knees, hands joined together as if in prayer.

Five minutes later the Stukas had had enough. They formed up again, steadily gaining height to escape the flotilla's fire and then swung round to make their return to Holland, leaving behind them the shocked survivors and the ever-widening patch of oil which marked the spot where Gibbs' MTB had gone under.

Grimly Peter Harding supervized the transfer of the handful of shocked, terribly burnt survivors down below and then realized, as he returned to the bridge, that their evasive action had taken them away from the sea battle. Drake's destroyers had vanished somewhere beyond the horizon, as had the Germans. The heaving cold green sea was empty. They were alone, save for the dull, steady flickering pink glow of a ship on fire somewhere out of sight, a grim reminder that danger still lurked there, waiting for this pathetic handful of little boats.

As the cold winter sun started to sink beyond the horizon and the smudge, which was the Dutch coast, began to disappear into the ever-growing gloom, the *Scharnhorst* was shaken heavily.

Down below, there was immediate chaos. In the crew's quarters enamel mugs and great metal dixies careered everywhere. Hammocks discharged their blankets and the huge seven-kilo cans of jam and sauerkraut smashed to the floor of the galleys, causing the cursing white-

uniformed cooks to wade knee-deep through a gooey mess of spilt food. And from below came that sinister sound of hissing steam, as cold seawater came gushing in and swamped the red-hot boilers of the engine room.

As the alarm bells started to shrill their warning and officers began to run the length of the ship, shouting orders for the water-tight doors to be shut, while petty officers signalled by swift blasts on their whistles, the great ship, trailing a film of escaping oil behind it on the heaving green sea, started to slow down until finally she had come to a complete standstill and lay there wallowing powerlessly in the troughs.

Instinctively, a tense Admiral Ciliax realized what had happened, as the captain bellowed orders and enquiries down the voice-pipes. They hadn't been torpedoed. There were indeed no British ships in sight since they had warded off the destroyers' desperate attack. No the *Scharnhorst* had struck a Tommy mine. Now the question was – just how badly damaged was she?

Five minutes later he had his answer. Engineer Lt Commander Walter Kretzschmar, his overall and face stained with oil, reported to the admiral personally, wiping the black muck off his hands with a piece of rag as he did so.

'Boilers are out, sir . . . Some damage. Can't estimate exactly how much at this moment,' he rapped out the phrases in quick staccato bursts. 'Electricity supply cut. That means no power for our guns. Radio dead, sir.'

He stopped and waited obediently for the admiral's orders. They were as quick as his own report. 'All right, Kretzschmar, get to it. See what you can do. Off you go!'

Dismissing the engineer who ran back to his precious engine room, as if he were a young rating and not a middle-aged senior officer, Admiral Ciliax turned to the *Scharnhorst*'s waiting captain. 'You know what I am going to have to do, old friend?'

His grizzled old shipmate nodded. 'Leave us. If I were in your shoes, I'd do the same, never fear.' He forced a

smile. 'We'll manage on our own, don't worry.' He flung a glance at the sky. 'In half an hour . . . an hour at the most, it'll be dark, too dark for the Tommies to find us at least.' Without waiting for Ciliax's command, he swung round on the waiting signals rating. 'Signal *Z 29*, she's the closest, to come alongside and pick up the Admiral.'

'Ay ay, sir!'

Smartly the signaller began to flash the message to the destroyer steaming slowly off the crippled ship's stern, like an anxious expectant father waiting for news of his wife's condition from the doctor.

Ciliax snapped a command to his aides to begin packing the charts they would need and then said to the *Scharnhorst*'s captain. 'You realize that you're right into the shit with your hooter.' He used the old seaman's expression deliberately, as if he wished to shake his one-time ship-mate out of his apparent calm. 'You can't move and you have no fire power. If the Tommies catch you now, you'll be in for real trouble.'

'They'll have to catch me first. Kretzschmar's a first-rate officer. I don't doubt he'll get that port engine working again somehow or other. Then we'll soon have steam up again. If the worse comes to the worse, I'll beach her off the mouth of the Scheldt,' he indicated the horizon to the east where the estuary of the Schledt lay hidden in the gloom.

'I'll need the escort for *Prinz Eugen* and *Gneisenau*, you understand,' Ciliax said, letting his aide help him into his heavy greatcoat, while the staff waited, their brief-cases packed, as if they could not get off the stricken battle-cruiser quickly enough.

The *Scharnhorst*'s captain nodded his understanding. 'Naturally, I understand fully.' Then for the first time since his ship had run into the mine and he had learnt the extent of the damage, his weathered face furrowed into a worried frown, as if he had just realized just how vulner-able he was. 'Admiral', he said, as Ciliax accepted his personal flag from an officer, 'what about sparing some

sort of protection – the E-boats perhaps?'

Ciliax made a quick decision. 'All right, old friend, you can have Hartung's flotilla. As soon as I get over to the *Z-29*, I'll have the signals officer whistle them up for you. How's that?'

'Excellent.'

Hastily the two men shook hands and then Ciliax and his anxious staff were going over the side as if they already knew what the fate of the *Scharnhorst* was going to be, stranded out there and alone, and had no intention of sharing it.

Ten minutes later, the great battle-cruiser with its two thousand man crew was alone, wallowing in the waves as the wind from the land started to heighten, every man on board her from captain to the youngest mess steward knowing that she was in mortal danger. The *Scharnhorst* was a sitting-duck.

The signal electrified the middle-aged men who manned the machines in the Nissen huts that surrounded the pompous, red-brick Victorian house in that remote little town, which held Britain's most precious secret.

'It must be a trick,' one of them said, fingering his dog-collar, excitedly.

'But why?' another, who in a previous existence had been an internationally famed chess player. 'What purpose would a trick serve, eh?'

'Check the source again,' the professor said in a voice that had always commanded respect and silence in the senior common room.

And they did, and again they were electrified by the couple of lines printed on the flimsy piece of paper with its bright red codename 'ULTRA' stamped across the top. 'But can we take the risk of forwarding it to the Admiralty?' the reverend objected again, biting the end of his pipe-stem in tense frustration. 'Remember the old legal maxim – one witness is no witness.'

'Bollocks to this,' the petty officer signaller watching the debate contemptuously to himself. 'The sod'll escape before these ruddy boffins can make up their mind.'

Unnoticed as the group of dons and maths wizards who made up the staff of this strange, remote place continued to argue, he slipped out and into the radio hut. Encoding took him five minutes. Expertly he began to tap out the details of the signal on his morse key, telling himself he'd either get a gong or lose his rating for sending an Ultra without permission of an officer. In the event he received neither. He was killed that very night, knocked down by a staff car in the blackout as he was leaving, slightly unsteadily, his favourite pub in Bletchley.

As was customary, Admiral Godfrey received it first, and as was his custom he sent Fleming out of Room 39 while he read it; for Fleming was not one of the select few who knew of the great secret. Thus it was that an astonished Fleming was privileged to see something which he had thought impossible: a full admiral, red faced with excitement, running down the august corridors of the Admiralty, scattering Wrens and staff officers as he did so, crying at the top of his voice, while doors flew open everywhere, 'Get me the Chief-of-Staff . . . *For fuck's sake, get the Chief-of-Staff.* . . .'

As he tried to dab the rating's wound, the man sprawled out on the oil-soaked deck yelped with agony. Peter bit his lip, the sweat trickling down his forehead with tension in spite of the increasing cold, now the sun had gone down. Grimly he tried again, trying not to see that the poor devil's upper body was startling pink, as if he had roasted on an old-fashioned kitchen-spit. But it was no use. The cotton wool, soaked with iodine, the only antiseptic he had, simply tore away the man's tortured flesh to reveal the gleaming white bone beneath. He nodded to the petty-officer, assisting him, and he handed the captain the morphine syringe. Harding had no idea where the

man's main veins were under that shocking, blood-dripping pink. He stuck the needle home blindly, hoping for the best.

Next to him the petty officer held up another hypodermic and whispered. 'Put the poor sod out of his misery, sir. He ain't got a sodding chance.'

Without a word, Harding took the proferred needle and injected its contents. The tortured man's head lolled to one side and his breathing immediately became shallow and very hectic, as his eyes rolled upwards to reveal only the whites. In five minutes the fellow would be dead.

Slowly Harding rose to his feet, letting the syringe drop to deck next to the gasping sailor. He supposed he had just committed murder, but it didn't matter. Nothing mattered much now. It was just then that Sparks came running down the deck to where the dead lay, sprawled out in a nauseating slick of blood and oil, some of them shrunk and charred to half their original size, split open from crotch to chin by that tremendous searing heat. 'Sir . . . Sir,' he cried, face glowing with excitement, 'an immediate . . . It's from Winnie . . . *WINNIE HIM-SELF* . . . sir!'

Spluttering excitedly, he thrust the message-form into Peter's reluctant, blood-stained hand. Dully he looked down at the words, reading but not yet understanding them until he came to the signature. 'Churchill.' Then he blinked several times, as if waking up from a deep, deep sleep and read it again: 'SCHARNHORST LOCATED OFF MOUTH SCHELDT . . . APPARENTLY HAS SUFFERED DAMAGE AND IS STATIONARY . . . PROCEED AT ALL SPEED AND FINISH HER OFF . . . ALL ENGLAND IS WATCHING YOU . . . CHURCHILL.

Sparks could not contain himself any longer. 'I was right, sir, wasn't I? It was old Winnie . . .' He looked at the petty officer and the dying man at his feet, as if he could not comprehend why the two men did not exhibit his own tremendous excitement. 'To think of it, Chiefie,

me taking a signal from Winston Churchill himself!'

'Don't wet yer knickers now, Sparks,' the petty officer said sourly and waited attentively for Peter's orders.

They were grim and sombre. 'Throw the dead overboard, Chief,' he commanded in a low voice. 'Can't burden ourselves with them now.' Leaving them standing there, Peter Harding strode back to the bridge, and started rapping out orders. The last phase of the great escape had begun.

Hartung stood at the side of the signaller as he started to jot down the message coming from the stationary battle-cruiser, wetting the lead of his pencil after every group of words in a way that somehow irritated Horst for no reason he could fathom.

Now, as their own engine noise was reduced to a minimum, he could hear the sound of hammering coming from the *Scharnhorst* and the hiss of welding arcs, as the engineers tried to repair the damage in frantic haste before the Tommies located the stricken ship. Somewhere down below a rating was singing mournfully, '*Auf einem Seemannsgrab, da blühen keine Rosen**'.

'Be quiet down there!' Hartung snapped angrily.

The seaman stopped in mid-stanza and stared up at his captain, eyes smouldering with resentment. They fear me and hate me, Hartung told himself. Sailors were a suspicious breed at the best of times, especially those from the northern coasts. Words like 'fox' or 'pig' were never mentioned because they brought bad luck. Putting a hawser cover on upside-down or placing a broom across a hawser had the same effect, according to their simple minds. Now a woman, Anna, had been killed on what was theoretically a ship and that was the greatest jinx. They knew it and Hartung did too. He dismissed them and waited impatiently as the signaller licked his pencil for the

---

*No roses blossom on a seaman's grave.

last time before beginning his reading of the message from
the *Scharnhorst*.

'They signal, sir, that the flotilla should swing out to
port and give the *Scharnhorst* anti-aircraft cover. Her
guns are out of commission temporarily.' Hartung
whistled softly but said nothing. 'Early warning of any sea
attack is also required,' the signaller continued, using the
stilted jargon of his calling. 'No acknowledgement of this
signal needed.'

Hartung nodded. 'All right, dismiss . . . Kaese!'

'Sir?'

'This is an emergency. We are justified in breaking
radio silence.'

'But we have no specific orders to do so, sir. It might
well endanger –'

'I'm giving the orders, Kaese!' Hartung interrupted
Kaese's protest harshly. 'For the time being, I'm respon-
sible for the *Scharnhorst*'s safety and I'm going to do it my
way, *verstanden*?'

'Yessir.' Kaese said unhappily and listened to the rest
of Hartung's orders in silence.

'So in essence,' Hartung concluded, 'we adopt a semi-
circular stance at a sea-mile's distance from the *Scharnhorst*, closing in if attacked from the air, but maintaining
our positions in case of sea-attack. At all costs we must
prevent any attacker from getting close enough to launch
his torpedoes accurately.' He paused and threw a quick
glance at the long grey stationary shape of the *Scharnhorst*, every detail of her superstructure starkly outlined
now. 'And remember, Kaese, one of our most important
ships and the lives of some two thousand men depend
upon us now. If we have to sacrifice *our* lives in order to
that purpose, then,' he shrugged slightly, 'it must be
done. . . .'

Now the February cold was intense. On watch, exposed to
the biting, bitter wind, Peter felt the chill creep up his legs

into his thighs and from there into his guts and chest, so that his body seemed one large block of ice, despite three sweaters and the heavy duffel coat he wore. But he persisted, crouching there, bent like an old man, forcing himself to take his frozen hands out of his pockets at regular intervals and sweep the swaying dark-green horizon to his front with his binoculars. He knew that soon it would be completely dark. He had to find the *Scharnhorst* before that happened; *he had to*!

For the last half hour they had been smashing their way through the rip tide that ran off the estuary of the Scheldt, a wide V of hurrying little ships, with to their rear, their unhappy Tail-End Charlie wallowing heavily in their boiling wakes, every man tense and anxious, knowing that their commander was determined to find the great enemy ship and fight to the death, some of them praying secretly that he would never do so.

Time passed. Night started to sweep across the sea from the west more rapidly now. Here and there in the little ships, a cook sneaked back to his galley to prepare a snack and a cup of tea for the crews, telling himself that there would be no action now and they could safely light the galley fires. The gunners relaxed, closing their eyes against the keen icy wind which made them water all the time. They had missed her. It was pretty obvious. Somehow the *Scharnhorst* had got away and even if she hadn't, they wouldn't find her now. It was too dark and the Jerries would have the battle-cruiser blacked out perfectly; they knew their very lives depended upon it. Some of them risked a quick 'spit-and-a-draw' behind cupped hands. It looked as if it had been a wild-goose chase after all. The hard-pressed sailors started to smile softly. Another hour and the commander would call off the search; then it would be back to Harwich and the boozers. They would live to fight another day, thank God!

'Craft, port-bow!' the look-out's shout shattered many a dream that late afternoon. Immediately skippers everywhere threw up their binoculars.

Harding did the same and gasped, focusing the glasses with a frenzy of fumbling to make quite sure that his eyes were not letting him down. But there was no mistaking that long lean grey shape which he had first glimpsed as a raw young officer back in what seemed now another age. It was the *Scharnhorst*, absolutely motionless, the destroyer screen which he anticipated would have been protecting her gone. She lay there in the water quite alone; then the clouds, which had parted momentarily and betrayed her position, closed again and she disappeared. The sea was empty again.

The first German shell caught Tail-End Charlie directly behind the bridge, sending Kelly flying against the stanchions, all breath knocked out of his body, ducking frantically as red-hot shards of steel sliced through the air, cutting great gleaming holes in the superstructure and felling men everywhere.

He swung round groggily, and gasped with surprise.

Lean, white shapes were knifing through the waves at a tremendous rate, their guns chattering crazily. *E-boats*! Kraut E-boats – he had been caught completely by surprise.

The MTB heeled again under the impact of a salvo of cannon shells stitching the length of the boat. Almost immediately she started to slow down; her engine room had been hit. Kelly flung a despairing glance at the other boats of the flotilla, knowing instinctively they were too far ahead to help him. He'd have to help himself. His mind racing furiously he started rapping out orders, as one of the speeding E-boats, a white bone in its teeth, started to peel off for another attack, while the rest pursued the MTB flotilla.

'Sparks, send out SOS in clear . . . say we're sinking!' he yelled above the roar of the racing E-boat's engines, 'that might fool 'em! Petty Officer!'

'Sir?'

'Light the smoke-pots. The Krauts might believe we're really on fire. And toss the Caley floats overboard, as if we're abandoning ship!'

The PO doubled away to carry out the sweating, ashen-faced American's orders. Kelly turned to face the man at the wheel and it was only then that he realized that the man had been terribly wounded, his hands still gripping the controls seared to blackened claws by the burning impact of the first burst of shells. 'Swing her round to port . . .' he began and stopped short, knowing that the dying rating couldn't carry out the order.

But he was wrong. His face rent by absolute agony, sobbing with the effort, the blood streaming down a wound at his side and forming a thick steaming pool on the deck at his feet, he brought the crippled MTB round, while below the men threw floats over the side, coughing and retching horribly with the smoke streaming up from the pots.

Kelly forgot the rating who hung over the wheel, which now dripped long, bloody strips of his flesh, eyes closed and softly dying. The E-boat, glimpsed every now and again through the billowing smoke, was only five hundred yards away at the most. He could see the twin torpedo-tubes being swung round in their direction. *Was this it?* He tensed and waited for the end, while the rating who had gone mad sang a frightening rendition of the old dirty ditty. '*Oh, up came a spider, sat down beside her, whipped his old bazooka out and this is what he said . . . Get hold of this, bash-bash, get hold of that bash-bash, I've got a lovely bunch of. . . .*'

Suddenly there was a flurry of furious white water at the E-boat's stern. Her knifelike prow rose from the sea immediately. With a contemptuous swerve, the German set off after the rest, hitting each new wave with an audible thump-thump. In a matter of minutes, it had virtually disappeared.

Kelly slumped against the bridge next to the dying man, his shoulders heaving in dry gasping sobs, his head

cradled in his hands, utterly and completed exhausted emotionally. God had spared them this time. Why?

But there was no answer this day to that overwhelming question and on deck below the inanely grinning sailor sang on as he clambered and staggered through the wreckage, '*Big balls, small balls, balls as big as yer head, give 'em a twist around yer wrist and sling 'em right over yer head. . . .*'

'Bearing green three-oh!' Peter called out the bearing himself, as the smoke cleared and the bright white shapes of the racing E-boats appeared from the gloom, heading straight for the MTBs which had swung round in a wide white circle to meet the challenge from their rear. 'Range eight hundred . . . Deflection – zero!' He waited barely a fraction of a second as the gunners bore their weapons to rear, then cried: '*FIRE!*'

The bridge shook violently as the twin Oerlikons started to hammer away, as if it might fall apart at any moment. The red tracer shells chased each other in a crazy race across the dark water, making it glow ruddily for an instant, while on the deck the steaming yellow shell cases clattered down in a great heap at the feet of the gunners. '*A hit . . .!*' someone screamed fervently. '*We've got a hit!*'

The leading E-boat staggered visibly. Smoke started to pour thick and white from its shattered boiler room. Slowly but surely she began to slow down, a sitting duck, as the MTBs concentrated their cruel fire on the stricken vessel.

Peter's boat flashed by, the crew lining the decks to toss grenades and incendiaries into it, as it began to list swiftly to port, riddling the milling panic-stricken crew. The grenades blasted great holes into them, sending bodies flying everywhere in gouts of bright scarlet, the normal comradeship of the sea forgotten now, as they were seized by an unreasoning, all-consuming blood-lust.

Now the MTBs were in among the E-boats, each side manoeuvring for position, swerving and curving round at tremendous speeds, throwing up huge white waves through which their opponents were briefly glimpsed, guns blazing, deck crews hanging on for grim death, as their craft heeled and wheeled violently, the radio masts almost touching the wave-tops time and time again.

Peter swung the wheel to port. Just in time! In an angry flurry of compressed air bubbles, the torpedo which had been heading straight for his bows hissed by. An instant later there was a tremendous explosion to his starboard and a boat, whether it was German or British, he had not time to check, heaved right out of the water, its screws still churning and went under immediately, taking its crew with it.

Peter cursed and flung the wheel to starboard. The MTB heeled violently. Icy-green water surged over the bow and obscured all vision for a moment. He hit the wiper button. The powerful blades slicked the water to both sides and there, directly ahead, was the E-boat which had just tried to wreck him. 'Gunners –'

His cry was drowned by the frenetic chatter of the twin Oerlikon. At this range, the sweating gunners, the gleaming cartridge cases clattering to the deck in a golden rain, could not miss.

The E-boat was ripped apart. Her superstructure disappeared in a flash. Her own gunners reeled from their cannon, their twisting, writhing bodies flayed a bloody scarlet by the exploding shrapnel. The bridge shattered. Peter caught a glimpse of the skipper's dying face, with what looked like a red cap where the head had once been, and then they were flying by the E-boat, already beginning to settle swiftly into the heaving water, panic-stricken survivors throwing themselves into the sea, to be churned to pulp by the screws of the other boats racing onwards.

Peter had had enough. Leaving the confused melee behind him, knowing now that his own flotilla was

doomed, just as the E-boats were – for both sides the
only outcome could be a defeat – he headed for the open
sea, giving himself time to think.

The real target was the *Scharnhorst*, not the E-boats,
that was why they were sacrificing themselves: to keep the
MTBs away from the crippled battle-cruiser. But he
couldn't let them get away with it. He ordered half-speed,
the sounds of battle dying away behind him now as he
considered the problem. Now he knew where the *Scharnhorst* lay and would be able to find her easily enough again
in spite of the darkness, lit here and there by the pink
flashes of explosions and gunfire. But dare he attempt to
attack her from the sea? Wouldn't one of the E-boats be
able to break away and attempt to stop him if he did?
What about coming in from the estuary side? There was,
of course, the chance that he might run aground there, for
he had no accurate charts of the Scheldt. Besides, there
was the chance of mines and the risks that the coastal
batteries, known to be in position between the exit and
South Beveland, might spot him. Yet as he considered the
possibility, it dawned on him that it was the only one that
was viable. . . .

It was a possibility that had occurred to Hartung too.
Backing out of the confused fighting to his front, the
darkness stabbed by the scarlet flame of Oerlikon fire,
with here and there searchlights sweeping across the
waves to momentarily illuminate the weaving, tossing
boats and the wrecks, slowly sinking below the waves, his
boat circled the still stationary battle-cruiser. Not a light
showed along the entire length of her hull, and it seemed
as if she might have already been abandoned, though
Hartung knew quite well that she was filled with sweating
anxious men, waiting for her engines to start once more
and let her escape from the terrible trap in which she
found herself now.

Slowly the E-boat, her superstructure scabbed with

shell-fire, one radio-mast trailing behind her in the still water to the lee of the *Scharnhorst*, headed for the estuary, while Kaese signalled the battle-cruiser his commander's intentions and asked for details of the progress of her repairs.

'An hour at the most,' he reported to an impatient Hartung, coming up from the radio cabin. 'The Chief Engineering Officer is confident that he can get her under way again under her own steam, but it'll take time.'

'*Ausgezeichnet!*' Hartung snapped and dismissed the *Scharnhorst*. 'I want every spare man on look-out, Kaese. There can be no slacking now. Every man must pull his weight.'

'They will, sir, believe you me. But you must realize –'

'There can be no buts!' Hartung again cut him short gruffly. 'See to it.'

'Yessir.' His second-in-command turned without another word, and stalked off in a huff.

Hartung didn't care. Nothing was important now but saving the *Scharnhorst*. After that, he didn't care.

Slowly the lone MTB sailed along the mud-flats, edging in and out of each cove, taking advantage of every bit of cover, advancing on the unsuspecting *Scharnhorst*, outlined a stark black against the lighter sea, like a predator stalking its prey. As far as Harding could judge, he was about a mile and a half away from her; too far to be sure that his torpedoes would hit her – and he had only two to play with. He *mustn't* miss!

Up front, the torpedo-rating, crouched over his deadly fish, waiting for Peter's orders, as the MTB stole ever forward, its engines barely ticking over and surprisingly quiet in spite of the stillness of the evening. The distance between the enormous battle-cruiser and the little MTB narrowed by the minute. Now Peter, by craning his head to one side and holding his breath, could hear the faint hammering from the German ship. They were obviously

busy at their repairs. For a moment, he wondered whether they had managed to repair the ship's defective electrical system yet. If so, those massive guns of hers could well play havoc with his vessel. But then he dismissed the thought and concentrated on the task on hand.

Slowly but surely the MTB eased itself forward, until now it was facing the almost exact centre of the ship, with Peter, straining his eyes, heart thumping painfully, hearing acute, tensed for the first sign that their presence had been discovered. Minutes crept by leadenly.

'Range six hundred and fifty' the torpedo-rating said in a low hoarse whisper.

Mentally Peter could visualize just how he was feeling up there; just like the rest of his men, pulses racing wildly, nerves jingling electrically as they all wondered whether they were going to be able to sink this pride of the German Navy and get away with their lives.

'Six hundred, sir!' the rating said.

Peter threw a last glance at the metal colossus towering up in front of him and in the very same minute that the first searchlights snapped on above him and he was suddenly blinded by that intense white light, he cried *'Full ahead! Fire number one. . . .'*

'There they are, Captain!' a frantic look-out cried, as the night silence was broken by the roar of a high-speed motor and from the direction of the *Scharnhorst* icy-white fingers of light parted the darkness with startling abruptness.

'Heaven, arse and cloudburst!' Hartung cried. 'One of the Tommy bastards has sneaked through after all . . . Full ahead. Come on, engine-room . . . *FULL AHEAD!*'

He grabbed the bridge stanchion as the E-boat's prow lifted straight out of the water and she began to fly towards the *Scharnhorst*, veering towards port as the helms-

man caught the tell-tale white wake of the Tommy MTB
and steered in that direction.

Harding's fingers tensed into set, dripping claws as he
counted off the seconds, his face drenched in that unreal
icy white light. 'One . . . two . . . three. . . .'

He started. There was the hollow boom of steel striking
steel. He prepared for the great explosion that must
come, his every limb rigid.

Nothing happened! The fish had failed to explode.

In a curve of jetting white water, the MTB broke to the
right, in the same moment that the whole length of the
Scharnhorst erupted with fire that almost drowned the
sound of her great engines whining and coughing, as
somewhere in her bowels the sweating, angry engineers
tried to start them once again.

Frantically Peter held on, as his vessel heeled and
reeled under the shock of the shells exploding all around
her, rushing through the air like a locomotive through a
tunnel, deafening him, sucking the very air out of his
lungs, so that in a flash he was gasping like an asthmatic.
And then they were away, the gouts of boiling water
falling to their rear, heading for the estuary, every man of
the crew waiting for the young captain's decision: would
he attack again or not?

The decision was made for him by Hartung. At over seven
hundred metres' distance he engaged the lone MTB,
knowing that she still had one more torpedo left and that
she could still sink the stationary *Scharnhorst*. The MTB
staggered under the impact as the rapid burst of 20mm
shells ripped the length of the craft.

The bridge was torn apart. At the wheel the helmsman
howled in agony, as a steel splinter cleaved his neck so
that his head fell on his chest, supported only by a frag-
ment of flesh like that of a broken doll. Peter sat down,

sick and shaken, hardly able to realize that the MTB was drifting out of control now, her engines smashed, the crew lying dead and dying in the mess of escaping oil and hissing steam.

For a moment there was an uncanny silence, as Peter remained slumped there, seemingly unable to function, as if he had all the time in the world; and then it all came back to him and with it the knowledge that he must act. He staggered to his feet and pushed the dead rating away from the wheel. He tugged at it violently. There was little response. But his bows did turn again towards the *Scharnhorst*. With his boot, he cleared the splintered glass away and cried, ignoring the destruction and the dead men sprawled everywhere like bundles of abandoned rags, 'Somebody get on to that torpedo! Do you hear me . . . the torpedo!'

'Ay, ay, sir.' A rating detached himself from the bulkhead against which he had been holding himself and staggered drunkenly towards the last torpedo, supporting the shattered stump of his left arm with his other, like a mother might cradle a child.

Slowly the dying ship with its cargo of dead men began to drift towards the *Scharnhorst*, prepared to do battle for the very last time.

'Oh the brave bastards . . . the silly brave bastards!' Hartung cursed, his voice a mixture of anger, awe and respect, as he saw the MTB, lying low in the water, begin to drift towards the *Scharnhorst*, trailing smoke after it. 'They haven't got a chance in hell. . . .'

'They still have one torpedo left,' Kaese reminded him coldly.

'Holy strawsack, of course! Come on, Kaese, what are we waiting for? Engine-room – *FULL AHEAD*!'

'But Captain,' Suddenly there was fear in Kaese's voice. 'We'll run straight into the *Scharnhorst*'s fire! It'll be suicide. If the Tommy wants to kill himself, let him.

But why should we do the same? *Sir*,' he screamed, voice high and hysterical like a woman's, 'let the *Scharnhorst*'s gunners tackle the Tommy!' Suddenly, crazed with fear, he grabbed the controls from the helmsman and wrenched the boat round violently, sending Hartung staggering against the bulkhead. 'I won't let you kill us all for nothing!' he cried, spittle forming at the corners of his mouth. '*You goddam crippled glory-hunter*!'

The words stabbed Hartung's senses like a knife. So that's what even Kaese thought of him! It wasn't difficult to understand his logic. Everything, even the shooting of a woman, was part of his overweening desire for the glory, which would compensate for the fact that he was a cripple, with a claw of a hand that made him an outcast, a pariah. That was what the crew believed of him. Were they right?

For what seemed a long moment, Hartung hung there at the bulkhead, while Kaese swung the E-boat round in a great wide sweep away from the shattered MTB, drifting ever closer to the *Scharnhorst* whose gunners would discover it soon and blast it out of the water. Or would they?

The overwhelming question roused Hartung out of his reverie. He raised himself and snapped. 'Kaese, get away from that wheel!'

The other officer, his face contorted with fear and rage, ignored him.

Hartung clapped his hand to his pistol holster. '*Leutnant* Kaese,' he commanded, his voice icy and full of menace. 'I am ordering you to relinquish the wheel, at once!'

Kaese seemed not to hear.

Hartung drew his pistol. The rating cowered against the bulkhead, muttering meaningless sounds.

'Kaese!'

The lieutenant looked over his shoulder at the hard-faced blond captain and sneered, 'You wouldn't dare, Hartung! The crew'd throw you over the side. They hate your guts, don't you know –'

His words ended in a howl of agonized misery, as Hartung's bullet caught him squarely in the stomach, blowing him back against the bulkhead, arms outspread. Slowly, very slowly, he began to slither to the deck, trailing blood along the bulkhead after him, cursing to the end.

Hartung grabbed the wheel and swung it round. The lone MTB came into sight again, as the *Scharnhorst*'s searchlights swept down on it and her guns started to thunder again. But Hartung knew they were firing to no purpose. The Tommy was already into dead ground right underneath the metal monster. Soon the Tommy would fire that one remaining torpedo and this time she wouldn't miss. He had to stop her before it was too late. He had to! If he didn't, it would be the end of the battle-cruiser. '*Full ahead!*' he bellowed thrusting the ashen-faced rating back to the wheel. 'Gunners, are you listening down there, gunners? Prepare to fire. . . .'

The E-boat raced forward for the final battle.

Frantically Peter and the one-armed rating, the blood jetting from his ragged stump, hammered at the jammed torpedo controls, while above their heads towered the massive steel wall of the *Scharnhorst*, its guns thundering ear-splittingly and tracer hissing into the night, dragging its blood-red lights after it across the surface of the green water.

The rating slumped to the deck, mallet falling from his nerveless fingers. 'Sorry, Captain,' he gasped, shoulders bent in defeat. 'I'm knackered.' He keeled over and fell dead.

Peter hammered on, the sweat dripping from his brows and blinding him, alone now on that ship of death, motivated by the crazed urge to free the torpedo and fire it, as if nothing else mattered, aware already of the commands above him and the dark figures armed with machine guns and rifles beginning to man the rail.

He smashed another blow against the jammed mechanism.

'*Halt, du verrucktes Schwein . . . HALT!*' a voice called down '*Eis ist genug . . . enough, you crazy man . . . enough, Tommy, or we fire!*'

Peter hammered on.

'*FEUER!*' the angry voice cried and a ragged volley of small arms erupted from the deck high above. Desperately Peter slammed his mallet against the catch, as the slugs howled off the deck all around him, and cried through gritted teeth. 'Move you bastard. *Move!*'

The E-boat heeled as a salvo of shells from the *Scharnhorst* dropped to the vessel's front. The helmsman screamed with fear as a great torrent of water swamped the boat. For one horrifying moment, Hartung thought she was going to go under, as the bow disappeared under tons of raging white seawater. But then she was up again, surging through the maelstrom, shell-splinters the size of a clenched fist hissing everywhere, slicing through man and material, ripping open the superstructure, leaving the metal a mess of gleaming twisted gouges.

'There she is!' Hartung gasped as he glimpsed the stalled boat dwarfed against the side of the *Scharnhorst*. 'Helmsman –'

He stopped short. The man was leaning over the wheel, as if he were taking a little nap. 'What in three devils' name, do you think you're about?' he growled and grabbed at the man's arm. It came off in his hand and the helmsman dropped to the deck, dead, leaving him staring in white-faced horror at the bloody limb he was holding in his hand.

For a moment he could do absolutely nothing. He was too transfixed with unreasoning terror. Then he dropped the limb and wiped the blood from his hands with a shaking gesture, strange little incoherent sounds coming from his abruptly slack lips, his eyes filled with crazed

wildness, as the E-boat heeled once again under a near miss and screaming men fell everywhere on the wrecked deck.

Hartung was again blinded by a roaring torrent of falling spray, his mouth and lungs full of acrid cordite fumes. He hung on to the wheel with the last of his strength, shaking his head to be able to see and realized that most of the front of the E-boat had gone now and she was losing speed rapidly. A rating, completely naked save his sea-boots, was perched up the wreckage of the shattered mast like some strange human bird.

Crazily Hartung cackled at the sight. 'Pretty birdie,' he croaked, completely mad now. 'Come to Daddy, pretty birdie'.

The burst of machine gun fire caught him in the shoulder, with a blow like that of a sledgehammer. He staggered back under that tremendous impact, still cackling crazily, not feeling the pain one bit, although his left arm hung now by shreds of scarlet flesh, specked with the brilliant white of broken bone fragments. 'Birdie. . . .' he sighed, aware of the great roaring darkness that was threatening to overcome him at any moment, his eyeballs rolling wildly, hardly able to comprehend the other wrecked boat with the strange white ensign hanging limply at its shattered stern and the lone man kneeling at its bow apparently hammering something. 'Birdie . . . what you doing . . . hammering,' Hartung gasped, swaying violently like a drunk. 'Not time to be . . . hammering. . . .'

Now the two crippled boats were bound on a collision course. Above, the sailors lining the rails of the *Scharnhorst* had stopped firing and were gazing down in awed silence at the spectacle below, as the two craft were outlined in the stark white light of the myriad searchlights converging on them. Now the heavy guns had ceased firing and there was no sound save the loud echoing boom rolling towards the land and the dying putt-putt of E-boat's crippled engines, plus what seemed like the laughter of some crazy man.

'My God,' one of the awed watchers gasped, 'it's un . . . unbelievable! It can't be happening . . .'

Peter gave one last blow, feeling the strength ebb out of his shattered body, as if someone had opened a tap, his mouth full of the salty taste of blood, peering down with his one remaining eye.

There was a click. The sound penetrated the fog of redness which surrounded him. The torpedo was activated. Slowly, infinitely slowly, he raised his head. The torpedo slid into the water with a splash. Bubbles started up from its fins. The motor was working. 'Thank God!' he croaked and sat back on his heels among the dead sprawled everywhere. He had done it!

Peter knew he was dying. There was no hope for him now. But he willed himself to stay alive until the job was done. He laughed suddenly, feeling absurdly light-headed, as he recalled for no apparent reason the look on Howling Mad Lucas's face so many years before, when he had reported what he and Horst had done with the Hell-Cat. God, hadn't he thrown an act, tossing back his bearded head and baying with infuriated rage? He had been scared stiff.

Abruptly his confused mind cleared for a moment. A strange white shape was heading straight into the path of the torpedo surging towards the *Scharnhorst*. 'Hey,' he called in a cracked voice, the bright red blood seeping out of the corners of his mouth, 'get . . . get out of the way, will you?' He tried to wave the intruder away, but found he couldn't raise his right hand. He looked at it and laughed wildly, then looked for his left one. It didn't seem to be there. 'That's funny,' he whispered, staring at the bloody, shredded stump uncomprehendingly. 'Very funny. . . .' He fought to keep his eyes open and see the impact of the torpedo. It was a tremendously difficult task. His eyelids were awfully heavy.

The strange white craft was getting close now. If the

lone fool standing crouched at her bridge, surrounded by what looked like corpses – for some reason he couldn't quite understand – didn't get out of the way soon, he'd . . . The thought vanished and he couldn't seem to be able to find it again. Instead he sat there, listening to the drip-drip of his own blood, watching, not fighting the blackness now. He was very tired, he told himself. It would be good to sleep. He yawned and blood spilled out of his mouth in a rich-red torrent. *Tired . . . very tired*, he mused, eyes almost closed.

The torpedo slammed into Hartung's craft. The E-boat reared right out of the air, her screws churning madly. With startling abruptness she disintegrated. Her oil tanks exploded and the weary lone observer felt the shock of that tremendous explosion, as if a gigantic hand had just squeezed his stomach.

Peter tried to open his eyes, but found he couldn't. All the same, a weak little smile crossed his pale young face as a hundred yards away, the E-boat's stern, consumed by a monstrous funeral pyre, started to slide under in a hissing and spluttering of the sea, as the greedy water recoiled angrily, as if surprised by the searing heat.

Then the angry tumult was over. There was no sound but that of the sudden waves lapping against the bow of the sinking MTB. Peter nodded his head faintly, as he lay slumped face forward on the debris-littered, holed deck, as if in approval. An instant later he was dead. . . .

An Afterword

Of course, the reader must realize that I knew Lt Commander Peter Harding, for a mere month or so in that winter of 1942, and naturally I never knew *Kapitänleutnant* Horst Hartung and the girl Anna at all.

Besides, at that time I was a terribly naive young man. It would take the North African landings, a year in E-Boat Alley, the Pacific, perhaps even Korea to make me understand what kind of folk they all were.

Some people would say that their sacrifice was in vain, I guess. The *Gneisenau* survived till 1943 and the *Scharnhorst* until 1945, though neither ship ever played any significant role in the naval history of World War II. So what was the value of Peter and Anna's efforts to destroy them – or indeed Horst's to save the two great ships?

But I don't quite agree. It wasn't the achievement – or the lack of it – which counted, but the attempt. To my way of thinking their belief – mistaken or otherwise – that something, a cause if you like, is worth fighting – *and dying* – for is of significance. But then, I guess I am an old man now with an old man's sentimentality about the past. And they are long gone, dead these forty years now. So perhaps I ought to just leave off there with those words from John Pudney's poem *FOR JOHNNY*:

'Do not despair
For Johnny-head-in-air
He sleeps as sound
As Johnny underground.

Fetch out no shroud
For Johnny-in-the-cloud

And keep your tears
For him in after years.

Better by far
For Johnny-the-bright-star
To keep your head
And see his children fed.'

Kelly, Rear-Admiral USN, (retd). San Diego, California
Spring 1980.